The Wheels of Change

SANDY APPLEYARD

Copyright © 2015 Sandy Appleyard

Proudly self-published by Sandy Appleyard

All rights reserved.

No part of this book may be reproduced in any way except with written
authorization from the author.

ISBN-10: 1507529848
ISBN-13: 978-1507529843

DEDICATION

For the real Jason Bourne, not the character.

OTHER TITLES BY THE AUTHOR

THE MESSAGE IN DAD'S BOTTLE
BLESSED AND BETRAYED
I'LL NEVER WEAR A BACKLESS DRESS
THE WIFE OF A LESSER MAN
NO THANKS, MOMMY, I PEED YESTERDAY
DON'T MESS WITH DADDY'S GIRL

ACKNOWLEDGMENTS

Special thanks goes to Ian Jedlica for editing this novel, and to John T. Sonne for introducing us. I'd also like to thank all my fellow indie authors who have supported me through my journey in this jungle we call independent publishing. Jan Romes, Katie Mettner, John T. Sonne, Ian Jedlica, John Dolan, Alison Waines, and so many more I'll catch you on my next book!

CHAPTER 1

Mark took the last bite of his sandwich, listening to the police radio chirping quietly from the other side of the room. He had just wrapped up a case and promised his wife Shelley this would be the last supper he would miss for a long time.

Richard, his partner in crime, popped his head in the door. "Finished all the paperwork?"

Mark nodded, swallowing. "Yep. You?"

Richard saluted a goodbye and turned to Lisa, his wife and Mark's assistant, who was locking up her desk for the night.

Suddenly the dispatcher's voice came on the radio. "We've got shots fired on Delta Ave. South of the freeway. All officers on deck. Repeat. Shots fired on Delta Ave. All officers on deck."

Another voice chimed in. "Copy that. This is Nelson. I'm on patrol a couple of blocks from Delta. I'll check it out. Requesting backup."

"Copy."

Richard glanced at Mark, already adjusting his gun in the holster and sliding his jacket over his shirt, bloated from his bullet proof vest. "My car or yours?"

Mark closed his office door. "Whichever is closest."

Sliding into the driver's seat of his patrol car, Mark switched on the overhead lights and activated the siren while Richard fired up the laptop.

THE WHEELS OF CHANGE

The police radio chirped. "Copy. This is Noonan. I'm approaching Delta Ave."

Mark lifted the receiver to his mouth. "Noonan. This is Chief Tame. Is Hobbs with you?"

"Yes, sir."

"Good. Nelson and Wendell are already there. Stand fast until Officer Matthews and I arrive. ETA three minutes."

Richard mumbled. "Not the way you drive."

Mark glared at him.

"Copy that, Sir," Noonan replied.

A few minutes later, Mark squealed the tires as he turned onto Delta Ave., parking crooked yet swiftly across the driveway, adjacent to Constable Nelson's patrol car.

Mark lifted his eyebrows. Richard frowned. "Not bad for an old timer."

"Smartass."

The house sat on a quaint street. There were no dead cars parked on the lawns, no smell of marijuana and no screaming babies. Neighbors were peeking out their front windows while some stood on their porches, chatting quietly. Overall, this wasn't the type of neighborhood you'd suspect to have gangs or drug dealers. There was no reason for shots to be fired there.

Mark approached the front door with his right hand firmly on his holster. The door was slightly ajar; he gently touched it with the end of his boot. Richard stood behind him, mirroring his stance.

"Drop your weapon!" Constable Nelson shouted. Mark and Richard entered, readying their pistols to fire.

The man standing in the center of the room dropped his gun on the floor, hands shaking. "Don't shoot!" he yelled as his hands rose above his head in surrender.

There was another man lying in a pool of blood on the floor, his neck had been slashed. The murder weapon, a knife, lay askew a few inches away.

Richard kicked the man's gun away. "Identify yourself!" he demanded, holding the gun near his face.

"I…I'm Rick Cranston. I live next door." He nodded to his left.

Richard quickly patted him down unnecessarily, since the man was standing in boxer shorts and a tank top. The only place he could hide another weapon was in his dark blue sport socks.

Satisfied Rick was unarmed, Richard put his gun back in the holster. "What happened here?"

"My neighbour…um…Jake Campbell." Rick gestured to the victim. "I heard him yelling and there was banging. Jake's a quiet guy, so it was unusual."

Mark checked the victim's pulse and rose, frowning. "He's dead."

"Did you see who killed him?"

"Yeah. I'd have shot him if it weren't for the damn safety sticking. Talk about a delayed reaction." He looked at the floor and lowered his hands.

"Would you be able to describe him to a sketch artist?" Mark asked.

"Sure. He was tall, slim and dark haired."

"Did you see his vehicle?"

"No, but there's a catwalk behind the house, it runs onto Steeple street. He ran that way."

Mark shot a look at Noonan and Hobbs in the doorway. "On it," Noonan said.

"Go on." Richard prompted Rick.

"Um…like I said, I heard yelling and banging, like Jake and the guy were fighting. So I grabbed my gun and came over to look in the window." He pointed to the small window beside the front door. "Anyway, I saw the guy coming at Jake with a knife, so I barged in and as soon as I pointed the gun at him, he grabbed Jake and sliced his throat like he was cutting a hunk of ham off a hock." Rick sniffed, wiping his nose with the back of his hand. "Then he ran off like a bloody coward."

"Did you call the police first?"

"Nah, I imagine that was Mary across the street. She's the paranoid type."

"What can you tell me about Jake?" Richard asked as Mark called the coroner on his cell phone.

Richard offered Rick a seat on the chair furthest away from the victim, as he pulled out his notebook.

Rick sighed as he sat, pulling his boxers up for slack. "Jake? He's a good guy. Never been married, though. That's all that's strange about him."

"What does he do for a living?" Richard pencilled in comments.

"I think he works at a bank? He's always dressed up for work. Real professional-like. Works late and all. He's not home much."

"How long has he lived here?"

"A couple of years maybe?"

"Does he have any family?"

"Err...I think he does. Sisters...or maybe they're cousins. Not sure. They're always dressed nice like him, though. Same age I'd guess."

Richard's brow lifted. "Not girlfriends maybe? Or colleagues?"

Rick's face scrunched slightly. "It's possible they're colleagues. But this is a Christian neighborhood. There ain't any funny business going on here." He waved a disapproving finger at Richard.

Mark looked downward at Rick. "Then why the gun?"

Rick looked at Mark matter-of-factly. "That's how I *keep* it Christian," he answered pointedly.

CHAPTER 2

"Clara!" Max Dunphy yelled as he opened the front door of his modest home. His boots were caked with mud and his pants were lightly dusted with dirt. He removed his hard hat and placed it on the console table by the door. Removing his boots, he faced the street as he put them on the welcome mat outside. When he turned back around, he closed the door.

"Clara? You home?" He put his keys inside the tray on the console table, looking from left to right expectantly.

As he ran his hands through his greasy, sweaty hair, he trotted upstairs. When he opened the bedroom door, he found Clara lying on the bed. Her limbs were sprawled open, like she'd been pushed down. He smelled the alcohol on her breath and shook his head in disgust. She'd missed a button on her cashmere blouse. Her hair was dishevelled and her eyeliner was smudged. There was a trail of black mascara from the corner of her eye down to her ear.

She snorted and turned over, and as she did, her cell phone fell to the floor with a soft thud. He picked it up and looked at the screen. The blood drained from his face.

The text message said, *"Fuck you, asshole."*

It had been sent an hour ago from Clara to a guy named Simon Cross. Max thought for a moment and recalled exactly who Simon was; a high profile womanizing advertising executive whose office was just up the street from the construction site where Max was currently working.

He scrolled up to the message history; the first message was sent two and a half hours ago to Simon from Clara. *"My husband has slipped out for an hour. You wanna meet up? Same place?"* His lips pursed as he continued reading. *"Looking forward to it. See you in ten."* And the final message, *"I can't wait to feel your manliness, baby…I've missed you."*

His heard this heart beating in his ears. He placed Clara's cell phone in his back pocket and grabbed a change of clothes from the drawer. As he showered quickly, adrenaline pumping in his veins, he contemplated his next move. Clara was still passed out on the bed as he dressed and headed out the door.

The 'Mars Construction' truck was too conspicuous, so he grabbed the toolbox out of the back of the truck and put it in the trunk of his car. As he slid into the driver's seat, he engaged the seatbelt, thinking about his next step. He knew exactly where to go, and he knew exactly what to do.

He waited alongside a strip mall at the construction site. His destination was around the corner and he pulled up just before the driveway leading into Cross Advertising, praying that the building was as quiet as the side street.

Based on Clara's message, if Simon left her less than an hour ago, there was a good chance he was back at the office. He pulled over to the opposite side of the street and watched a lady leave the building and get into her car. Her vehicle and only one other were in the lot. The remaining vehicle was a late model BMW, parked in a spot that said 'Reserved for Simon Cross'. Max smiled sickly from ear to ear.

As the lady turned out of the lot, Max pressed on the gas and slowly pulled into the driveway of Cross Advertising. Craning his head into the glass entrance doors, he peeked into the building. You could have shot a cannon through it. There was nobody in the waiting room.

Make it fast. He coaxed himself as he exited the vehicle, pressing the button to pop his trunk. The toolbox was beckoning him as he loosened the hinges and opened the lid. He took what he needed and slowly walked over to the black BMW. Lying on his back, he took his small flashlight and pointed it at his intended target.

Within two minutes, he had done what he'd planned and hoisted himself back up, dusted off his pants and shirt, replaced his toolbox and closed the trunk. Pleased with himself, he walked to the office entrance and opened the door without looking back.

CHAPTER 3

EARLIER THAT SAME DAY

Sandra set the tray down on the console table alongside the wall in the boardroom. She quickly placed a mug from the tray on each place at the large table and sat the coffee urn on a doily in the center.

"Are we all set?" Simon asked, entering the boardroom.

"Just need cream and sugar." Sandra watched Simon adjust the overhead projector on the screen. The green light beamed on the white screen with the 'Simon Cross Advertising' logo noted clearly.

"They're here," Sandra whispered to Simon.

He nodded, adjusting his tie and exited the boardroom, walking confidently across the tiled waiting room floor. When he saw the account executives from Mansfield, the clothing account he was hoping to win, his hand was immediately drawn, offering a handshake to Mr. Stockton, the head account executive.

"Wonderful to see you, sir," Simon said proudly, giving the man's hand a solid pump.

"Likewise," Mr. Stockton said pleasantly.

"Simon, how do you live with all this traffic? It took us two hours to drive here!" Mr. Wakeman exclaimed good naturedly, offering Simon a handshake.

THE WHEELS OF CHANGE

Simon shrugged. "March Break in LA…it's the place to be."

Three others accompanied Mr. Wakeman and Mr. Stockton. They were introduced as the junior account executives: Mr. Blake, Mr. Klein and Ms. Redding. Simon offered both men a handshake and swiftly took Ms. Redding's hand, chastely kissing it, noting the shiny gold ring.

Mr. Stockton cleared his throat. "Shall we?" and gestured to Simon to lead the way.

Simon blushed and dropped Ms. Redding's hand. She reacted blandly, like his flirty gesture was no big deal.

Sandra scurried into the boardroom before Simon, carrying the milk and sugar.

"And this is my assistant, receptionist, and miracle worker, Sandra," Simon announced as the middle-aged woman blushed.

She waved off the compliment. "Buzz if you need anything."

Simon's nerves were showing. Mansfield was a huge account, one that he had wanted to win for some time. This meeting was very important as he stood to gain valuable information about their business's sales goals, and with that data he could put together possibly the most powerful advertising campaign in his company's history.

In the last week, Simon had been aptly working on the most compelling sales pitch. He'd outlined why his top accounts had chosen Simon Cross Advertising, and what returns he brought in comparison to their closest competitors in the last year. If this meeting went well, Simon would hopefully be supplied with key numbers and plans for Mansfield, allowing him to create a winning campaign pitch for them…and so far Simon had never lost.

Mr. Stockton sat quickly. "So, Mr. Cross—"

"Please call me Simon, sir."

Mr. Stockton adjusted his tie and cleared his throat. "Sure, Simon. What have you got to show us?" he said as though it was an accusation.

Simon touched a button on the projector and quipped, "I'm glad you asked."

The green logo appeared on the second frame and showed Simon holding a poster board with numbers marked on it; his projected account wins and his actual account wins for the past year. All his junior executives stood alongside the board like soldiers.

The next frame was a mock mission statement. "Choose Simon Cross Advertising; your competitors will never *cross* you again."

There was a brief chuckle in the room. Simon watched Mr. Stockton closely but his face remained tight. "Sorry, just a little humour to demonstrate we're not all about being serious. Some of our biggest clients get a kick out of that statement."

"Who do you represent, Simon?" Mr. Wakeman asked, pouring himself some coffee.

"Well, our biggest client is Crabtree Jewellers. Do you remember that commercial with the kid proposing to his little girlfriend? That was us," Simon answered humbly.

Ms. Redding smiled. "I remember that. My niece ran to the television whenever she saw the little boy with the bubble-gum-machine ring."

"Yep. Their sales tripled in a month after that commercial aired."

"Impressive," Mr. Wakeman said half-heartedly as he sipped from his mug. Simon wasn't sure if he was speaking about the coffee or the commercial.

Mr. Blake, one of the junior executives sat forward, suddenly interested. "Do you have any clients that sell apparel?"

Suck up. Simon thought to himself. "Er. Not at the moment. But our clients sell a myriad of different products and services. There isn't anything we can't advertise successfully."

Blake scribbled something on his notepad and relaxed in his chair.

"So far," Mr. Stockton corrected.

"Yes," Simon conceded. "But we're very confident we can put together an excellent campaign for your products. Almost every client of ours has a unique product and we've always delivered an unbeatable advertising strategy for each."

Mr. Stockton sat upright, as if he was suddenly poked. "Well, I think we've seen enough for now."

Simon's brows furrowed; he was about to fire up the shots from some of his most popular commercials.

Stockton continued. "We'll talk numbers and then meet again in a couple of days. Do you think you can put something together quickly, Simon?"

Simon nodded emphatically. "Absolutely, sir. In fact, my partner and I have several ideas in place already."

"Good."

Mr. Blake quickly scratched more thoughts onto his lonely piece of paper. The rest of the entourage rose and headed for the boardroom door.

...

Simon's phone beeped, breaking him from his reverie of the previous night with Tamara. He leaned forward in his leather desk chair and pushed the call button. "Yes, Sandra?"

"Sir, your four o'clock just called. Ryder is running late; about a half hour."

Simon paused while his cell phone vibrated on the desk. The screen said, *"My husband has slipped out for an hour, you wanna meet up? Same place?"*

His smile reached his ears. He hit the call button. "Tell him to reschedule."

"Sir," Sandra confirmed.

He keyed into his Blackberry "Looking forward to it. See you in ten."

The intercom beeped again. "Yes, Sandra."

"Sir, it's Ryder, will you take the call?"

He sighed. "Yes, put him through."

The voice came on the line much too perky. "Simon, my boy! You pissed at me?"

"No," Simon muttered as his Blackberry vibrated again. It was Clara. *"I can't wait to feel your manliness, baby...I've missed you."*

His face flushed as he watched the tent in his pants form. "Something's come up."

"Yeah, I'll bet," Ryder sneered good-naturedly. "What's her name? Kayla? Barbara? Or is it that redhead from Wichita...fuck, she was hot, wasn't she?" Ryder was referring to the three women Simon was seeing when he lived in Kansas a few years ago, before his advertising business took off and he moved to California.

"Those were the days," Simon agreed. "A woman from every city."

"How do you survive now? You're not a one woman man, are you?" Ryder teased.

"Hell, no," Simon urged. "Two now."

"Really?" Ryder was impressed. "Hell, you definitely live vicariously, Simon."

"Ah, it's nothing," Simon waved, standing up to adjust his hair in the mirror beside the door. His short dark waves hadn't moved an inch since morning. "It's easy to fuck around."

"For you," Ryder retorted. "I'm married."

"That's your problem. Listen, I'll be back in an hour or two. You think you'll be around then?"

"Nah. Stacy wants me home tonight. Her mother's coming over. Raincheck?"

"Tomorrow, then. We've gotta get the numbers together for Mansfield," Simon said firmly.

THE WHEELS OF CHANGE

"For sure. I've got a few ideas in mind. You?"

Simon opened Mansfield's file on the desk and looked at the story boards he had put together. All their products stared back at him: shoes, jackets and hats. Made for a king. "I think I've got an angle. That rap star Jonas wears their stuff. Maybe we can get an endorsement."

"Awesome. We'll chat tomorrow then. Say, nine?"

"Check with Sandra, but I think that's good. See you then."

Simon patched him through to Sandra and grabbed his keys, Blackberry and the half full pack of condoms inside the desk drawer. Smoothing his pants, he stuffed the box in the inside pocket of his nylon jacket and opened the door.

"Be back in an hour or two," he mouthed to Sandra. She was on the phone, but saluted him and smiled briefly, keying something into her computer.

The chairs in the front reception were empty, having been full most of the day. His BMW was parked at the first reserved spot. Disengaging the alarm with the fob, he slid into the driver's seat. The warm leather stung his backside and he was thankful he closed the sunroof as the afternoon sun peeked through the back window. Ray Ban sunglasses that his mother bought him were hung from the rear view mirror. He put them on, watching himself in the mirror.

He put the car into reverse and made his way out of the empty parking lot. Sandra sent him a text message, letting him know his schedule was clear the rest of the day, but tomorrow looked very busy. Simon responded with a smiley and let her know he'd be back to review the client list for tomorrow and go through the story boards for Mansfield.

Life for Simon couldn't get any better, in his opinion. His advertising business had been successful for well over a year, with a roster of prestigious clients he'd worked very hard to obtain, and his list was growing each month by about fifteen percent; so much that he was thinking of expanding.

Gus Ryder, the guy he blew off, was his first client. He owned a bike shop in Santa Barbara, very well known for selling top of the line Harley

13

Davidson motorcycles. Gus lived up to his ironic surname. He came to Simon about five years ago, before he was well known, when Simon opened for business. Simon was cheap and new and Ryder was desperate for visibility, having just moved to Santa Barbara and newly married.

They became close, sharing knowledge and money. It was a joint decision to move to Los Angeles. Ryder opened another shop with Simon's help and Ryder loaned Simon money to open his business in LA. Ryder still managed the shop part time, but the market for bikes in LA was huge, they almost sold themselves. So Simon and Ryder typically worked together most days.

Simon received a Bachelor's degree from UCLA, and it was then that he ultimately decided California living was for him. That was his plan after University, to move back home to Santa Barbara and open a small advertising business, establish himself, and then move to California and thrive there. He had been very successful.

Simon's name and face was recognized everywhere in LA: billboards, commercials, internet and newspapers. The mere mention of the name Cross and he was treated like royalty. It was very heady.

His cell phone rang and he fished it out of his pocket, thankful he was at a stoplight.

"Mother?" he said, pressing the button for speakerphone.

"Simon, is this a bad time?"

"Er...no. I'm just heading to a meeting. I've got a few."

"Good. Um...I got your cheque."

He listened as his eyebrow lifted.

"I thought you would send more," she stammered. "Remember we talked about that repair the pool needs?"

His lips pursed, recalling the supposed rip in the pool liner. It was nothing pressing.

"Did you get an estimate?"

THE WHEELS OF CHANGE

"Um...no. I can't get them to come out this time of year just for an estimate. You know how many Californians have pools, Simon?" Simon hated it when his mother begged.

"But what happened to the money I sent you last month? Is that all gone?"

"Well...yes. Remember I had Auntie Barbara come stay with me?"

His eyes rolled. "Yeah. I thought you were going to keep your distance from her."

She sighed with frustration. "Yes. I did. I hadn't seen my sister in over a year, Simon. Besides, I've been clean."

Simon realized he was one turn away from the hotel where he was meeting Clara. "Fine. Listen, I gotta go. I'll have Sandra wire transfer the money to you tomorrow."

"Good boy, Simon. Thanks."

As he pulled up to the Hilton, he saw Clara's Audi A4 parked in the back inconspicuously beside a large Winnebago with Canadian license plates. He parked on the other side of the camper. It was peak tourist season in LA: March Break. Simon hated this time of year and almost wished he'd arranged to have his late afternoon tryst somewhere closer, but it was too risky. Clara's husband worked at the Mars construction site too close to their second-closest lodging option: The Prince George Hotel.

Thankfully Clara was standing in the waiting area, which was unusual. Simon drank in the sight of her. She had legs up to her neck. Her white linen skirt kissed her ankles but was slit all the way up to the top of her thigh. As she stood on an angle, her left leg was almost completely revealed. Her sunglasses were large, concealing most of the upper half of her face.

He approached, kissing her chastely on the cheek. "Been waiting long?"

"I was about to leave, I've only got forty five minutes left," she said under her breath, which Simon noticed smelled of alcohol.

He winked and gently led her with his hand on the small of her back. When she was drunk it was no challenge. Forty five minutes would be

15

plenty. As they waited by the elevator, Simon discreetly ran his hand down her behind. She looked at the floor and returned the sentiment by moving forward a step and caressing his groin with her hand. His hardness jerked slightly and she smiled.

The light pinged that the elevator was arriving, and they relaxed. As the door opened to the empty elevator, they stepped in and silently waited for the door to close again before attacking each another like animals.

When they arrived in the room, Clara opened the bar door and offered Simon a glass of wine. He looked at her and furrowed his brows, removing his shoes. "I came here to fuck, not to drink," he growled.

She was snide. "Yeah, but you'll be done in ten minutes...this'll help."

Clara took the two supplied wine goblets off the top of the bar and poured. Simon's face was red with anger at her insinuation. As she sipped her wine, she gently pulled at a button on the side of her skirt. It fell to the floor, revealing her white laced thong panties, garter belt and stockings. His anger dissipated as she handed him his wine and he removed his jacket.

Simon gulped it back at once. She did the same and proffered him another glass. His empty stomach lurched at the acidy liquid pouring into it, and he instantly felt warm. The second glass he took slower as he watched Clara undress herself seductively. Out of all the women Simon had been with, Clara was the best at strip tease.

His rear end found the side of the bed and he sat, watching her with awe as she removed her blouse and bra. When her breasts were free she put down her glass and began rubbing them slowly. As her nipples puckered he licked his lips; the effects of the wine made her look even sexier.

Clara removed the last of her garter; her thong remained and she stood in front of him with her hands on his shoulders. He couldn't help take her breasts in his mouth, but as he leaned forward, she stepped back, shaking her head. Teasing him.

She sat on the guest bed an arm's length away and opened her legs, moving her thong to the side, revealing herself openly. Simon quickly removed his shirt and opened his fly, letting himself free. She waited. His hand quickly found his hardness and she put her hand out to stop him.

"You forgot something," she said softly, and wet his hand with her tongue. He gasped.

Sitting on the bed opposite Simon, Clara began to pleasure herself and urged him to do the same. It was thrilling to watch and moments later, Simon found his release. As he groaned her name, she rose and pushed him over onto the bed. She left him while she retrieved the box of condoms from his jacket and removed one, tossing it on the bed. When she grabbed another, she coquettishly looked at him with one brow arched.

"You're ambitious," he commented.

"You have no idea, baby. It's been weeks." She ripped open the packet with her teeth and slid it on him.

"How the fuck do you survive?"

Ignoring the question Clara climbed on top, filling herself with his hardness. Simon fondled and sucked her breasts as she rode him. Her breasts bobbed up and down as her head arched back and she groaned, finding her release, screaming profanities so loud Simon feared the neighboring rooms would hear.

"Done so fast?" Simon was worried.

Clara answered breathlessly. "Oh, Cross, I'm not done with you yet."

Suddenly she was on her back, spread eagled and waiting. She arched her pelvis up and grabbed his rear, forcing him into her. When she wrapped her shapely legs around him, he lost his mind.

"Fuck, Clara!" he hissed, pounding in and out of her so fast his head started to spin.

"Oh, yes!" she yelled. He tried not to notice the smell of her breath, thankful she wasn't a kisser.

A moment later she climaxed again. "Are you finished?" she asked blankly, as if it didn't matter to her either way.

He returned the unimpressed look. "Um...yeah."

Simon lifted up and started dressing as Clara scurried to the washroom.

"Is the room on your tab?"

"Uh…yep."

"Good. That's a vintage wine, it's all they had decent on the list," she huffed.

He shook his head.

When she re-entered the room, her hair was smoothed and her makeup refreshed. Simon was fully dressed and she approached him with the faint smell of mouthwash. He tried not to recoil but failed.

Clara caught the reaction. "It's bad enough I smell like you," she said as though Simon was a disease.

Her pupils were dilated and she'd missed a button on her blouse. For a moment, Simon wondered what happened to her, and then he dismissed the thought.

"Clara, I think it's over," he said softly, almost apologetically.

Her eyes met the floor. "You're unbelievable, you know?" she hissed.

As she looked up, Simon swore he saw a tear puddle at the corner of her lashes. Then she sniffed, turned around and said with her back to him. "Never mind. You're not worth it."

Absently, she slide her feet into her shoes and retrieved her purse from the bathroom. Simon watched, expecting a rebuttal.

As she opened the door and walked out she said coolly, "See ya," as if they would meet up later.

He watched the door close and she disappeared.

CHAPTER 4

Richard walked into Mark's office and tossed a file on the desk. "Just as we suspected. The victim bled out. Severed carotid artery. No mystery there."

Mark opened the file and briefly looked at the coroner's notes. "So Jake, what brought this guy to you?" he said to himself, fingering through the victim's information.

Richard chewed the end of his fingernail. "I couldn't say. He's pretty clean. Rick Cranston was right."

"Any forensics show up on the knife? Any prints on the victim?"

"Paul's saying there was nothing. No sign of a struggle. He's still testing for any DNA on the body, but so far there's nothing. Let's keep our fingers crossed."

Mark's lips pursed. "Noonan and Hobbs canvassed the area on Delta and Steeple, behind the catwalk and everything. Nobody saw a thing."

"Rick's just finishing up with the sketch artist now. Shall we call up Peggy over at WNYU?"

"I already did. Lisa's going to send her a copy of the composite and it'll hit the headline news at eleven o'clock."

Richard nodded, noticing the blank look on Mark's face. "What're you thinking?"

Mark rose. "The victim is too clean."

"That's what I was thinking, too. What's the motive?"

"We've gotta dig deeper on this one, I'm afraid. There's gotta be a reason some yahoo comes over and slashes a guy's throat in broad daylight."

"I'll call Jones."

Cameron Jones worked directly with the Federal Bureau of Investigation. He was the key technical analyst and could hack into any information system to gather pertinent data about a suspect or victim worldwide.

Within an hour, Cameron appeared through the front door, wearing his signature Bermuda shorts. Richard tried unsuccessfully to hide a smirk, observing the Mickey and Minnie Mouse pattern. "You should see how my mother used to dress me," Cameron said, popping a gum ball into his mouth.

"Is she blind?" Richard scoffed.

"Nah. She used to smoke loads of pot though. Sixties brat," Cameron explained, opening his laptop on the console table in Mark's office.

Richard rolled his eyes. "That explains a lot."

Cameron was matter-of-fact. "She still grows it…but to make clothes. These shorts are made from hemp."

Richard smirked.

"So, what's the victim's name?" Cameron asked. His fingers strummed the keys while he searched his bag for something. Richard watched in awe from behind.

Mark looked at Richard and cleared his throat. "Jake Campbell."

Cameron typed in the name and blinked twice. "Thought so. Too common. You got anything else?"

Richard eyed Lisa from the other side of the door. "Hey, love. You got the victim's property there yet?"

Lisa winked, handing Richard a manila envelope. "Just delivered it two seconds ago sweetie."

Richard kissed her on the cheek. "Did you call Little Rickie's sitter to tell her we'd be late?"

Cameron was listening to this exchange, meanwhile Mark was oblivious; he was so used to it. Cameron's discomfort showed as he started strumming the keyboard, mumbling to himself, "Okay...next screen...F1 to minimize..."

"Yep. Lilly said no problem. She's watching a movie, anyway." Lisa released the envelope and kissed Richard chastely on the lips, confident the office was empty at that time of night.

"F2 to scroll..." When Richard winked and handed the envelope to Cameron, he paused. "F4 to ...get a room..."

Richard laughed but couldn't hide the heat on his cheeks. "Oh, sorry. Judging by your shorts there, you're more into PG stuff."

Cameron ignored the comment. "I'm not here for your viewing pleasure. Read off his SSN or whatever else you can find."

Richard reached over and grabbed the rubber gloves Mark offered him. He struggled to get them on.

"Do you need to shower?" Cameron joked.

"Very funny."

As Richard pulled out the Social Security Number and relayed it, Cameron keyed it in and pulled up all the employment information pertaining to Jake.

"Works at a bank. Been there fifteen years. Loyal," Cameron read. "Let's see what else we've got." He pressed a bunch of keys and viewed licensing data, criminal records, last known address and a slew of other personal information.

"Looks real clean, boys. I don't know what to tell you."

Mark sighed and rubbed his head. "Dammit. There's gotta be a motive."

"Bank first or hit his folk's place?" Richard asked.

Cameron popped another gumball into his mouth. "Co-workers will squeal a lot easier than grieving parents."

"Good point," Mark agreed. "We'll hit the bank first thing in the morning."

...

Simon's jacket lay untouched on the bed. The pack of condoms was scattered across the floor. He bent down to pick them up, and when he placed them back in the box his Blackberry vibrated in his pants pocket. He checked the message. It was Clara. The text read, *"Fuck you, asshole."*

He laughed under his breath, sickly impressed. That was the most eloquent break-up message he'd ever received. He navigated to his address book and quickly deleted Clara's number. Simon informed the receptionist at the registration desk that he wouldn't need a tab for the room anymore. She looked at him kindly and took his credit card, updating it for current charges.

It was almost quarter past five and the thought of sitting in rush hour traffic frustrated Simon. All he wanted to do was get something to eat and head back to the office. His stomach gnawed at his spine and his head still felt fuzzy from the wine. The office was ten minutes away; he sent a message to Sandra to let her know he was on his way back and to order him something to eat from the deli up the street.

Every tour bus and minivan on earth seemed to be in LA. Traffic was backed up for miles on the Rosa Parks Freeway, only Simon realized this too late. He sat unmoving for ten minutes, watching relentless drivers weave in and out of lanes, trying desperately to advance an inch, and he lost his patience.

The next car that pulled out in front of him, Simon honked at loudly. His eyes rose up to the rear view mirror as the driver behind showed Simon his favourite finger. Simon returned the sentiment. His foot found the gas pedal and he rammed right up the car's tail end. Then Simon backed off, noticing he had handicap plates. They were both in the far right lane and the next exit was less than a quarter mile away. Up ahead, Simon saw

THE WHEELS OF CHANGE

flashing lights and the secondary cause of the bottleneck in traffic.

A glance in the rear view mirror showed more flashing lights approaching from behind. The ambulance was almost at Simon's passenger side door when he felt the car jerk forward. "What the FUCK!" Simon seethed as he unfastened his safety belt and exited the car.

The driver in the car behind, the one that rear-ended him, was a woman. As he inspected the damage she opened her door and reluctantly joined him. Her hair was blonde and tied back in a tight bun. She was wearing powder blue nursing scrubs and a noticeable gold cross pendant necklace. Simon didn't bother to read the name tag pinned to her right shoulder.

Tutting to herself with her hands on her cheeks, she explained. "I'm terribly sorry, sir. My foot hit the gas instead of the brake pedal." She bent over to assess the damage. "Well, it looks like it's just a small dent in your license plate. Do you want my insurance details?" she offered, searching his face.

The woman backed away, giving Simon a chance to take a closer look. It was nothing but a small scrape in the paint and a barely noticeable dent. His temper eased slightly.

He sniffed. "No, that's okay."

She put her hand briefly on his upper arm. "You're not hurt are you?"

"No."

"Oh thank god." She put her hand on her chest, touching the cross pendant hanging on her necklace. "I'm Grace." A car passed, drowning her out so Simon was unable catch her name. He didn't ask her to repeat herself.

"Simon." He gave her proffered hand a swift shake without eye contact.

She waved her index finger at him. "You look familiar."

Simon's lips curled slightly. "Simon Cross Advertising." Removing his wallet from his back pocket, he handed her a business card.

"I knew it. Your billboards are everywhere." She looked at his card and removed a pen from her breast pocket. "I'll write my number down in case you change your mind."

As she wrote her number she explained diplomatically. "My mother raised me to be honest. If I damaged your car I'll pay for it. That's my way."

She handed Simon the card and as he looked at it, she hesitated. "It's my work number."

He nodded, understanding.

"Again, I'm so sorry for this." She shook his hand again. "It was nice meeting you, despite the circumstances."

"No harm done," he murmured. "Safe driving."

Traffic was finally moving as they headed back to their cars. Simon chucked the business card with Grace's information into the garbage bag hanging between the seats without glancing at it.

He put the car into gear and began driving, saluting Grace from the rear view mirror. There was room to pass, so she slid beside him and drove ahead, waving at him from the passenger window.

The interruption had done nothing to help Simon's hunger and fuzzy head. He was still feeling frustrated about Clara and this delay. When Simon finally entered the office, Sandra was packing up her desk. "Your sandwich is in the fridge. I ordered you the usual and a large coffee," she said, switching off her computer.

"Thank you." He headed to the kitchen. "I'm famished."

"I've got that appointment at Josh's school, so I'm leaving now," she reminded Simon.

"See you tomorrow," he called back, opening the fridge.

Simon unwrapped the sandwich and stuffed half of it in his mouth before he even reached his desk. Sitting down at the desk he didn't bother closing the office door. There was a clear view of the reception area from his vantage point. While he perused his emails, he finished the rest of his meal. Just as he took the last sip of coffee, the front door opened.

THE WHEELS OF CHANGE

The man entering wore black jeans and a white t-shirt that hugged his large biceps. He didn't stand at Sandra's desk waiting to be served. Instead, he boldly walked over to Simon's office and looked at the name tag on the door.

Simon rose. "Can I help you?" The man towered at least two heads above him.

He nodded, pointing at the door. "You Simon?"

"That's me. What can I do for you?"

His face was like stone. "You son of a bitch," he said under his breath.

Simon's eyes widened and his brows furrowed. Then he noticed the 'Mars Construction' logo on the arm band of the large man's shirt and swallowed. *Oh shit.*

He came closer to Simon as Simon gripped his desk, not sure if he should run or listen to what he had to say.

"Look. I don't know who you are," Simon lied. "But I'm not looking for any trouble."

The man without a neck crossed his arms over his wide chest and laughed while glaring at Simon. "You fuck a man's wife and that's not looking for trouble?"

"I don't know what you're talking about," Simon lied again.

"Clara told me what happened," he said with his chin pointing upward. "She came home drunk as a skunk and well fucked."

Uh oh.

He laughed again without a trace of humour. "And I wasn't home, so I know it wasn't me."

"H…how do you know she wasn't lying?" Simon ventured, trying not to blink.

The man's hand rustled inside his back pocket as he pulled out Clara's cell phone. He punched in a few key strokes and the screen lit up. Simon

25

knew what he was about to show him, but he looked anyway, trying to keep a poker face. He read the text conversation they had before the hotel, and then the one after. Simon looked at him, stared at the floor a moment and took a step back.

The visitor put the phone back into his pocket and took a seat in front of the desk, proffering Simon with his hand to do the same.

Watching Simon hesitantly sit down, his hands folded onto his chest he leaned back, not taking his eyes off the ad exec. Simon waited, wondering what he was going to say next. He wanted to offer him a coffee to try to ease the moment, but was too scared to move.

The man spoke matter-of-fact as he lifted his thumb and slowly traced his bottom lip. "Construction business has been real slow lately."

Simon waited, wondering where he was going with this, when suddenly he cleared his throat. "The way I look at this, we've got two options here." Lifting his index finger, he continued. "One. I can beat the shit out of you and spread the word across town that you're a wife fuckin' whore...and of course, your face will make great evidence." The middle finger rose. "Two. You can give me fifty thousand dollars to keep my mouth shut...and Clara's too."

Simon wondered why there wasn't a third option, but didn't press. His palms were sweating and the sandwich he ate moments ago was slowly creeping up his esophagus.

Without hesitation Simon reached into the desk drawer and pulled out his cheque book, making it out for fifty thousand dollars. The man watched him intently, with a funny grin on his face. His eyes were dark.

When Simon finished writing the date and amount, he hesitated. "Um. Wh...who do I make it out to?"

The man winked. "You can make it out to Clara."

Simon wrote 'Clara' and then stopped. *I don't know her surname.* His lips pursed and he could feel a bead of sweat crawling between his shoulder blades. *If he hasn't hit me yet, he'll hit me now.*

The burly man's eyes were laughing. "Is there a problem?"

THE WHEELS OF CHANGE

"I don't know how to spell her last name." Simon lied.

He blinked slowly and smiled, but the smile didn't reach his eyes. He seemed to be enjoying this, so Simon kept quiet.

"D-u-n-p-h-y." He enunciated each letter carefully, snidely, like they had been through this a thousand times.

Simon tore the cheque out of the book and handed it to Clara's husband. He took it but his eyes didn't leave Simon's face.

As he rose out of the chair his gaze was locked on Simon. A chill ran down the rich man's spine. Instead of leaving he slowly strolled through Simon's office, stopping to look at every picture, all the advertising plaques, Simon's diploma from UCLA and even the picture of his mom he had on the desk.

Simon followed with his eyes only; he stood stock still. When he was finished perusing the office, he walked out to Sandra's desk and stood with his hands on his hips. Simon reluctantly followed as Mr. Dunphy stared out the window enclosure, and drew in a deep breath, then let it out slowly.

"You know," the large man said. "It's too bad you didn't ask about the third option."

Simon felt the blood drain from his face. He stole a quick glance at the man's hands, which remained steady, calming the younger man's nerves.

He walked closer to Simon, speaking quiet and even. "I know scumbags like you." Pointing to the cheque still in his hands, he said, "You'll have this cheque cancelled by sunrise, won't you?" His voice was matter-of-fact.

Simon shook his head quickly. "No. I swear. Take it."

Mr. Dunphy gave a throaty laugh and headed to the door. Before exiting he turned to Simon. "People who live in glass houses shouldn't throw stones, you know."

Once on the other side of the door, Simon watched him crumple up the cheque and shove it in the cigarette receptacle outside. Standing like a stone, Simon remained, watching the man as he pulled out of the parking lot. As soon as the small sedan turned toward the highway, Simon bolted to the door and locked it.

He wiped the sweat off his face with the back of his hand. *Jesus Christ. What the fuck was Clara thinking?*

Taking a deep breath, Simon tried to shrug it off. The next couple of hours he reviewed his client list and story boards, trying to take his mind off what happened with Clara's husband. It worked well. He was pleased to look at all his hard work laid out on the desk. Months of planning, preparation and dedication was finally paying off. The story boards were vibrant, eye catching and his best work.

Looking at his watch, Simon realized he'd been working for nearly four hours, it was going on nine o'clock. He'd completely forgotten that he was going to try and hook up with Tamara. His Blackberry had been quiet, so he picked it up and glanced at the blank screen. Smirking, he navigated to Tamara's number. She picked up on the third ring.

"Simon," she purred.

"Tam, baby. Whatcha up to tonight?"

"Well," she sighed. "I've just had a bath and I'm lying here alone on my couch watching television." Her voice was sleepy yet sultry.

"Hmmm," he spoke smoothly. "Sounds lonely. You feel like company?"

She hesitated. "It's late...But...I don't have anything going on until ten tomorrow."

Simon laughed softly. "Thirteen hours of passion. Sounds like heaven to me."

"We could fuck thirteen times, baby."

"Give me a half hour. I need to pick something up at home," Simon explained remembering he needed to wash off from being with Clara earlier.

"Can't wait," she whispered.

"Me neither. Wait in the bedroom..."

THE WHEELS OF CHANGE

...

The sky was darkening but Simon could still see the faint outline of clouds in the sky. The street lamps were just beginning to illuminate and as he stepped outside to lock the office door, he looked to his left and saw the cheque he wrote to Clara's husband sitting crumpled in the cigarette receptacle. He picked it up, tore it into bits and placed the remnants into the small opening in the center for garbage.

Echoing in Simon's head were his words, *It's too bad you didn't choose option three.* He shook his head, trying to forget the man's stony face glaring into his eyes.

The street was quiet, but Simon still looked over both shoulders before getting into his car. A car passed and then another but they all keep driving. *You're being paranoid* he said to himself. *Clara's husband was pissed; you'd have probably done the same in his shoes. He was just trying to scare you. Message received!* He laughed. *I'll be sure to keep my hands off your wife!* He smiled, sliding into the car.

The engine purred soundly and Simon exhaled slowly. He gently placed the car into gear, backed out of his spot and exited the lot.

Exiting the ramp to the highway he stepped on the gas, thankful that it was clear sailing. No Winnebagos weaving in and out of lanes, no traffic jams, no overworked nurses to rear-end him again. Turning the radio up, Simon heard one of his favourite songs, ironically, 'Life is a Highway' by Tom Cochrane, and he began singing. Just as he reached the chorus, he noticed red lights ahead, and then a full stop at his exit.

He pushed softly on the brake but there was no slack in the pedal. The singing suddenly ceased. Absently, he pushed harder, but his foot reached the floor, yet the car's speed has not changed. He could hear his heart pounding in his ears. Simon's eyes darted down to his feet. He tried the pedal again, pushing with all his weight. Nothing. The traffic was steadily approaching. "Oh Fuck!" he cried out loud, weaving around a car, his tires squealing as he just barely made it without losing control. Neighboring cars were honking in protest.

His breathing quickened like he was running a marathon. *What the fuck is happening?* He asked himself as he saw the cars getting closer, pushing on the pedal desperately and repeatedly, like when you're pushing an elevator call button in hopes that more effort will bring the elevator faster. The car was still travelling at highway speed.

His hands were shaking and he felt his throat closing up from sheer panic. *I'm going to die! I'm going to FUCKIN' DIE!* Brake lights quickly reached his windshield and all he heard was breaking glass and a long sickly scream from the horn. He saw the vision of Clara's husband in his head, mouthing *It's too bad you didn't choose option three* right before the world went black.

CHAPTER 5

Richard poked his head inside Mark's office. "Hey buddy, it's 8:45. The bank opens at nine. Do you want to head out or shall we round up Noonan and Hobbs?"

Lisa overheard and hung up the phone, calling out. "That was Noonan. He's got the stomach flu."

"Where's Hobbs?" Mark asked.

"Over with Nelson at a B & E on Forty Sixth Street."

"At this time in the morning? Where's Wendell?"

"That's where Hobbs got the flu from."

"Christ," Mark muttered.

Lisa held up her hands. "As long as I don't get it, I don't care."

"Amen," Richard added.

But Mark wasn't griping about the flu bug being tossed around. Mark knew that when they were short staffed, that was the time when trouble always started.

Mark grabbed his hat and placed it on his head. "Alright. Let's make this fast."

"You want to split up?" Richard offered.

THE WHEELS OF CHANGE

Mark gave him a knowing look. "Sure. We're short staffed. *Now's* the time to go against protocol." He shook his head and opened the door.

Richard's brow rose. He looked at Lisa and she mouthed 'grumpy' and blew him a kiss.

There were only two tellers on site at the bank, three people were waiting in line and nobody was using any of the three ATM machines. If Mark or Richard farted, everyone would know.

"Geez. Maybe they're all wiped out with the flu, too," Richard said, half joking.

Mark ignored the comment and approached the customer service desk.

"Can I help you, Officer?" the lady behind the desk asked. She'd spent way too much time on her makeup and not enough time on her hair. Her makeup looked painted on with a magic marker in an attempt to mimic a cat's eye, and her hair sat messily in a ponytail, like she'd forgotten to brush it.

"I'm Chief Mark Tame, and I'm here to speak to someone regarding Mr. Jake Campbell."

She turned toward her desk, looking up the name on a list, and Mark noticed her nametag.

"Excuse me, Suzie? Can you tell me who his supervisor is, or who he works closest to?"

Mark watched Suzie's red fingernail shake nervously down the length of the page. When she reached the bottom, she bit her lip and looked at the switchboard. "I know he isn't in yet, his light is still on." she explained with the same red fingernail shaking, pointing to Jake's line on the board.

Richard intervened gently, sensing her nerves. "That's fine, ma'am. Who does he report to?"

"Well the only person I know who's here is Red Fisher. Shall I call him for you?" she said, like she was asking their permission.

Mark nodded good-naturedly. "That would be helpful."

31

A moment later a tall, stone faced man opened the door behind reception and peered out. Suzie turned around with the phone still in her hand. "Oh, I was just about to call you, Red. These officers are here to see you about Jake...err...Campbell."

Without coming fully into the room, Red said simply, "He's dead."

Suzie's gasp was audible. Mark pursed his lips. "Thank you. Can we speak to you privately?"

"I've only got a moment. Come through here." He gestured to the door without eye contact.

"I thought bankers had more tact," Richard said under his breath.

"Not this one."

As they walked through a small, enclosed corridor of empty offices, Red began. "I don't know what to tell you about Jake. He was a good guy, a reliable employee. He and I hung out here and there for drinks after work."

Red stopped at his office and gestured them in, in a practiced manner.

"So you hung out with him after hours? What was he like?" Richard asked, observing Red's receding hairline and bloated waistline.

"He was cool, you know. Just a regular guy."

"Are you married?" Mark asked, noting there were no pictures to tell that tale. "Single," Red said like it was an affliction.

"How long have you known Jake?" Richard asked.

"Hm. I'd say two years maybe? Since I started working here, anyway. We didn't hang out until about six months ago though."

"Was Jake seeing anybody?" Mark asked.

Jake picked up a pen off his desk and placed it back into the cup sitting next to the keyboard. "Not that I'm aware of."

Richard watched Red's finger strum his lower lip. "Did you know if he was in any trouble?"

Red shook his head and drew a breath. "Can't say he was. But I didn't know him that well...like I said."

Richard was about to ask another question when Red interrupted. "Have you checked with his family yet? I hear his mom fell to pieces."

"No. But that's where we're headed after this."

Mark and Richard rose and Red hesitated a beat, then rose with them, gesturing them out the door in the same practiced manner as before. "If you think of anything, please contact me," Mark said, handing him a business card.

Red nodded, "You know your way out?"

"Yep. Thanks," Richard said, following Mark down the corridor.

When they reached the reception desk, Mark handed Suzie a card. "If anyone else can offer any input about Jake, can you please have them call me?"

Suzie rose quickly. "Oh sure, sir. I didn't mean any disrespect. I didn't know he was...err...deceased."

"That's quite alright dear, thanks for your help." Mark tipped his hat. Suzie blushed slightly and sat back down.

...

There was a muffled voice in the background and Simon tried to ignore it, feeling tired and weak. From what, he couldn't remember. *It must be the television. I've forgotten to turn it off so many times before.* The voice he heard in the room struck him as familiar. He listened carefully and then shrugged it off, drifting back to sleep. A few seconds later it was quiet again and Simon felt someone gently caressing his hand. He flinched as he realized he was not at home.

"Simon?...Simon?...Can you hear me?" the voice said softly. His eyelids felt heavy, but he managed to open them. His mother, Nancy, was staring deeply into his eyes, the way she used to suspiciously eye him when she suspected he was doing pot in high school. Simon said nothing to her at first, trying to process where he was. When he saw the room and medical equipment surrounding him, his eyes opened wide.

"Shh...shh...It's okay Simon," Nancy soothed. "You're okay. You were in an accident. Do you remember?"

He blinked, and placed a hand on his head. "My brakes failed," he explained weakly, clearing his throat.

Her face scrunched. "Really? The cops thought you might have fallen asleep at the wheel. You had some alcohol in your blood, too."

Simon recoiled. Nancy caught the reaction. "It's okay, it wasn't over the limit or anything. You're fine." She looked down. "Your car's a right off, though."

"Great," he murmured.

Nancy chuckled. "It's just a piece of metal, Simon." She sat up and gestured with her hand. "Be more worried about your legs."

His eyebrows furrowed. "What do you mean?"

Nancy's explanation was flat. "The doctors say you had a spinal cord injury. Go ahead." She encouraged again with her hand. "Try to move them."

He looked at her as if she was playing a sick joke. Clearing his throat again, he attempted to move his left leg. Sure enough, nothing happened. His heart beat faster. He tried to move his right leg. Same thing. Nancy nodded disapprovingly, like he failed a test. The colour drained from his face.

Nancy opened her mouth, about to speak, just as a doctor walked in.

"Oh, hello, Mr. Cross. Nice to see you awake," the doctor said. He instantly reminded Simon of Mr. Potato Head. He had a big, fat red nose with a dark, hairy moustache under it, a smattering of dark hair on his head and a body shaped like a potato.

He smiled at Simon. "How are you feeling? I'm Dr. Bennett"

Simon cut to the chase. "I...I can't move my legs."

Dr. Bennett frowned nervously. "Err...yes." He looked cautiously at Simon's mom. "Would you mind giving us a few moments please?"

Nancy looked displeased but crossed her arms and left.

After the door closed, Dr. Bennett took a seat in the chair Nancy vacated.

He placed his clipboard on the bed and looked at Simon plainly. "I do apologize. It must be quite a shock." He looked at the floor and gently kicked away an imaginary piece of dust. "There is a chance you'll get the feeling back. We're going to let the tissue surrounding your spine heal for a few weeks and perform surgery to try and fix the nerve damage."

Dr. Bennett waited a moment and looked at Simon, waiting for his reaction.

"What are the chances it'll work?"

"Pretty good." He squinted slightly. "As long as the swelling goes down, there's a pretty good chance."

Simon observed the cables and tubes surrounding him. "What do I have to do?"

"Just sit tight. Rest. You'll be in here for a couple more days—"

Simon cut him off. "A couple *more* days? How long have I been here?"

Dr. Bennett chuckled. "You've been out for five days, Simon. We had to keep you sedated so you wouldn't move your spine."

Simon looked up at the ceiling and sighed, shaking his head.

"Is there a problem?" the doctor asked softly.

Simon swallowed and licked his lips, still staring at the ceiling. "I...I have a business."

Dr. Bennett smiled. "Yes, I know." He pulled his chair up closer. "Simon, it's very important that you rest. Right now it is critical that you stay immobile."

Simon looked down at his legs, a puff of air escaped from his lips. "That won't be a problem."

There was a small bag hanging off the side of the bed. "What's that for?" Simon asked.

The doctor rose. "Ah, yes. That's a bag for your urine," he said, lifting the sheet slightly so Simon could follow the trail of the line leading to it. The tube led right into a catheter that was tucked inside his penis. Simon cringed.

"Jesus Christ," he muttered.

"It's temporary," the doctor said. "You fractured your lumbar spine. L-11, which will cause you to lose sensation in toileting."

Simon huffed but listened as Dr. Bennett continued. "We'll do an operation in a week or so to decompress the fracture, which will help it heal faster."

The ad executive was not impressed. "Great."

"I know this is difficult, Simon. But everything happens for a reason, and if you do as you're told, there's a good chance you'll be fine. The choice is yours."

The doctor rose and lifted his clipboard. "I'll be back in a couple of hours with the neurologist. We'll do an evaluation and see what the best course of treatment is."

Simon pasted on a half smile. "Thanks."

The doctor nodded and exited the room, inviting Nancy to re-join Simon.

She scurried to her son breathlessly. "So what did he say?"

Simon took a deep breath and rubbed his forehead. "I've gotta have surgery in a week."

"So what happened?"

Exhaling, he plopped his head on the pillow, looking upward, as though the fluorescent lights had all the answers. "Shit, I don't know. I was driving home from work and my brakes failed."

"I just spoke to Ryder and he says the brake lines were cut."

Pursing his lips, Simon seethed.

Nancy's foot tapped on the floor. "What son of a bitch cut them, Simon?"

"Shit, I don't know. I'm not everybody's favourite, I guess." He lied.

"Cut the shit, Simon! Was this professional? Did someone have a hit on you?" Nancy rose and began pacing.

Simon scratched the scruff on his chin. "No, it wasn't professional!" he shouted. "You're being ridiculous, mom! How the hell does Ryder even know?"

Nancy pointed a finger at Simon. "You wouldn't lie to your mother would you? Because so help me God, if someone tried to kill you...!" she said through gritted teeth.

He gently grasped Nancy's hand. "Mom, go for a coffee, okay? You need to relax."

"Fine." She paused and looked at her watch. "Ryder should be here soon anyway."

He watched her visibly relax as she grabbed her purse off the side table and walked out, kissing his forehead before she left.

A few minutes later, Ryder walked in and lifted his hand like he was going to high five him. "Simon, man, good to see you!"

He sat in the chair. "How are you feeling?" His face was red, like he just ran up a flight of stairs.

"Well I can't feel anything from the waist down. But doc says it's temporary. I fractured my L...something."

Ryder chuckled and shook his head, like Simon just told him a joke.

"Only you. You should tell her to take it easy next time." Then he got serious. "You know your brake lines were cut?"

"Yeah. I suppose that was thanks to Clara's husband."

"Shit." Ryder's eyes widened. "You should see your car. Be thankful you're alive man, it's bad. No jokes."

"Seriously?"

Ryder pulled the chair up closer. "You rear-ended a fuckin' transport, my friend. You're just lucky your head's still attached."

"Holy fuck." Simon was incredulous. "I didn't even see a transport in front of me."

"Well he was there. Full load, too. Buddy walked away without a scratch." Ryder changed tack. "So you gonna press charges on the fucker?"

Simon hesitated, and then waved it off. "Nah. I fucked his wife. I suppose we're even."

Ryder howled. "Jesus Christ! You learned your lesson then, huh?"

They had a laugh and then Ryder wiped his eyes with the back of his hand. "Seriously though, seems a little harsh, don't you think? I mean adultery's one thing, but attempted murder's another, no?"

"Ah. How would I ever prove it?"

"You've got cameras set up at the office don't you?"

"Yeah. But then everybody will know his motive."

"What does that matter? He'll be in jail anyway."

Simon shook his head. "I appreciate the concern man, but I don't need my mother knowing." He craned his neck toward Ryder. "And what the *fuck* possessed you to tell her my lines were cut anyway?"

Ryder put his hands in the air like he was surrendering. "Dude, she asked. I can't lie to your mother man, sorry."

THE WHEELS OF CHANGE

Simon went silent. "Cat got your tongue? What's on your mind?" Ryder touched his friends arm. "Simon. Listen. It's none of my business and you can tell me to piss off if you want. But I think you should press charges."

Ryder watched his friend open his mouth in rebuttal. "Hear me out for a minute, man." Ryder said solemnly. "You don't exactly have a reputation for celibacy around here, and I'm willing to bet your mother isn't going to care either way. She's your mom, she probably has a clue or two. Don't let this guy get away with it, man."

He let Simon digest for a beat and then continued. "Let me ask you something. Did you know she was married?"

Simon swallowed and looked at Ryder. "It didn't matter to me."

Ryder looked at him and said matter-of-factly. "It mattered to him."

CHAPTER 6

"Oh my gosh, Mr. Cross," Sandra whined. "You poor thing."

"I'm okay Sandra, have a seat." Simon gestured to the chair by the bed. Ryder was standing by the bedside table, examining all the dials and buttons like a curious child.

"Jesus, Ryder told me what happened. He's been taking care of everything for you sir, and everyone wishes you well." Sandra glanced at Ryder and he winked at her warmly.

"What happened with Mansfield?" Simon asked.

"Well, they won't sign without you," Ryder explained. "But they had a look at your story boards and were impressed."

"That's right," Sandra confirmed. "Melinda's been calling every day asking about you. They're good people."

Melinda was the Executive Marketing Director at Mansfield. Sandra ran down the list of all the other contacts that called and Ryder filled Simon in on meetings and upcoming events.

"Have they got wifi in here?" Ryder checked behind the bed stand. "We can hook you up with Skype and do some online meetings. If the doctor okays it, that is."

Sandra was pleased. "That's a great idea."

"Great," Simon muttered. "A meeting in my pyjamas."

The forty-something woman gently grasped his hand. "You'll be back at the office before you know it. Just be thankful you're okay. From what Ryder says, you're lucky to be here."

He looked towards the window, averting his glance from her.

"We'll be back later, buddy. No worries. Listen to the doctor and call me when he's been back to see you, okay?" Ryder tossed Simon his cell phone. "That's about the only thing that survived." He bent down so Sandra couldn't hear. "Be sure to delete those texts, eh?"

Ryder took Sandra's arm and led her out of the room. "I'll be in touch," she smiled weakly. Simon nodded, looking down at his hands.

The door clicked closed and Simon took a deep breath, staring at the phone in his lap. The display indicated several missed calls and texts and he pondered if he was even allowed to have his phone on. The few calls that were interesting were from Tamara, all the others were clients and Nancy. He first read the texts from Tamara, and then listened to her message.

"Thanks for standing me up last night. I waited until midnight and gave up. I hope there's a damn good excuse why you never showed up." Her tone was justifiably snide.

The line clicked off and there were no further messages from her. He looked down at his useless legs. Normally he would make up for failures in bed. It struck him that he would have to think of another way now. The thought rattled him.

He tried to lift his left leg. It was a phantom extension of his body, an appendage that he no longer had rights to. His hand fisted into a ball as he gritted his teeth. Up until now, he told himself that this was temporary, like a strange bout of flu that would be over in a couple of days. When he tried to lift his right leg unsuccessfully, he banged his head forcefully against the headboard in a fit of rage, sending a shooting pain down the back of his neck, which oddly stopped as it hit the middle of his back. The coppery taste of blood came to his mouth as he bit his tongue and breathed through the pain. He closed his eyes tightly and felt for the emergency call button.

Moments later a nurse trotted in. "Mr. Cross? Are you okay?"

"I'm…in pain," he winced. There was an intravenous bag hanging from a metal pole that wasn't attached to the tube leading to his arm. She re-attached it and adjusted the plastic switch at the top of the bag. Within seconds the pain dissipated.

"The doctor should be in to see you soon, but this should be good for now," she explained, watching the speed of the drip. Simon noticed she was very slender and blonde, attractive. Her breasts were large and her shirt could have been a size larger.

He ran his fingers through his hair in a vain attempt to look civilized. She didn't look at him as she adjusted the plastic switch once more and pushed a few buttons on the console above. Scanning her body as she checked the equipment, the pain medication had gone to work and suddenly Simon felt a twinge of audacity. "You think when I'm outta here you'd like to get a drink with me?" he slurred.

She turned towards him and he noticed her nametag. Her name was Nicole.

The smirk on her face wiped the medicated smile off his. "Simon...is it?" She lifted her left hand up so he could see her ring twinkling from the overhead fluorescent lighting. "I'm married."

Simon grimaced facetiously. "Makes no difference to me." Then he paused. "Err...how big is he?"

Nurse Nicole took a deep breath and released it quickly, blowing a sprig of hair out of her eyes, as she watched the drip work faster. She pasted on a smile. "He's *much* bigger than you...good night, Mr. Cross."

His eyes got heavier as he watched her tight rear walk away. Surrendering to the medicine, he fell into a deep sleep.

. . .

"Mr. Cross?" a familiar voice said. "Are you okay?"

Simon opened his eyes and saw Dr. Bennett at his feet and another doctor he didn't recognize.

"Mr. Cross, this is Dr. Flamborough. He's the neurologist I told you about?"

THE WHEELS OF CHANGE

Dr. Flamborough was tall and slender, the direct opposite of Dr. Bennett. He had uncovered Simon's feet and looked like he was playing 'This Little Piggy'.

"Mr. Cross, can you feel this?" Dr. Flamborough wiggled one toe and looked at Simon.

"No. Just in my hip a little."

Dr. Flamborough pursed his lips. "Vibration in the hip is good." His tone was not convincing. "What's your pain scale? 10 being the worst."

"I don't feel any pain, the nurse gave me something."

"Where was the pain before?"

"My neck…I…err…slammed my head into the wall." He fidgeted with the fold of his sheet.

Dr. Flamborough exhaled sharply. "Mr. Cross, it's very important that you remain as still as possible. The bones and surrounding tissue in your spine are swollen. Movement will interrupt the healing process and ruin your chances of ever walking again."

Dr. Bennettt intervened. "Would you like to talk to a counsellor?"

"You mean a *shrink*?"

"It isn't uncommon for people in your condition to require counselling. We have services available here if you'd like to talk to someone."

"There's no freakin' way I'm talkin' to no quack. It's bad enough I've got doctors poking and prodding me."

Dr. Bennett nodded. Dr. Flamborough looked up, letting go of Simon's big toe. "Suit yourself, Mr. Cross. But just beware of the risks."

Both doctors headed for the door. Dr. Flamborough looked back before exiting. "I'll be back in a couple of days to assess you. We're looking at surgery towards the end of next week most likely."

"Sure. Thanks."

43

He didn't hear the door close. Nancy's head poked in. "Simon. How are you feeling?" She sat on the chair and looked at him intently. "I came in a while ago and you were out like a light."

"The nurse gave me something."

Nancy looked up at the drip and nodded. "Feeling better now?"

"Yeah."

"So what did the doctor say?"

"Surgery next week."

Nancy looked at her feet. "Simon. I know this is a bad time. But I need to ask you a favour."

"What is it?"

"Well, I finally got in touch with a pool repair guy. I need a deposit."

CHAPTER 7

SIX YEARS EARLIER

When the last of his ten year old beard fell into the sink, he put down the clippers and reached for the razor. *The ponytail stays* he said to himself. Part of his reluctance was fear that it wouldn't grow back, the other part was simply that he wasn't going that far. The feel of naked skin on his face was very foreign, almost chilling.

Ryder checked his hair in the mirror as he finished shaving. Satisfied, he glanced at his watch. His appointment with Glen Somers was at nine thirty, it was almost eight and he had to travel across town. He had another appointment at three with Wendy Rogers, marking his sixth meeting with an advertiser that week. He switched off the light and threw some of his dirty dishes into the sink to wash later.

The bachelor pad was a total mess; he had a couple of friends over the previous night to play poker. His buddy Chuck was getting married the following weekend and his fiancé was strictly against strip joints, so he had to settle for his second choice. Ryder silently promised himself he would never marry a controlling woman like that. He met plenty of biker chicks at his shop, but none so far were marriage material. Ryder was looking for a sweet girl, one who wanted a family but who liked the odd cruise up the coast once in a while, not one who lived only for the road.

As he picked his crisp, new dress pants out of his closet, he hoped his junk food binge the previous night hadn't ruined the nice fit he'd achieved at the store. Thankfully, his stomach was forgiving, and he vowed to go easy on the breakfast buffet at the IHOP. His shirt gracefully concealed the slight beer belly.

When he was done dressing, he shuffled through the pile of business cards he acquired through the week and selected the two remaining advertisers he made appointments with. He picked Brett Carmichael's card and remembered the visit with him the previous day, before buying the suit.

"Nice to meet you, Mr. Ryder. Sorry for the wait," Mr. Carmichael had said, giving Ryder a firm handshake.

The office was huge and filled with stuffy leather chairs, mirroring the furniture style in the waiting room.

"Geez. All you need is a baby grand piano in here," Ryder said, straightening the torn belt on his jeans.

Mr. Carmichael pasted on a smile. "Err...yes."

"So what can we do for you? My secretary Bethany claims you own a bike shop?" he said like it was a bad taste in his mouth.

A woman, Ryder assumed was Bethany, suddenly entered the room and gracefully handed both men a cup of coffee without eye contact. Ryder smiled a thank you even though she didn't look at him. She turned on her heels and walked out, closing the door behind her.

"That's right," Ryder answered.

"And what kind of bikes do you sell?" Mr. Carmichael took a sip of coffee like he just graduated head of the class in charm school. He held the small cup delicately with two fingers, making sure his pinky was angled upward.

"Mostly vintage Harleys, but I also sell later models, and I do the odd repair." Ryder struggled with the small coffee cup and his large beard.

"And what does the average sale net you, sir?"

"Err...well, that depends. I have a model in the shop that just sold for $200,000."

"Really." Mr. Carmichael tried to look impressed. "And is that an average sale or is it rare for you to sell a bike worth that much?"

Ryder suddenly felt like the only monkey in a room full of peacocks.

"Well, that was a top of the line model. It took me over a year to sell that one. The others usually sell for around $20,000. That's why I'm here. I believe in karma."

He finally managed to take a sip of coffee, and got his beard inside the coffee cup. Coffee dripped all over his semi-white, sort-of-clean shirt.

"Y...Yes." Mr. Carmichael handed him a napkin out of a polished silver canister on the desk. His face was scrunched slightly, as if Ryder passed gas.

"Sir. If I may. Can I suggest another advertising agency?" Mr. Carmichael said, flipping through his Rolodex. "Tracy Stones is a wonderful advertiser. She's just over on the other side of town, actually. She'd be more than happy to speak to you about your...err...needs."

"Stones? Yeah. I've seen her already," Ryder said, mopping up the rest of the coffee from his shirt. He rose. "Thanks for your time." Mr. Carmichael did not extend his hand, instead he stood at attention and led Ryder to the door.

"Have a nice day."

"Thanks," Ryder said, looking at the man's hand. Then he pursed his lips and pasted on a smile, turning on his heels.

"I wonder if I'd get better fuckin' service if I'd paid for my goddamn coffee," Ryder said under his breath as he walked out the door and headed for the IHOP.

. . .

When Simon graduated from UCLA, he was knee deep in debt from student loans. He was also in the process of putting together a business plan and at the same time, shopping around for a business partner and a bank that would give him credit to get started. The stress was overwhelming.

Simon had to meet with the bank. He and Nancy were having breakfast at the IHOP and his nerves were showing. He heard laughter as he leaned over the toilet bowl. He knew there was only one other person in the bathroom.

"The food here isn't that bad, is it?" the voice asked.

"Nah. I haven't eaten yet."

The man laughed again. "Ah, you tied one on last night, did ya?"

"I wish," Simon scoffed, opening up the door.

The man was standing at the urinal off to the side. "Pregnant?" he joked.

Simon shook his head, smiling. "God, no." He washed his hands and pulled the bottle of Pepto out of his jacket pocket.

"I think I've got an ulcer or something. Burns like a son of a bitch."

"Jesus man, you stressed out much?" he asked, zipping up his pants.

As Simon sipped the last of his new bottle, the man stood beside him and washed his hands.

"You okay there, buddy?"

"Yeah." He tossed the empty bottle into the trash. "I've got a meeting with the bank."

Simon bent over and splashed cold water on his face.

"You in some kind of trouble?" he asked, and then checked himself as he lifted his hands up in surrender. "Pardon me for interfering." He extended his hand. "I'm Ryder."

Simon shook his hand. "Nah, that's okay. I'm trying to get a loan. I just graduated and I want to start up a business. Name's Simon Cross."

Ryder was impressed. "No kidding. What kind of business?"

"I'm in advertising. I've been working my pants off in school. I was on the Dean's list and did a ton of volunteer and part time work. My nerves are shot."

Ryder turned around, leaned against the sink and crossed his arms over his chest. "No shit. I got a bike shop here and I've been looking all over for advertising from someone who's *not an asshole.*" Then he laughed. "Somehow I don't think *you're* an asshole."

He offered Simon a paper towel from the receptacle beside him. "I try not to be," Simon admitted. "Although you'd have to check with my mother, she's at our table."

"Yeah. You're *definitely not an asshole.* Anyone who takes his *mom* out for breakfast at the IHOP is pretty decent in my book."

"I'm Gus," he said. "But everyone calls me Ryder, that's my last name." Ryder scratched his chin in thought and then extended his hand again. "Simon. You're hired." Ryder said firmly. "Does that help you out?"

"Kind of. Having a client doesn't hurt."

Ryder tipped his head. "What kind of money do you need?"

Simon rubbed his face up and down and sighed. "Like a hundred grand or so."

Ryder's face relaxed. "Cancel your bank appointment, my man." He put his arm around Simon's shoulder.

Simon looked at Ryder like he had suddenly sprouted cauliflower from his ears. "What the hell are you talking about?"

"I just sold a Harley Davidson 1932 DAH Hillclimber last week." He looked at Simon like he should understand.

Simon shook his head. "So?"

"It sold for $200,000."

His eyes widened. "Are you serious? What the hell do you need advertising for, then?"

"You said you just graduated from UCLA, right?"

"That's right."

"The market here in Kansas is okay, but I want to venture out...to LA."

Simon's eyebrows lifted.

"You see?"

"But we just met. So far all you know about me is that I puke and have breakfast with my mom. You're going to loan me a hundred grand out of the blue? Somehow I don't buy it."

His hand was still around Simon's shoulder and he gripped it harder, causing Simon's head to bob from side to side. "Simon, trust me. Let me treat you to breakfast and I'll tell you all about what kind of shitty advertisers are out here," he chuckled. "You're *definitely* not one of them."

...

Nancy was sitting at the table, gnawing at a hangnail. Her foot was tapping on the floor like she was waiting for bad news. When she saw Simon approach the table, she immediately rose. "Simon? Are you okay? I was about to get the waiter to check on you."

"I'm fine mom. This is Gus...err...Ryder."

"Nancy." She furrowed her brows. "What, you two met in the bathroom?"

"Yep. What a story we can tell the grandkids, eh?" Ryder chuckled.

"So what is it? Gus or Ryder?" Nancy sat back down.

"Everyone calls me Ryder. I own a bike shop."

Nancy nodded and then looked at Simon. "Are you feeling okay? You like kind of pale."

"I'll be fine now. I don't need to go to the bank." He looked at Ryder.

Nancy was confused and thought perhaps her son was joking. "What do you mean? Did you find money in the toilet or something?"

"No. Ryder here's going to loan me the money in exchange for my services," he said, trying the explanation on for size despite how ridiculous it sounded.

THE WHEELS OF CHANGE

Nancy laughed. "Really? Are you like a millionaire or something?"

"Not exactly, ma'am."

The waiter brought glasses of water and instructed them as to where the breakfast buffet was, like they had never been there before, even though they came every week and saw the same waiter.

"Well, how are you going to loan him the money?" Nancy asked Ryder.

"I have it. I've been in business for five years now and I'm looking to expand."

"How much can you loan him?" Nancy asked like it was a big secret, turning toward him as though she didn't want Simon to hear.

"Mom!"

She blushed. "But, Simon. I need money too."

"Don't worry, mom," Simon said flatly. "You'll get your money."

CHAPTER 8

Ryder walked into Simon's room carrying a large basket full of socks, scarves, sunglasses and various accessories. Simon's eyes popped open when he spotted the 'Mansfield' label.

"You're kidding, right?" Simon said as Ryder placed the basket on his lap. The sensation was odd, like someone had given him a large shot of novocaine in both legs.

"Nope," Ryder said. "Apparently Mansfield executives live under rocks." He pulled up a chair and sat beside him. "You know they never saw the commercial we did for Crabtree?" Ryder chuckled. "Melinda pulled it up on YouTube and showed Nancy, the head chair, and apparently they both cried their eyes out watching the kid proposing to his little girlfriend."

"You're joking," Simon smiled.

"No. They had a meeting this morning and sent this basket of goodies over for you. We're hired." He offered Simon a high five.

Ryder changed the subject. "So what's the doctor sayin'?"

"Surgery next week."

Ryder scratched his head. "Oh yeah? You stuck here until then?"

"Far as I know."

Ryder lifted his chin. "Hey, what are you going to do about your place? I mean, if...if um...if you can't walk? Don't you need to build a ramp and

THE WHEELS OF CHANGE

get some wheelchair access or something?"

"I haven't thought about it."

"Hmm. I can make some calls if you want."

He waved Ryder off. "Nah. Thanks. I'll get my mom to do that. She needs to keep busy, this place gives her the jitters."

The door opened and two police officers entered. Ryder rose and stood beside Simon. With his modest bulk, he met the height and frame of one officer, but the other was shorter and younger.

The older one looked at Simon. "Simon Cross?"

"Yes, sir. What can I do for you?" Simon was suddenly conscious of the fact that he was in his pyjamas in a room full of large, fully dressed men.

"I'm Officer Crow and this is Constable Garner. We have some questions regarding the recent motor vehicle accident you were involved in."

Officer Crow looked at Ryder. "Would you mind giving us a moment, sir?"

Simon interjected. "Err...this is my business partner, Gus Ryder. He probably knows more about this than I do."

Officer Crow nodded assent.

Constable Garner opened his black notepad and removed the pen from his upper left breast pocket. He looked at Simon.

"I have confirmation from our investigator that your brake lines were intentionally cut. Were you aware of that, Mr. Cross?" Officer Crow asked.

"That's what I heard from my friend Ryder." He glanced at Ryder, who nodded confirmation.

"Do you have any idea who might have done this?" Constable Garner lifted his head and began tapping the pen impatiently.

Ryder intervened. "Some yahoo apparently came into the office that afternoon and threatened Simon. We're pretty sure he's the culprit."

Simon looked at Ryder the same way he used to look at his mother when she used to speak for him as a child. Only this time he felt like saying *'I lost the use of my legs, not my tongue.'*

Crow looked down at Simon. "Do you know this person's name?"

He sighed and rolled his eyes up at Ryder. "I don't want any trouble, Officer."

The Officer crossed his arms and spread his feet apart slightly. "Mr. Cross, attempted murder is a felony in the state of California. Unless you cut your own brake lines in a suicide attempt, I suggest you cooperate."

Simon nodded. "I don't know his first name, but his last name is Dunphy. He's married to Clara Dunphy and he works for Mars Construction."

Constable Garner was writing feverishly. "Is that over by the Prince George Hotel?"

"Yeah," Simon said.

"And what is your affiliation with Mr. Dunphy?" Officer Crow asked.

"I don't have any affiliation with him. I met him once."

"Do you have any proof that he's the one who did this?"

Ryder intervened again. "We have security cameras in the parking lot. I can get the tapes for you if you like."

"That won't be necessary, Mr. Ryder. They'll be subpoenaed for evidence."

Ryder nodded and stared at his feet.

"Mr. Cross, if you don't have any affiliation with Mr. Dunphy, what do you think his motive is?"

This was the moment Nancy chose to storm into the room. The door flew open and she entered, breathless. "Simon! Simon, what's going on?

THE WHEELS OF CHANGE

The nurses said I couldn't come in, that you were being questioned by the cops?" She eyed both police men as Constable Garner made a ghost of a move toward retrieving his pistol, a natural reaction to the explosive interruption.

"Ma'am! Ma'am!" Officer Crow insisted. "Ma'am, if you'll please give us a moment. We're conducting an investigation here." He grabbed her gently by the shoulders and Ryder took her arm and directed her toward the foot of the bed, away from the two police men.

"Mom, I'm fine. Just relax."

Officer Crow watched Nancy sit and avert her glance to the window. He turned toward Simon. "Mr. Cross, once again, what motivation would Mr. Dunphy have to make an attempt on your life?"

"You find the bastard who did this to my son!" Nancy seethed.

"Ma'am. If you please. Keep quiet or I'll have to ask you to leave," Constable Garner chided, holding his hand up.

"Mr. Cross?" Officer Crow repeated.

Simon looked away from Nancy. He realized that either way he was sunk. "I had an affair with Mrs. Dunphy," he mumbled. Nancy didn't hear his response.

As Simon spoke, Nancy interrupted. "Who would want to hurt him? He's got such a good name around here!"

Officer Crow hadn't heard Simon's response, either. "Sir?" Then he turned as Nancy interrupted. "Ma'am, I'm not going to ask you again to keep quiet."

"Well, Simon, why would anyone want to hurt you? I'm afraid for your life, I'm afraid for mine. What if he had a hit put on you? People do crazy things like that around here!"

"Mom, it's nothing like that," he said flatly, feeling his face heat.

"Well then what is it, Simon? Why would some thug cut your brake lines in broad daylight?" Nancy rose and approached Simon with her hands on her waist. The rims of her eyes were pink and he couldn't tell if she was

55

angry or scared or both.

"Ma'am. This is the last time. Sit...down," Constable Garner stated firmly.

She ignored the officer. "Why, Simon? Why?" Nancy insisted, screeching in a tone Simon didn't recognize.

"BECAUSE I SLEPT WITH HIS WIFE, GODDAMMIT!"

Simon expected his mother to look horrified, but instead she looked at him snidely, like he just told her the expensive Rolex watch he bought her for Christmas was really a fake.

"Well, I should have known," she conceded. "The apple doesn't fall far from the tree."

CHAPTER 9

Officer Crow knocked on Mark's office door. Lisa wasn't at her desk. Mark was finishing up a phone call and he waved Crow in and hung up. "What can I do for you, Mitchell?"

"Sir, Constable Garner and I were just in to interview Simon Cross? The attempted murder victim?"

"The Ad Exec., right?"

Mitchell nodded. "Anyway. Something's fishy about it. He doesn't want to press charges."

Mark's eyebrows lifted. "Hmm. What did he say?"

"Apparently he had an affair with the perpetrator's wife. I guess he felt he had it coming or something."

Mark winced, remembering him and Shelley's challenges with adultery in the past. "Well, regardless, charges have to be laid in a felony. If he doesn't want to offer testimony that's his prerogative; he doesn't have to stand trial."

"That's what I thought, sir. But I just wanted you to know what was going on."

Mark nodded in appreciation. "So how is Mr. Cross? You think we'll see any of his annoying billboards up anymore?"

"Not anytime soon, sir. He's in a wheelchair. Not sure what the prognosis is."

"Well, I guess being a pompous, self-fulfilling man-whore doesn't warrant being killed...but it comes close," Mark said, half-jokingly.

Mitchell smiled. "That's exactly what Officer Matthews said."

"Spend too much time with someone and you start to sound alike."

"Apparently so, sir."

...

TWENTY THREE YEARS EARLIER

Nancy lit a cigarette and leaned against the sticky countertop. "Simon, eat your breakfast. Your dad is going to be here any minute to pick you up."

The twelve year old looked down at his cereal, Captain Crunch in milk that smelled funny. Suddenly he was not hungry. The wires in his braces were poking into the side of his cheek; Nancy had missed taking him to the orthodontist again the previous week.

"What's the matter? Is your mouth sore?" She came closer with her cigarette burning in his face.

"A little." He lifted up his spoon as though he was going to eat.

"I'm sorry, baby. I'll make another appointment on Monday, I promise." Then she changed the subject. "So, did dad mention where he's taking you today?"

"Um. No, not really. Maybe to play baseball or go to the movies or something."

Nancy turned around and started aggressively scrubbing the counter. "Yeah. Did Betty Boop go with you the last time?"

"Mom. Her name is Becky, and no, she didn't come." Nancy called her ex-husband's girlfriend Betty Boop because she had black hair and an amazing body.

THE WHEELS OF CHANGE

"Well, make sure he brings you home in time for dinner tomorrow. You need to finish your homework, remember?"

She looked out the window over the sink and saw James's car pull up. "Great, Betty's with him. I'll be in the bathroom."

Nancy stormed out of the kitchen, kissing Simon on the forehead. "Don't forget your bag. It's by the door."

Simon got up and dumped his cereal in the sink, peering out the window. Becky stayed in the car as his dad exited. He finished washing his bowl as James opened the door.

"Hey, Simon. How's it going?" He stuck his hand out, palm up. Simon smacked it. "Your mom around?"

Simon picked up his bag. "Bathroom."

"Why don't you go wait in the car with Becky? I want a quick word with your mother," he said warmly.

"Sure, dad."

. . .

James looked at the light at the bottom of the bathroom door and sighed, running his hand through his hair. He paused and then quietly walked over to the door. As he stood there, he could hear her crying, or so he thought. James was familiar with her sniffling, but not because she cried a lot. He opened the door and found her bent over a small mirror, snorting powder as he suspected.

"You couldn't wait until he left?" James asked coldly.

"What the hell do you want?" Nancy said casually.

"I wanted to talk to you, but clearly you're not able to have a conversation. Some things never change."

She stood upright, pinching the bridge of her nose. "What do you want, James?" It was more of an accusation than a question.

He shook his head and rubbed the back of his neck. "You know, I was starting to feel guilty for leaving you. I blamed myself for so long. How many times did I try to get you help and you just kept coming back, and for no good reason, Nancy?"

He began to roll back and forth on the balls of his feet, "I stopped travelling for work, we went away to Cuba nearly every year. Hell, I even bought you that goddamn car you always wanted. But nothing was ever good enough Nancy, nothing."

Nancy stood, listening while her eyes slowly glazed over. "I asked what you wanted James, not for you to rehash how much of a horrible fucking wife I was."

James laughed without a trace of humour and shook his head again. "Well I guess there's never going to be a good time to tell you this. So what the hell...Becky and I are getting married."

Silence.

Nancy was stunned. James stood with his hands in his pockets, looking at the floor. Suddenly Nancy lunged at him. "You son of a bitch!" she yelled, throwing a punch at him.

He blocked her with his wrist and took hold of her hand. "Nancy! Control yourself!" he said as she tried to hit him with her other hand.

"Why are you doing this to me? You fucking asshole! After all I did for you!"

James grabbed hold of both her hands and she stopped. Her breathing was rapid and her hair was all over her face. "I'm going to let go of you now, but you have to calm down," he said softly. When he released her she stood there and he wiped the hair out of her face. She watched him, confused. He looked at her like the sick person she was, like he was about to ask if she needed to lie down. A tear fell down her cheek and she folded herself into his arms. James put an arm around her and stroked her hair with his other hand.

"Why don't I take Simon for a while? So you can get some help."

Nancy sobbed. "Don't ever take my son from me. He's all I have."

James gently took her shoulders in his hands. "I would never take him

THE WHEELS OF CHANGE

from you. But you can't look after him when you're like this."

She swallowed, blinking, and took a step closer. "Promise me something?"

"Anything."

"He looks so much like you, James. Every time I look at him I see you. It's bad enough you have to look at me the way you are; I don't ever want him to give me that same look," she sniffled. "Please don't tell him."

James brushed a tear from her face. "I never have."

CHAPTER 10

The faint sound of a chair scraping across the floor caused Simon to open his eyes. "Err...sorry, Simon. I didn't mean to wake you," Ryder said.

He rubbed his eyes. "What time is it?"

"Nearly seven." Ryder cleared his throat. "How are you feeling? Any news from the doctor?"

"Nah. I've been sleeping a while and nobody's come in. I'm having some screwed up dreams, though."

"Oh yeah? Good or bad?"

"The one I had earlier was a hot one about Tamara. But the one just now was really fucked up...about my parents."

Ryder screwed his face up. "Have you heard from your dad lately?"

"No. He went on vacation. I think he should be back now."

"Well, brace yourself." Ryder pulled his chair closer. "Anyone who doesn't know about what happened to you will know now."

"What do you mean?"

"Max Dunphy was arrested. It's all over the local news. It hasn't hit national yet, but it won't be long."

"Jesus Christ," Simon muttered. "So I guess the cops got hold of the

THE WHEELS OF CHANGE

tapes."

"Yep. Sandra said they came earlier. It wasn't hard to pinpoint him," Ryder explained. "Dumb fuck wore his Mars Construction shirt and there was a big sticker with the logo on his toolbox. At least he was smart enough to leave his truck at home."

Simon shook his head in disbelief.

"You know he has priors?"

"No. What for?"

"You name it: assault, carrying an unregistered weapon, a couple of restraining orders. This is his first felony though," Ryder chuckled. "You broke his cherry, man."

"And his wife's, too," Simon joked.

Ryder lifted a finger, mocking disapproval. "You better watch that, mister. You nearly got yourself killed."

"Ah," Simon grunted and waved.

Ryder changed the subject. "I called a couple of places to get your house retrofitted for wheelchair access."

"Oh yeah?"

"They say it'll take a couple of days. Apparently it's nothing major, just a ramp at your rear entrance, some grab bars in your bathroom and bedroom. I've already been through to move stuff around. Thankfully, your house is pretty big so access won't be a problem."

"Good. Thanks."

The door opened and Nurse Nicole entered, carrying her caddy. "Ah, you're awake."

"Very much so, now," Simon said silkily, running his fingers through his hair.

She glared at him as she unravelled the cuff for the blood pressure

SANDY APPLEYARD

monitor.

"This is my buddy, Ryder," Simon said. Ryder nodded and smiled.

Simon watched her pull his arm toward her and attached the cuff to his upper left arm. He resisted the urge to cop a feel of her breast. As she pumped up the pressure on the cuff, Simon inhaled deeply, smelling her light floral scent. "You smell divine."

She watched the dial on the cuff. She was nonplussed. "It's Bounce..."

He eyed her up and down. "Would you?" he joked.

Ryder rolled his eyes. "You'll have to forgive my friend, ma'am," he explained apologetically. "Since his accident, Simon lacks...tact."

Nurse Nicole was not impressed. She removed the cuff roughly and smirked. "It's a dryer sheet, Mr. Cross. We're not allowed to wear perfume in the hospital."

She checked the level of his urine bag and the saline drip, as well as the other liquids they had pumping through him. "How's your pain?" she asked, with her hand on her hip. Her face was still sour.

He looked at her breasts. "Fine, sweetheart."

"My face is up here, Mr. Cross," she pointed.

"Call me Simon."

"I'll call you whatever you want, Simon, if you'll stop flirting with me. Don't you know how to take a hint? I told you I'm married, and even if I wasn't married, I still wouldn't be interested in a filthy...invalid like you." She gave him an evaluating glance.

The smile wiped off his face like he'd been slapped.

She wasn't finished. "I've got news for you, Simon. Women don't like to be treated like playthings. I don't care how much money you have; yeah, I know who you are, I watch local television. You think you're some big wig advertising exec. and you can get into any girl's pants you want. But some women value their marriage and don't appreciate being pawed at by some home wrecking pig like you."

She stormed out, letting the door slam behind her.

"She must have watched the news today," Ryder surmised. "You better lay low for a while."

"She had no right to talk to me like that," he argued.

"You *asked* for it." Ryder's voice raised an octave. "Look, I'd do anything for you, you know that. But this shit *has to stop*. Haven't you learned *anything?*" He paused, his face was upturned and there was a blue vein popping out of his neck. "I hate to tell you this, but…look. I *love* my wife. If someone ever fucked around with her *I'd kill him, too.*"

Simon stiffened. "So then why the FUCK did you tell me to press charges?" he yelled.

Ryder rose. "Because it's YOU, Simon. Even though I don't agree with your lifestyle, it doesn't mean I won't protect you." His finger pointed at Simon. "If that guy tried to kill you and failed, you can be damn straight he'll try it again. If it wasn't *you* I wouldn't give a shit. Let the *fucker* get away with murder. I would have done the same!"

The door opened slowly. They stopped yelling at once. A tall, large breasted woman walked in. Ryder took a breath and ran his hands through his hair. He recognized her from the office, it was Tamara.

She eyed both of them. "I…is this a bad time?"

Simon waved her in. "Hey, what are you doing here?"

"I saw what happened on the news." She hesitated. "I haven't heard from you in days."

"I'll leave you two alone," Ryder said. "See ya later." He glared at Simon but nodded to Tamara.

She waited for the door to close. "So tell me…what the hell happened? Some guy tried to kill you?" Her voice was cold and flat.

"Yeah, apparently."

Tamara looked at Simon and smiled, but it didn't reach her eyes. "Well,

I guess you had it coming…seeing as you fucked his wife."

Shit.

"Are you mad at me too?" he scoffed.

"Simon, I know we weren't exactly exclusive, but Jesus Christ!"

"You've got nothing to worry about. It's over with her."

"I guess it is." She waved her hand down the length of his bed, demonstrating the predicament he was in.

Simon glared at her. "I meant I ended it…*before* this happened."

"So were you with her the other day? Before you called?"

"What difference does that make?"

"I don't like to be second choice, Simon."

"Well you're not anymore. I told you it's over with her."

Tamara stared at the floor. "So, what happens now?" she asked quietly.

"What do you mean?"

"Well, are you paralyzed now? Does anything *work* anymore?" her voice quivered.

Simon drew in a deep breath. "Not at the moment."

She swallowed. Her eyes looked glassy.

"Are you okay?" Simon asked.

She sniffed and blinked tightly. "Simon, I can't do this."

"What? What can't you do?"

Tamara waved her hands up and down the length of the bed again. "*This,*" she explained. "I can't do *this.*"

Simon bobbed his head up and down. "I never asked you to."

Silence.

She was about to say something, but Simon cut her off. "Goodbye Tamara." He looked at her and nodded.

Tamara walked out, looking at the floor. The door slammed behind her. There was a pitcher sitting on the nightstand, within arm's reach, half full of water and semi-melted ice cubes. Simon picked it up and threw it across the room in a fit of rage. It banged into the window and the water splashed across the glass. The pitcher landed on the floor with a thud. Water dripped down the wall and that's when Simon realized that he couldn't get up to clean it.

It hit him. This was what his life might be like forever.

CHAPTER 11

"Well, it looks like the swelling has almost disappeared, Simon." Dr. Bennett wheeled Simon back to his room after an MRI scan. "We can do the surgery first thing tomorrow. Does that sound good for you?"

"Sure. What's the prognosis?"

"Well, we'll go in and try to decompress and repair the injury in your spine."

Dr. Bennett parked Simon in the room and adjusted the side bars and head rest so he could sit up properly.

He wiggled himself up higher. "And if that doesn't work?"

"If that doesn't work, we'll do stem cell treatment."

"What's that?"

"Good question. We take healthy stem cells from our donor bank and inject them into the parts of your spine that have been damaged. This helps to promote movement and sensation in your body. Hopefully the result will be a return to normal mobility and function."

Simon was impressed. "Hmm. Sounds interesting."

"It is. It may take several injections, but the therapy has been proven very effective in spinal cord injuries. You're an excellent candidate seeing as your injuries are still fresh."

THE WHEELS OF CHANGE

"So how quickly can I go home?"

"After we decompress the spine and adjoining structures, you can probably go home in a day or two. Stem cell surgery can't happen until everything is healed and all the swelling has disappeared."

"How long will that take?"

"Probably a month. Maybe less. We'll do weekly follow ups to see where you are."

Simon nodded.

"Do you have somewhere to stay? You'll need someone to care for you."

"Great," Simon murmured.

The doctor grabbed a char and sat next to Simon. "Simon, you are going to need someone to change your dressings, your diapers..."

He shouted, interrupting him. "What? Diapers?"

"Simon, you have no bowel or bladder control. You know you've had bags for that since you've been here."

Simon's heart started to pump hard. "Will that be forever?" his voice cracked.

"There are no guarantees, Simon. But I'm hopeful you'll make a good recovery."

He swallowed, fighting the lump in his throat. Without numbing medication, reality was kicking in hard.

"What the hell am I supposed to do? I have a business to run, a life to lead...this is a fuckin' nightmare!"

The doctor reached for the side of the bed; he seemed afraid to touch Simon.

"Simon, to be frank, you're lucky to be alive. That transport truck you hit could've easily killed you. You could have suffered a severe head injury, or worse."

"Worse?" Simon hissed. "Worse than this?" He could feel his face heat up. "Doc. No offense, but I'm thirty five years old, unmarried, and a full fledged advertising executive. Nothing is worse than this!"

"Dead would be worse, Simon."

He chewed on his finger. "I think I'd *rather* be dead."

Dr. Bennett sighed. "Simon, lots of people lead very fulfilling lives from a wheelchair. There are very few limitations nowadays. The only limitations will be those you put on yourself."

Simon looked up at the doctor. His mind began to reel. He'd completely forgotten about a wheelchair. The thought made him want to wretch. *How the fuck am I going to get around in a goddamn chair? So much for my car, my life, sex…how the fuck am I going to ever have sex? What woman in their right mind is ever going to want with me…ever again! The words 'hang on a second honey, can I get you to change my diaper first?' come to mind. What the fuck!* "Will I ever walk again, I mean, what are the chances?" his voice trembled.

"Walk again? I would give you a twenty percent chance. But having your other functions restored, I'd give it fifty percent."

The way he answered was like he was announcing lottery statistics, and it made Simon want to punch him in the face.

"Twenty percent chance. That's just fuckin' wonderful!"

Dr. Bennett rose. "I should leave you alone. Let you think." He patted the bed twice and left.

As soon as the door closed, it opened again and Nancy appeared. "Hi, Simon," she said. "I hear there's good news?"

"Yeah," he scoffed unconvincingly. "Real good."

She looked confused. "The doctor told me your spine isn't swollen. You can have your surgery."

"A lot of good this is all going to do," he retorted. "I've only got a twenty percent chance to walk after it."

Nancy cocked her head to the side. "Simon. Be hopeful. I've spoken to the doctor and he says he doesn't want to get your hopes up."

He ignored her statement. "I need somewhere to stay mom." His tone was cold.

"Well, you can stay with me...but Ryder's getting your house ready, isn't he?"

Simon nodded reluctantly.

"Well then it's settled." She hugged him. "Oh, this will be fun! You haven't stayed with me since before you went off to college!"

CHAPTER 12

TWO WEEKS LATER

Mark's phone sat quietly on the dresser, both Shelley's and Mark's clothes lay in various piles on the floor and the bed sheets were knotted between them. The bed swayed gently in a rocking motion and the sound of passionate lovemaking was being overheard by nobody but Mabel, their nosey next door neighbor.

"Mark," Shelley breathed. "Did you remember to close the window?"

Mark opened his eyes as Shelley broke him from his reverie. "No..." He gently began sucking her nipple as she moaned.

"I think we've saved Mabel a lifetime of porn with all the stuff she hears." Shelley wrapped her legs tighter around Mark's waist.

"That's the best compliment I've heard in a while," he said, grinding into her deeper.

"Oh...Mark," Shelley cried. "I love it when you do that." She lifted herself up to kiss him deeply. "That's what you get for wearing that sheer nightie to bed." He surrendered his tongue to her mouth.

Shelley grabbed a handful of his salt and pepper hair and began sucking his neck. "Easy, Vampira. No marks please," he said, although his tone said *please don't stop*.

Mark's physique over the years had changed little. Shelley could still sit

THE WHEELS OF CHANGE

in his lap and ride him like she did when they first married nearly thirty years ago. Despite his past heart attack, his body was strong and agile. Being married to the Chief of Police certainly had benefits.

She found his nipples with her hands and mouth and sucked hard. "Marks are okay here, right?" she teased. Mark's head swayed back as his hands caressed her rear end and he pumped her up and down, finding her warmth and wetness. Shelley's physique also changed little over the years. Yoga classes and a strict diet were to thank for that.

Mark lifted Shelley up slightly and pushed his legs to the other side, so Shelley was on top. Pleased to find her breasts, Mark began sucking and fondling as Shelley bobbed up and down, feeling herself getting closer to climax. Mark could feel her insides tighten and he slowed down, enjoying the hugging sensation.

"Mmmm…god that's good," Mark whispered. He felt the depths of her as he slid all the way in and out again. She grabbed her breasts and began kneading them, desperate to find her release. "Hey, those are mine," Mark said, rising up and lowering Shelley back on the bed.

Shelley's back arched as Mark sucked and twisted her nipples gently and suddenly her breath became quicker as he felt the familiar pulsing inside her. He bowed his head as his eyes rolled upward and he climaxed with her. As the bed began to tap against the wall, the phone rang. The first and second ring was drowned out by the bed and their lovemaking, but the third ring Mark heard.

He took a deep breath. "Great timing." He leaned over to look at the screen. "Great," he griped. Shelley knew the tone.

Mark cleared his throat. "Tame here."

"Sir, it's Nelson. There's been another murder. I'm texting you the address."

"Thank you. Where's Matthews?"

"Err…I tried to get a hold of him, but there's no answer on his home or cell phone."

Mark looked at his watch. Wednesday was date night for Richard and Lisa. "I'll catch him on the way in."

He dressed quickly and gave Shelley a chaste kiss on the lips; she'd remade the bed and was half asleep. "I'll see you later, babe." Mark grabbed his phone and blew her a kiss on the way out but her eyes were closed.

The address was six minutes from Richard's house according to the GPS. Mark reached for the cherry out of the back seat and hoisted it over his head on to the roof. As he approached the neighborhood where the Matthews' lived he watched an otherwise quiet, sleeping block of houses turn lights on and neighbours peek out of their front windows. Richard's car was parked in the driveway and his house was still. Moments later, Richard appeared in his bathrobe. He was still looping the sash around his waist as he opened the front door, shielding his eyes from the red lights.

"Murder on Grillham St.," Mark called. "Get dressed."

Richard lowered his head and turned back into the house. Mark waved to Lisa, who was peering out of the master bedroom window. He couldn't tell if her face was red from embarrassment or from the reflection of the cherry beaming in her face.

Minutes later Richard walked up to the car. Sliding into the passenger side, his face was solemn. Mark put his hand on Richard's knee. "I got interrupted, too."

Richard looked up with a half a smile.

Mark mirrored his expression. "But I didn't shut my phones off."

Richard was about to argue when Mark put his hand up, cutting him off. "You went against protocol."

Richard sulked. "So what have we got?"

"Nelson called me. I don't have much to go on except an address."

Mark pulled out of the driveway and put the siren back on, sped up and watched Richard fire up the laptop.

"Chief Tame here. We're en route to Grillham St. ETA five minutes," Mark barked into the radio.

"Copy," said Nelson.

They pulled onto Grillham St., which was all but a vacant lot with one large home. There were only three houses on the parcel of land, covered by greenery and a small church.

"Hell of a place to murder someone," Richard commented.

Mark was thankful Richard had gotten over his huff. "I wonder if there's a cemetery behind that church."

"Makes murder more efficient."

The Crime Scene Investigation truck was already there along with two other cruisers, one belonging to Nelson.

"Paul, what have we got?" Mark asked the coroner as he entered the large house.

The body was right in the entranceway, like the victim tried to leave right before he was murdered. A small marble staircase led into the house; it had blood pooled in the shape of a kidney around the victim. Inside the house was a black baby grand piano with the lid up and a large, tear shaped crystal chandelier hanging above. The spiralling staircase leading to the upper floor was flanked by a balcony, allowing a view right across.

Mark whistled as he followed the marble tile into each room upstairs. "This guy is riiiiich."

"Chase McCann. Never heard of him myself," Paul commented, handing Mark the victim's wallet with his identification.

"He's in the media," Nelson volunteered. "Big time reporter on one of the sports stations."

The victim was lying on the polished marble floor, face down. He was slender and the knife edge was sticking out his back, like he'd fallen onto it. Paul, the coroner, turned the victim's head to the side. There was blood coming out of his nose and mouth. His nose appeared to be broken and there was a large bruise on his forehead. "The break and bruise is post mortem. He died before he hit the ground."

"Young guy," Mark commented. "Fit."

Richard chimed in. "You'd think he could run away from his attacker."

"He was probably taken by surprise," Paul added.

"Maybe it was someone he knew." Richard turned to one of the investigators dusting for fingerprints on the door jam. "Any signs of forced entry?"

"None so far. The security alarm was disabled."

"Maybe he used a ruse," Mark speculated. "See if the guy had a security camera. You'd think with a place like this he'd have one. Maybe we can get a shot of the murderer."

ONE WEEK LATER

"There you go, buddy." Ryder hoisted Simon up higher in bed. "Is that better?"

"Yup, thanks."

"So, they had a bail hearing for Max Dunphy. He was granted bail only because this was his first felony. The judge posted bail at $10,000"

"Yeah?" Simon said. "Do you think he's dumb enough to jump it?"

"Nah," Ryder waved. "But I'd make sure your mom locks all her windows and doors at night."

"No problem. Mom's pretty jittery lately, anyway. Besides, unless he plans on rigging my wheels..." He pointed to his shiny new wheelchair on the other side of the bed. "There's not much more damage he can do."

"You got a lawyer?" Ryder asked.

"No. Do I need one?"

"Unfortunately, yes. You probably won't have to testify, but what do I know?" Ryder changed the subject. "How's things going with your mom?"

"Why don't you ask her yourself," Nancy said, coming in the door, carrying a tray of food.

THE WHEELS OF CHANGE

"Sorry about that," Ryder chuckled. "I didn't hear you coming."

Nancy ignored the comment. "We're doing fine, aren't we Simon?" She handed Simon a glass of water and a pill.

He examined the yellow tablet. "What's this one for?"

"It's for pain," she urged, pushing his hand towards his mouth.

"But I'm not *in* pain," Simon argued, pushing back. "That's the problem. I still don't feel anything."

"Nothing?" Nancy said impatiently, like when he was a kid and she was waiting for him to do his business on the potty.

"No...*nothing*." He felt the heat on his face.

"I don't understand," Nancy whined. "The doctor said to give it a week or so. It's been a week. Why isn't anything *happening*?" Nancy was opening up the curtains, trying to hide the fact that she was pacing.

Simon sighed. "Mom, why don't you go relax...take a bath or something."

Nancy looked at him from the corner of her eye. "I'll do no such thing. You know I never take baths."

Ryder looked at Simon, ignoring her comment. "How does the back feel? I heard they did some pretty invasive shit back there."

Simon took a sip of water and answered. "It feels fine. I would have bet money it would have hurt a hell of a lot more. I almost wish I did feel pain, just so I would know there's something happening."

Suddenly Nancy turned around. "Simon. You just reminded me, um, I need you to write me a cheque."

Simon looked over as she folded up his laundered clothes and placed them into the dresser. "What for?"

"Well, I had to buy a bunch of medical supplies for you, all those bandages and diapers and things."

He winced when she mentioned the diapers. "Okay, okay mom." He held his hand out like he was trying to stop traffic. "How much do you need?"

"I don't know...a couple of hundred. I have to buy groceries, too. I forgot how much you can eat."

Ryder rose and pulled his wallet from his back pocket. He removed a wad of cash and gave it to her. "Here you go. Let me know if you need any more."

Nancy smiled a thank you and left the room.

"She okay?" Ryder stuffed his wallet back where it belonged. "Do I want to know why she doesn't take baths?"

Simon waved. "She's got a water phobia. Fell in a pool when she was a kid. Never learned to swim."

"Really?"

"Yeah, but don't mention anything," Simon said quickly. "She's real closed about it. I only found out when I was a kid and wanted her to take a bath with me. She never even told my dad." Simon changed the subject. "When's my place gonna be done?"

"Soon. Why? You need to get outta here?"

"Yeah. This is a fuckin' nightmare. She fusses too much, she's always in my face. It's like she's just waiting for me to get up and walk outta here."

Ryder chuckled. "Maybe you will."

"Believe me, nothing would make me happier."

Suddenly Nancy walked back in the room. "Simon, um, I'm going to need more money."

Simon rolled his eyes. "Fine. Should I just give you a fuckin' blank cheque?" he exclaimed.

Nancy looked up at the ceiling. "Simon. Really. After all I'm doing for

THE WHEELS OF CHANGE

you?"

"Jesus Christ!" he shouted. "Do you want me to get out? Believe me, I'd love to get out!" He reached for the wheelchair. It was too far for him, so he was just waving in the air. Ryder saw him struggling and walked over to the wheelchair.

"Relax buddy, I've got it." He helped Simon into the chair and fixed his feet so they were sitting on the metal plates.

"I need air, man," Simon said as Ryder wheeled him past his mom.

"You don't understand, Simon." Nancy insisted as they walked towards the door. "I need things. I've been busy taking care of you," she explained to deaf ears.

Ryder closed the door and wheeled Simon over to the swing on the porch. He parked the wheelchair beside the swing and applied the lock. Then he sat on the swing.

"What's up with your mom?" Ryder whispered. "She's edgy."

"I don't know." He scratched his head. "She hasn't had anyone stay with her in years. It's probably just the adjustment."

"I'll get the guys to rush on your place. I'd offer you to stay with me, but my place is too small, you wouldn't get your wheels through there."

"That's okay. I appreciate it. How's Mansfield coming along?"

"Good. Sandra's working on the idea boards today. I'll bring them over tomorrow."

Simon shivered. "Damn. One thing about being immobile, you sure feel the cold."

"You want me to get you a blanket?"

"Sure. Linen closet's right next to the bathroom." He rubbed his arms.

Ryder rose and entered the house. He listened first to see if Nancy was in earshot. Nothing. He walked over to the hallway beside the kitchen and remembered that all the doors in the house were identical. There were two doors closed beside the guest bedroom. Ryder took a guess and opened one.

When the door opened, he saw Nancy hunched over the counter, snorting white powder through a straw off a small mirror.

CHAPTER 13

"I don't want a nurse, doc," Simon said to Dr. Bennett. "Can't I get like an occupational therapist or something? I mean, I'm starting to get some feeling back. Can't someone just help me get mobile?"

"I suppose we could do that. They have occupational therapists that are trained in nursing as well." Dr. Bennett scratched his chin. "It would be awfully expensive though, Simon."

"I don't care," Simon urged. "Money's no object."

Dr. Bennett's eyebrows lifted. "Well then, I can look into it right away."

"Make sure it's not some old hag with a Ben-Gay addiction or anything," Simon advised. "I respond much better to women my age. Attractive women," he added pointedly.

Dr. Bennett shook his head, chuckling. "I have no control over the physical appearance of our staff, other than that they're dressed appropriately and carry themselves respectfully," he smiled. "But it is nice to hear you back to yourself again."

Simon looked up, confused. "How do you know anything about me before this shit happened?"

The doctor rose, patting Simon's leg. "Not to worry, Simon." He changed the subject. "Now, I've got you booked for a stem cell injection with Dr. Flamborough tomorrow. Do you have any questions regarding that?"

THE WHEELS OF CHANGE

"No. Not really. Do I need to stay in the hospital?"

"Just for the day. We need to ensure you don't have any adverse reactions to the treatment. It's almost like getting a transplant in that we'll inject the healthy donor cells into your spinal cavity. As long as you don't react in about twelve hours, you're free to go home."

"Will it work?"

"There's a possibility it will, Simon. But an equal possibility that it won't."

"Great," Simon grunted.

...

"Chief!" Lisa called over to Mark from her desk. Mark was walking back from the washroom. "Call for you. Some woman from the bank? Says she knew Jake Campbell?"

"That's one of our murder victims." Mark recalled. "We've already interviewed one guy over there, maybe this lady knows more."

"Line two."

"Thanks." Mark picked up his phone and took a seat, adjusting his collar. "Chief Tame here."

A confident, female voice answered. "Good afternoon, Chief Tame. I'm Laurie McDonald, a former colleague of Jake Campbell."

"Thank you for calling, Ms. McDonald. What can I do for you?"

"Please, call me Laurie."

"Sure, Laurie. My friends call me Mark."

"Mark. I'll level with you," she said in a firm voice. "I knew Jake. I'm not surprised Red didn't tell you much about him."

"Why's that?"

Laurie sighed. "Because Red's a loser. Although I'm sure you're already acquainted with that aspect of his personality."

Mark chuckled under his breath.

"Anyway, Jake was a good looking, kind-hearted guy." She cleared her throat. "A complete opposite of Red."

"Go on."

"Jake had one flaw."

"And what was that?"

"He liked to sleep around a lot...with women in the office."

"Interesting," Mark said. "And how is it that you're aware of this...may I ask?"

"Well, word gets around. It's high school-ish, I'm ashamed to admit. But I have nothing to lose. Most of the others are still married."

"Do you know who the others are? Would you be able to give me a list?"

"Sure. As long as you don't mention that I ratted them out," Laurie scoffed.

"Not a problem. We just need to ask them some questions about Jake. No names need to be mentioned." Mark changed tack. "Do you know anyone who would have had a personal vendetta against Jake?"

Laurie paused for thought. "Jake was a sweet guy; he got along with everybody. But I know he wasn't a favourite with the guys. All the ladies had a thing for him. I'd say just Red was the only one who was really fake with him. But that was more of an ego thing."

"Great. Thanks Laurie. When you have some time, email me that list." Mark relayed his email address and said goodbye.

Richard walked in just as Mark hung up the phone. "Hey, what's the story?" He sat down in the guest chair.

"Looks like Jake knew how to have some fun."

"Like how? Drugs? Drinking? Gambling?"

"Sex."

"Ah." Richard's finger was at his temple. "When ol' Ricky said he wasn't married, but he had lots of female guests...I had a feeling."

"A 'friend' of his," Mark air-quoted 'friend', "is emailing me a list of other 'friends' in the office we can interview."

"Whoa. Looks like someone's in search of a new 'friend'," Richard teased. "Sounds like she's sucking up to the Chief."

"Ha...ha," Mark scolded. "Have we found anything out about Chase McCann? Is the coroner done with him?"

"Yeah. Just like it looked." Richard leaned his right ankle on his left knee. "Knife went straight through. He bled out."

"Any prints on the knife?"

"Not a one."

Mark inhaled deeply and exhaled slow, interlacing his fingers behind his head. "I think we're looking at a serial."

Richard sat up straight, counting each item on his fingers. "Both young guys taken by surprise, one stabbed, one with a slit throat, clean crime scene. Yeah, I'd have to say I agree."

"The perp likes knives and young, unmarried guys," Mark added. "What do you know about Chase?"

"He's pretty clean, too. On television every night at six."

Mark frowned. "How is he with the ladies?"

"He keeps a pretty low profile, but I know he's not married."

"Hmm. Let's see if we can make any more connections," Mark suggested. "We'll need more if we want the F.B.I. involved."

"We better be fast," Richard said. "The third time's a charm."

...

"Pack your bags, my man," Ryder said. "Your house will be ready in a day or two, but all the essentials are in place."

"Oh yeah? Who'd you sleep with to get that done so fast?"

"Ah," Ryder waved. "They threw a couple more guys on the job, that's all."

Simon glared. "Did you tell my mom?"

"Nah, she's stressed out enough." Ryder avoided eye contact. The last thing Simon needed was to know his mom was off the wagon…again.

"Tell me about it." Simon changed the subject. "Dr. Bennett's got an occupational therapist lined up."

"Cool. And your whatcha-call-it injection is when? Tomorrow?" Ryder emptied out Simon's drawers into a bag beside the bed.

"Yeah." Simon did a double-take on Ryder's method of simply shoving the clothes into the duffel bag. "You want my mom to get that or something?"

"Nah, it's done." Ryder zipped the bag with one hand, while forcing the clothes to stay behind the zipper, causing the bulging bag to look like it was about to explode.

"Do me a favor?" Simon said. "Make sure this OT is at least *good looking?*"

Ryder gave up on the zipper three quarters of the way through. His face was red from exertion. "Simon," he grunted. "Your idea of good looking and mine are completely different. I'm afraid I can't really help you there."

"What do you mean? You drooled over half the women I've slept with in the past year."

Ryder ignored the comment. "I'm not sure I'm as comfortable with ogling as you are, Simon. Besides, isn't it more important that the woman,

THE WHEELS OF CHANGE

assuming it *is* a woman, is qualified and competent?" Ryder sat on the chair, leaving the half-open bag on the floor. "You're going to be spending who knows how long with this person. I think you're better off taking Dr. Bennett's recommendation. No offense."

Simon's lips pursed. "Fine. But if she's a dog, you're going to be the one to fire her."

Ryder shook his head. "No problem."

...

Nancy paced the hospital room. "Simon, I'm not at all comfortable with this idea."

"There's nothing to worry about, mom," Simon argued. "The injection was successful. All I have to do is listen to what the OT says and all is well."

"Have you even *met* this 'OT'?" Nancy's voice raised an octave as she air quoted 'OT'. "And will she stop you from doing something stupid? Like working?"

"Mom, I'm an adult. Quit treating me like a child." Simon gritted his teeth. "If she's not up to my standards, then I'll fire her. And as far as working, Sandra and Ryder have something figured out."

Ryder interjected. "We've managed to convince Mansfield to meet at Simon's place. His living room is large enough for that. Anything else can be done online or over the phone. Plus, I've been fielding most of the work since the accident."

"And the doctor says as long as my occupational therapy works well, I can start going into the office in a couple of weeks or so," Simon added.

Nancy scoffed, gesturing towards Simon's legs. "And how are you going to manage that? You can't walk!"

"Dammit, mom! Cut it out! I have to live my life! I have a business to run!" Simon's face was red and a vein in his neck was popping out.

Ryder was standing in the corner of the room, watching Nancy with concern. He'd just written her another cheque at her request. He was battling with a decision. Should he tell Simon about it or not?

...

Mark walked in the door and placed his cap on the console table by the door. The house smelled fragrant, a combination of pot roast and apple crumble wafted through his nose, and he smiled. "Mmmmm...smells lovely, baby." Mark called upstairs as he heard the toilet flush.

Shelley strolled down the steps and wrapped her arms around Mark's neck, kissing his lips. "Mmmm...I'll have some of that for dessert."

"I made apple crumble," Shelley giggled. "But that's for the kids."

"Kids?" Mark held Shelley by the waist. "Are we having company?"

"Jessica and Michael are coming by." Her face looked guarded. "She says they have news."

Mark grimaced knowing that could mean anything. Michael's stock portfolio skyrocketed last year when they got married, and they took an extended honeymoon in the Greek Islands. Since then, they always had news. Every month it was something different. They bought a new car, and then they bought a cottage near Mark and Shelley's cottage. A few months ago Jessica was promoted to Senior Executive Assistant. The list went on and on.

"Who knows," Mark chuckled. "Maybe they're flying to the moon."

Shelley waved her finger at Mark. "I don't think so. This time she was different on the phone."

Mark cocked his head to the side. "Different how?"

"She asked Jennifer and Mick to come over, too. She almost convinced me to go pick up my mom, but she's down with the flu."

Mark lifted an eyebrow. "What do you think it is? Did she give you a hint?"

"I don't want to jinx it," Shelley kissed Mark chastely. "But I doubt this time it's about money."

THE WHEELS OF CHANGE

Mark's cell phone started to ring. He checked the screen. It was police dispatch. Shelley walked away, knowing the familiar look on Mark's face.

He answered, patting Shelley's rear end playfully. "Tame here."

"Chief Tame? Rick Cranston. Remember me? I was the guy who found Jake Campbell stabbed?"

Mark walked to the living room and sat on the couch. "Sure, I remember you, Rick. What can I do for you?" he said cheerily.

"I hate to bother you at home, but I remembered something about one of the girls Jake had over at his place."

"What did you remember?"

"Well, all the girls were gorgeous, but I remember one with extremely long black hair, pin straight, like Cher's."

"Do you remember any distinguishing marks?"

"No. I can't say I do. But there was something else I didn't think of."

"Go ahead."

"I felt kinda stupid when I remembered, but Jake's been in a couple of bank commercials. The Cher look-a-like was in one of them with him. Both were good lookin' people. It's not a wonder they were on TV. I saw the commercial again earlier today, just on local TV though."

"No need to feel stupid, Rick. Any information is helpful, no matter how silly it may seem."

Rick paused. "Can I ask a question?"

"Shoot," Mark said flatly.

"He wasn't running a brothel or pimping or anything like that, was he?" Rick said under his breath, like it was a big secret. "I guess those girls weren't sisters or cousins after all, like I'd originally thought."

Mark chuckled. "No need to worry, Rick. It's my guess that most of his guests were colleagues of his. We have a few leads we're checking out shortly."

"Phew!" Rick whistled. "I didn't think Jake was the type. I'm usually a pretty good judge of character. Didn't want to believe my instincts were slippin'."

"Still sharp as a tack," Mark commented, then Rick interrupted.

"Say, they gonna clean that place up soon? The neighbors keep askin' when the damn place is goin' up for sale."

"I'll follow up for you personally," Mark promised. "Thanks for calling."

"Not at all, Chief. Take care."

CHAPTER 14

"Thanks, man." Simon took the glass of water Ryder gave him, along with two pills.

"Feeling okay?" Ryder asked casually as he grunted back into the chair beside the bed.

Simon nodded. "So, when's Mansfield coming? Were you able to set that up?"

"Yep. The day after tomorrow. It's just Stockton and Wakeman coming though, I think."

Simon smirked, remembering his last encounter with the account executives of Mansfield. The junior account executive, Ms. Reding, in particular. "Ah, they'll bring at least one gopher."

"Down boy," Ryder teased, knowing Simon's intention. "Off limits. This is our bread and butter, man."

"Relax. A little flattery never hurt anyone."

"Yeah. I've seen your flattery." Ryder gestured to Simon's legs.

Simon rolled his eyes. "So when's this OT supposed to be here?"

Before Simon finished his sentence, the doorbell rang. "Speak of the devil," Ryder said.

"I like her already," Simon commented. "Punctual is good."

Ryder rose to answer the door, but before he left the room, he pointed at Simon. "Now behave yourself," he warned, "or you're on your own tonight. You'll have fun crawling around in your Buzz Light Year pyjamas in the dark."

Simon laughed and waved him away.

Moments later, Ryder entered Simon's bedroom with a tall, dark-haired, flat-chested girl who smiled, revealing adult braces. "I'm Darla." She pronounced her name "Dawla" with a slight British accent.

Simon extended his hand for her to shake. "Nice to meet you, Darla."

"My last name is Daringer. My friends nicknamed me 'Da-Da', but you don't have to call me that." Her accent rolled off her tongue. "And don't worry about these hideous things." Darla pointed to her mouth. "They'll be out in a week."

Darla has promise. Simon smirked.

Ryder caught the look. "So how long have you been an occupational therapist, Darla?"

"About five years," she nodded. "I just came from England a couple of years ago. Accreditation is the same there though, no worries." Her hand came up, as if to fend off any argument.

"That's quite all right," Simon said. "You came highly recommended by Dr. Bennett."

Darla's face lit up. "Oh yes, Dr. Bennett. He's wonderful. Despite his similarity to Mr. Potato Head." She giggled. "No offense to him, of course."

Simon's face turned red with embarrassment. "I hadn't noticed," he lied.

Darla wasn't convinced. "Really...So what's your pain been like, Simon?"

"Not bad at all. I'm actually avoiding the pills as much as possible."

"Good." Darla was satisfied. "It's much easier to rehabilitate someone

THE WHEELS OF CHANGE

who isn't suffering from much pain. Not to mention one with such a sense of humour. That'll come in handy when I've got you in compromising positions." She winked good-naturedly.

"Simon likes being in compromising positions," Ryder joked. "That's how he got in this mess."

"Oh dear," Darla chuckled. "I've got my work cut out."

. . .

Mark sat on the couch and opened his laptop. "You're not working, are you?" Shelley chided.

"Just checking emails, love."

"Good. The kids will be here soon. Jessica will bust a vein if she sees you're working."

"Not to worry," Mark said, logging in. Laurie McDonald hadn't sent him the list of bank employees to interview yet. He closed the lid and turned around. To his surprise, Shelley was standing right there.

"Thought I'd come over and get some sugar while we're still alone," she purred.

"Checking up on me, are you?" Mark embraced her. Shelley planted a seductive kiss on his lips, then a second.

"How long have we got, exactly?" Mark whispered, turning his head to the side and offering her a taste of his tongue.

"Everything's in the oven." She kissed him again and ran her hand down to his pants. "Pie's cooked." Her hand caressed his hardness. "Wine's chilled."

Mark groaned. "How long?"

Shelley lifted her shirt, revealing her braless state. "Long enough. Twenty minutes?"

Mark lunged at her breasts, sucking her nipples voraciously as Shelley unzipped his pants and grabbed his manliness. Both began to pant hungrily. Shelley was wearing a long, flowing skirt that Mark lifted easily. His eyes bulged as he realized his wife was also not wearing underwear. "I'll give you one thing Shelley," he breathed. "You're one hell of a planner."

He gently tossed her on the couch and slid on top of her. "Door's locked, right?" he asked before parting her legs.

"Yes, and chained," she sighed, wrapping her legs around him. Shelley and Mark both groaned as he filled her. "God, I never get enough of you," she said, arching her back.

"Amen." He quickly pumped in and out of her. The springs on the couch were squeaking relentlessly as his pace picked up.

"Oh, faster baby!" Shelley panted as Mark interlaced his hands with hers above her head. His body was angled upward and she cried out continuously, begging him not to stop. Skin was slapping rhythmically. The force of her release drove Mark over the edge and he grunted as she mewled from the wave of sensation.

When they both finished, Mark lowered himself on her. "I think that was a record."

Shelley laughed, kissing him chastely on the lips. "For me, too."

...

Shelley passed Jessica the platter of meat, watching the look of contentment on her daughter's face. "So how come you guys changed the locks when we moved out?" Jessica asked. "And why don't we get a key?"

Shelley and Mark exchanged glances. "The only person who has a copy of our key is Mabel next door, and she knows to knock first," Mark said in a matter-of-fact way.

Jennifer scrunched her nose. "Oh god, I don't want to know."

Shelley tried to keep a straight face, changing the subject. "So Jessica, what do we owe the pleasure of this visit?"

Jessica's eyes bulged as she was taken by surprise. "Well, I said we had some news."

"Please share. I need to get an image out of my head," Jennifer laughed. Shelley slapped her playfully.

"I'm pregnant," Jessica blurted. Michael took her hand from the table and interlaced it with his.

Shelley bolted up from the table and grasped Jessica by the face. "Oh! My baby! I'm so happy!" she cried, kissing her from cheek to cheek.

"Mom! Take it easy!" Jessica laughed.

"Give the child some air," Mark chuckled. "This can't be good for the baby."

Shelley rose, composing herself but her face was still flushed. "Congratulations you two."

"Here here!" Mark, Jennifer and Mick cheered, raising their wine glasses.

Jessica was about to raise hers when Michael sheepishly removed the glass from her hand. "Sorry, babe."

As Jessica feigned pouting, Mark's cell phone started to ring. Shelley gave him a warning glance he tried to ignore. He looked at the screen and pursed his lips, rising from his chair and leaving the room.

When he was out of earshot, he answered the phone. It was the Deputy Chief, Andy Kerrington. "What's up, Andy?"

"We've got a jumper," Andy said evenly.

Mark's jaw dropped. "What? Where? Who?"

"Says she's McCann's girl. She's completely lost it. Noonan's been trying to talk her down but she ain't budgin'."

"Jesus Christ," Mark muttered. "I'll be right there."

. . .

Mark shielded his eyes from the twilight sun as he angled his head to the top of the skyscraper. "How the hell did she get up there?" he said to Richard.

"Chase's office is in the penthouse," Richard explained. "There's access from a service elevator."

"How'd she get a hold of the key?" Mark was incredulous.

Richard shrugged. The surrounding noise was incomprehensible. There were three full sized fire trucks, two ambulances and half a dozen police cruisers in the area. Constable Hobbs had just cinched off the last of the yellow caution tape around the perimeter.

"Did somebody call Elizabeth?"

Elizabeth Marx was the Head Behaviour Analyst with the F.B.I. and helped them solve their last serial murder case. Sergeant Lipkus, Elizabeth's boss, and Mark, had had a decade long vendetta against each other.

"Yeah. ETA ten minutes, Lipkus said," Richard answered.

Mark's eyes bulged, "Lipkus?"

"Shocked the hell out of me, too," Richard said.

"So what have we got so far?"

"Michelle Pinchot, thirty-two. Apparently she and Chase had a thing for about a year. She wanted more, he didn't, so he ended it. They still fooled around casually. She's a reporter and got sent away to do a cover a story on endangered rhinos in Africa. No doubt Chase pulled some strings on that one."

"Go on."

"Anyway, when she came back a few months later, she got wind of his canoodling with other office females and became mighty pissed."

"Why was she pissed? He broke it off."

Richard looked expectantly at the top of the building and lifted a brow. "Maybe she has issues."

"So when he died, she completely lost it," Mark commented.

THE WHEELS OF CHANGE

"Think she's a suspect?" Richard asked.

"Why would she kill him, then two days later commit suicide?"

"She's not dead yet," Richard added, cocking his head to the side.

...

"Ma'am? I'm Elizabeth Marx. I'm a psychologist with the F.B.I. I just want to talk to you," Elizabeth called from the door leading to the roof from the penthouse floor.

"Go away," Michelle answered. Her voice quivered, and her arms hugged her midsection. She was standing about three feet from the edge of the roof. Only a six inch curb separated her from her demise.

The door where Elizabeth stood was about twenty feet from where Michelle was. Harsh winds blew from the twenty-five storey altitude, causing the door to shut tight behind her.

Elizabeth took a step closer. "Michelle. Michelle, you don't want to do this."

"What the hell do you know about me?" Michelle growled. "And stay the hell away or I'll jump!"

Elizabeth put her arm out and lowered her head, not taking another step. "I know you're upset about Chase, Michelle, but this isn't the way to deal with it."

She rounded on her and bounded forward. "What do you know about Chase? Did you fuck him too?"

"No. No, I didn't know the man personally."

"Liar!" Michelle shouted. Her eyes were blazing.

"I swear. I'm a married woman." Elizabeth lifted her left hand. Michelle inspected her diamond ring from afar.

Michelle stepped back and scoffed. "Wouldn't matter."

Elizabeth studied Michelle's face, she was pale, her green eyes were puffy and there were beads of sweat on her brow. Michelle's short sandy-coloured hair was cropped at the neck, like a pixie cut, and her trousers hung unnaturally around her waist with the pant legs rolled at the bottom. Her dress shirt was stuffed into her pants with the sleeves rolled up to her elbows.

Elizabeth stared at her from top to bottom and paused. "You're wearing men's clothes." she observed.

Michelle sniffled, wiping her nose and turned around so her back was to Elizabeth. "They're Chase's."

"Where did you get them?"

"From his office."

"Why?"

Michelle ignored the question. "He's dead."

"I know he's dead, Michelle. I'm sorry for your loss."

"He sent me away, you know." Her voice quivered. "He didn't want me."

"Men can be insensitive," Elizabeth said evenly. "He's not worth ending your life for, though."

Michelle looked up to the sky and visibly began to sob. Her shoulders shook as her head bowed down towards the ground. Elizabeth thought she was making progress so she slowly inched her way to Michelle. Her plan was to embrace her from behind, hoping all she needed was to be held. Before she reached her destination, Michelle turned around to face her, five feet away.

"I want to be with him," she said simply and turned around again, running toward the edge. Before Elizabeth had a chance to stop her, Michelle's arms angled out as she dove off into oblivion.

. . .

"Code red! Code red!" Mark yelled into his walkie-talkie, watching

Michelle's body fly through the air towards the ground. Elizabeth's conversation with Michelle had been overheard with the use of a bug planted inside Elizabeth's shirt.

"Go to her," Mark ordered Richard, nodding toward Elizabeth on the roof top.

Despite the Emergency Response Team's quick movements, and due to the angle of Michelle's jump and the wind force, they were unable to save her. She landed six feet away from the ERT canopy.

The ambulance and ER Team were quick to get to her lifeless body. Blood quickly pooled around her as she lay face down. Marty, the head of the ERT placed his hand on her neck and nodded. "She's gone."

One person from the Crime Scene team began taking photographs and another started erecting a tent around the body so they could conduct their investigation discreetly. There wasn't much to record, but it was protocol.

Richard and Elizabeth joined Mark, who was standing beside Marty.

Elizabeth sighed. "She was deeply disturbed. She's wearing McCann's clothes and from the looks of her, she cut her hair like his, too."

"Think she could be a suspect?" Mark asked.

"It's tough to say. I couldn't get an alibi. If she hadn't been dressing like him, I would say no, as she was clearly in love with him. But then again, she could have thought that if she couldn't have him, nobody could. And we don't see any dead women around, do we?"

"We'll need to check forensics on McCann's place and see if her prints show up anywhere," Mark said. "His office will need to be checked out as well."

"She was in his office though, so that complicates things," Elizabeth offered.

"We'll look for signs of struggle between him and her," Mark said.

"Could be tough," Richard intervened. "If she liked things rough, we could find more than normal."

"We'll cross that bridge when we come to it," Mark conceded.

. . .

"I hope you didn't eat a lot of breakfast," Darla said to Simon.

"Nah. Ryder brought some coffee and donuts," Simon answered, nodding at the table beside his bed.

"I thought we'd start with some stretching this morning." Darla lowered a duffel bag onto the floor beside his bed. "Are you in any pain today?"

"Not one bit."

"D' you have any feeling anywhere?" She took a small square sheet of rubber, like a mat, and placed it on the bed.

"A little in my low back." He pointed.

"Good." Darla leaned on Simon's bed, left knee on the bed, right foot on the floor. "Now it's important for you to let me do the work. I'm going to take your left arm and place it over my left shoulder."

Simon complied while Darla knelt on the non-skid material under her knee and gently pulled Simon toward her.

"Do you feel a pull anywhere?" she asked.

"Yes. Just in my arm."

"Good. We'll do five repetitions and hold for ten seconds each, then switch to the other side."

As Darla worked, Simon couldn't help but inhale her scent and revel in the feeling of having a woman close to him, even if it wasn't sexual. Her touch was firm yet nurturing, something he'd never felt. He found himself relaxing in her embrace. When they finished with the stretches, Darla rose and removed the non-skid mat.

"We'll do some leg stretches next. Are you up for that?"

"So far, so good."

THE WHEELS OF CHANGE

"Good attitude, Simon."

Darla sat beside him. "I'm going to remove your bedding, are you decent under there?"

"I am."

"Excellent. Now I'm going to lift up your left leg with both my hands and gently stretch your hamstrings. It shouldn't hurt, okay?"

"Got it."

Simon watched Darla peel down his bed sheets and turn around to grasp his left leg. When she slowly lifted it, she asked, "Do you feel a pull or pain?"

"Nope. Nothing." Simon was growing rather fond of her accent, finding it soothing.

She held his left leg for ten seconds and as she lowered it, she asked, "So if you don't mind my asking, this motor vehicle accident you were in, were you hit by a drunk driver?"

Normally Simon would think of a cheeky or flirtatious response, but he was so relaxed by Darla's touch, he couldn't help but answer honestly. "No. Nothing like that." He licked his lips and closed his eyes, enjoying the movement. "I hit a transport truck. My brake lines were cut."

Darla didn't flinch. "Be thankful you weren't hurt worse," she said, focusing on the stretch.

Each repetition seemed to be gaining further flexibility and Simon, despite the numbness in his legs, was beginning to feel refreshed. The room was completely silent save for their breathing and the barking of a small dog outside.

"So why did you leave England?" Simon asked.

Darla exhaled and lowered Simon's right leg down, having finished stretching the left. "I came here during placement in my last year of university and ever since then I wanted to come back," she answered simply.

"What about America made you want to come back?"

"I met someone."

"Ah. That's what I figured."

"What gave it away?" Darla asked, sitting next to him.

"You look the type is all." He opened his eyes. "Young, smart—"

Darla interrupted. "Geeky?" she giggled.

"A little," he admitted. "I don't see a ring. Have you given him an ultimatum yet, or has he not hit the deadline?"

Darla looked down and smiled, nodding. "Ah. So you didn't figure it out after all."

Simon cocked his head to the side. "What do you mean?"

"Some people are more than meets the eye, Simon."

Simon stared at her, waiting.

"I said I met someone. I never said it was a he."

CHAPTER 15

"I think we're looking at this case all wrong," Mark said to Richard.

"Why do you say that?" he asked, taking a bite of his sandwich.

"We have to find the link if we're going to prove this is serial."

"I thought we already established it was serial." Richard wiped his mouth with a napkin.

"Let's look at the facts again." Mark pulled the stack of files on the edge of his desk toward him.

"Both victims are men. Both seem to have issues with the women around them."

"Did Ms. McDonald send you the list of possible women Jake Campbell had affairs with?"

"Yeah. But I think the list alone proves the point. He liked to sleep around. So did McCann."

"And there aren't any other murders we're investigating," Richard added.

Mark hesitated. "What about the attempt murder? The guy in the wheelchair?"

"What about him?"

"What's his story?" Mark rifled through papers.

"Simon Cross; he's the Ad. Exec., isn't he?"

"That's the one."

Mark buzzed Lisa. "Hand me the file for Simon Cross when you have a moment, would ya?"

Lisa rose and opened the door, handing the file to Richard, who took her hand and softly kissed it.

Mark ignored the gesture and opened the file, leafing through the papers. Lisa walked out and Richard pulled his chair closer to Mark's. He watched Mark's index finger run down the sheet where Constables Crow and Gardner took his statement.

"Relationship to perpetrator Max Dunphy stated 'had affair with Clara Dunphy'."

"So he liked to sleep around, too," Richard said.

"And he's high profile. Just like McCann and Campbell," Mark added.

"But he didn't try to stab him, and Simon is still alive," Richard said. "Do you think they're related?"

"Too alike to discount it." Mark took down Max Dunphy's address. "He's out on bail, right?"

"Believe so."

"Let's go see if he's got an alibi for the murders."

. . .

The Dunphy house was a mid-size home on a busy street. It was one of those streets where there were more people than homes to accommodate. There wasn't anywhere for the boys to park their patrol car, so they had no choice but to park directly in front of Max's 'Mars Construction' truck. There was another car parked in the driveway and the lights were on in the living room.

THE WHEELS OF CHANGE

Mark knocked on the door and a tall slender lady opened it, holding her cell phone in her hand. Her hair was swept up in a clip and her eyes were glassy. "Can I help you?" she said a little too casually, like Mark and Richard were selling Girl Guide cookies.

"Are you Clara Dunphy?" Mark held his credentials up.

"I am," she said with a slight eye roll.

"Is your husband home?"

"I certainly hope not," she said, as a younger male exited, shrugging on his jacket. His cheeks turned pink and he avoided eye contact with the boys. He walked down the street and disappeared around the corner.

"When was the last time you saw your husband, ma'am?" Richard asked.

"Last night." She keyed something into her cell phone. "He got a call from a friend and left."

"Do you know where he went?"

"I don't know. He was screaming on the phone earlier last night, something about money."

"Are you and Mr. Dunphy having financial problems?" Mark asked.

Clara rolled her eyes. "My husband is no business man. He could have had any amount of money from Simon Cross but the imbecile tore up the check to prove some macho point." She shook her head. "His goddamn lawyer is costing us a king's ransom and chances are he'll go to jail anyway."

"Ma'am, we need to contact your husband. Do you have any guess as to where he is or a number where we can reach him? He is forbidden to leave the state, you know, right?"

"He knows," she said. "But he hasn't called or anything."

"And you haven't tried to contact him?"

Clara was incredulous and said like it was the dumbest thing she'd ever heard, "Why?"

103

"Can we come in and take a look around?" Mark asked.

"Sure. Whatever." She walked down the hall to the kitchen, where there was a half empty bottle of wine on the counter. She poured herself a glass and stood by the sink.

Mark and Richard followed her and Mark gestured to the stairs leading to the second floor. "Is the bedroom upstairs?"

She gulped down her wine and nodded. "Don't mind the mess."

As they headed upstairs, Richard joked. "Max Dunphy is a lucky man."

Mark shook his head.

The bedroom door was open, clothes were lying on the floor and the bed was almost completely devoid of sheets, they were all on the floor. Richard inspected the headboard on both sides and commented. "She likes it rough. Bed's been moved."

"Never mind that. Get over here and help me with the dresser," Mark growled.

They both opened the drawers and didn't see any large gaps in clothing. Nothing looked like it was missing. Mark yelled downstairs to Clara. "Does he have spare clothes in his car or at the office?"

Clara didn't answer but made her way up the stairs. "Yes. He's usually got a couple spares and some spare coveralls, both in the car and at the office. He gets pretty dirty with his job as you can imagine."

"Show me where you keep your luggage," Mark instructed.

Clara opened the closet door on the wall opposite the bed. There were two large brown leather suitcases on the floor and a smaller bag on top. "It's all here," she confirmed.

Mark fished out a business card from his pocket and handed it to Clara. "Mrs. Dunphy, if your husband calls or makes contact, you need to let us know."

"Is he in any trouble?"

THE WHEELS OF CHANGE

"If he's left the state, yes. But for now he's just wanted for questioning."

"Questioning? Didn't you already get a statement from him? Can't you go through his money-sucking lawyer?"

"Ma'am, we need to question him on another case," Richard explained.

Her eyes widened. "Another case? What do you mean?"

"There have been some murders recently and we need to know your husband's whereabouts when the murders occurred."

The colour drained from her face. "You think Max killed these people? He just went after Simon for revenge, he wasn't thinking clearly! My husband is no killer. I don't think he even realized what he was doing when he hurt Simon."

"Does your husband ever carry a knife, ma'am?" Richard asked.

"Just a pocket-knife. Why?"

Richard ignored the question. "Are there any knives missing? In the kitchen? Maybe in a workshop?"

Clara sat down on the bed, rubbing her reddened eyes. "He doesn't have a workshop, and we don't own any knives other than the cheap steak knives his mother bought us for a wedding gift."

"Are any of them missing?"

"No. Not that I'm aware of. They've hardly been used."

"We'll take a look," Mark said, heading for the bedroom door.

"They're all here." Clara pointed to the butcher's block on the counter. All slots were full and the knives all matched. Richard opened the utility drawer and inspected it. There was a bunch of glass shot glasses, a corkscrew, salad tongs and a soup ladle in the drawer. Mark frowned as Richard closed the drawer. Below the drawer was a wine cooler and after perusing the rest of the cabinets, the boys deduced that they must eat out a lot.

105

"Thanks for your time, ma'am." Mark tipped his hat. "Be sure to call if Mr. Dunphy makes any contact."

Clara nodded, leading them to the front door.

"Why'd you put her through all that?" Richard asked when Clara closed the door. "The knives were still on the victims, and they were both hunting knives."

"I wanted to see if she'd sweat," Mark explained. "She's definitely not hiding him anywhere."

"That's for sure," Richard scoffed. "It seems when the cat's away the mice will play."

"We'll check out Mars Construction and see if any of *them* sweat."

. . .

"Well, his truck's clean," Richard said, peering through the window.

"That's the cleanest work truck *I've* ever seen," Mark said suspiciously.

"Maybe he's one of those neat-freak guys or something," Richard surmised.

"Doubt that." Mark shone his flashlight on the floor. "Since when do construction guys vacuum?"

The floor in the two-seated van was spotless. Even the black dashboard and grey cloth seats were white-glove friendly.

Mark sucked his teeth. "Let's get over to the construction site. I'm curious to find out if Max is as clean as he's making himself out to be."

. . .

"Can I help you?" said a large, burly man with oversized, dark sunglasses and a cigarette hanging from his mouth. He approached the gated entrance to the construction site. His voice was gravelly from years of smoking and yelling over noisy equipment.

THE WHEELS OF CHANGE

Mark flashed his credentials. "I'm looking for Max Dunphy."

"Max?" The burly man scoffed, removing the cigarette from his mouth. He flicked it on the ground and mashed it with the toe of his boot. The metal from the steel plate on the toe was exposed. He didn't remove his sunglasses. "He ain't here. Called in sick."

Mark didn't like the smirk on his face. "Any idea where he is?" he raised his voice over a bulldozer.

"None," the burly man said, shaking his head.

Mark decided to probe a little. "Does he take his work van home?"

"Yessir."

Richard eyed a couple of Mars Construction trucks lining the exit on the other side of the fence and he walked over to take a look. They were all filthy. He walked back and stood beside Mark.

"When's he expected back?" Richard asked.

"Didn't say. Said he'd call."

"Are you his supervisor?" Mark asked.

"Yes I am. I manage all the folks here."

"I didn't catch your name," Mark said.

"Calvin. Wayne Calvin." He didn't offer his hand to shake.

Mark fetched a business card and handed it to Wayne. "When Max calls, let me know."

Wayne took the card but didn't glance at it. "What's this all about anyway? He in some kind of trouble?"

Mark's head cocked to the side. "Mr. Dunphy was arrested for attempted murder last week. He's out on bail, but he's suddenly disappeared."

"How many days has he missed?" Richard asked.

107

"I was away last week, but I think he was here," Wayne explained, seemingly dodging the question. "What's today...aw, hell." He shifted his weight. "See, the problem here is that these guys swap time cards so they can mess with the system. One guy punches in for another guy, the other guy punches out for the first guy and so on."

"Have you got security cameras?"

Wayne clucked his tongue. "Nope."

"Are your employees bonded?"

Wayne laughed out loud. "We have three months to build this God-forsaken hotel. It's going to be named after royalty, see? But the pay's for a pauper. The only way we make ends meet around here is overtime."

"So you hire anyone who will do the work for the piddly pay, right?"

"That's right."

"Even someone who's got a record."

"Long as he ain't no murderer, he's welcome to work a bulldozer."

"Thanks for your time, Wayne," Mark said. "Call me if you hear from Mr. Dunphy."

Mark and Richard walked away. Richard muttered. "Looks like Max's days here may be numbered."

"Seems to me like if you've got something to hide, working at a construction site is the place to be."

...

"She's gotta go," Simon said to Ryder.

"What? I though you liked her." Ryder's brows furrowed.

"She's a fuckin' dyke!" Simon hissed.

"What? How do you know? And why do you care?" Ryder's hands

THE WHEELS OF CHANGE

rose from his sides, like he was lifting barbells.

"She told me. And *I* care because I don't want any dyke touching me."

Ryder started to chuckle. "How did *that* conversation start? Did you ask her to sleep with you? There's a first 'Gee, sorry Mr. Cross, I'm a lesbian.' Bet you never heard *that* one before!"

"Fuck...off," Simon said, giving Ryder the finger.

They both heard the door knock. "I'll get it," Ryder said, ensuring the brake on Simon's wheelchair was solid.

Ryder opened the door and Nancy walked in. "Hey Nancy, I didn't know you were coming over."

Nancy ignored Ryder's greeting. "Can I have a word with you, Simon?" Her tone was clipped.

"I'll be in the other room," Ryder said, looking at the floor, hands in his pockets.

Nancy watched Ryder enter Simon's bedroom and close the door. She knelt down to Simon's level.

"Simon, honey. Something's come up. I have to go visit Auntie Barbara for a while."

Simon's brows furrowed. "Is she okay? What happened?"

"She got herself messed up with that goddamn artist again."

Raphael Lavernier, a French Canadian artist, who prided himself on his love for women and art, had Aunt Barbara smitten the last time he came into town. She followed him around like a puppy dog for months while he was on tour in California, doing god-knows-what. Then he dumped her and went back to Canada, leaving her in an expensive hotel, with an expensive hotel bill among other things.

"Are you kidding me?" Simon was incredulous. "Is she stupid? The last time she got mixed up with him I got hosed for five grand!"

Nancy stared at the floor. "Simon, it won't be that much, I promise."

Simon's lips pursed as he looked up at his mother through glaring eyes. "How much?"

"Well, I need some money for food and accommodations and, well, I don't know what else." Nancy avoided eye contact.

"Mom, I don't want you going there. Auntie Barbara is trouble."

"Simon, I'm a big girl. And she's my sister. She's been there for me many times."

"Yeah, I recall." Simon seethed, remembering how many times Barbara pushed Nancy off the wagon after months of being sober.

"Are you sure she's not just on another bender?"

"I'm positive, Simon."

Simon grumbled. "My cheque book's in the drawer." He nodded toward the bureau by the kitchen. Nancy walked over, shuffled a few things around and removed the cheque book, grabbing a pen off the kitchen table.

"Here you go." She handed him the book and pen.

Simon wrote the cheque and tore it off. He hesitated before letting go of the cheque. "I want you to call me every day. Any sign that Auntie Barbara is using, I want you back her pronto." He glared at her.

"I promise, Simon." Her index finger traced an 'x' over her chest. She kissed him on the forehead and walked out, slamming the door behind her.

"What was that all about?" Ryder said, appearing after having heard the door. "Everything okay?"

"Yeah. She's fine." Simon wasn't in the mood to get into it with Ryder, so he changed the subject. "When's the Mansfield guys getting here?"

"This afternoon," Ryder said. "Right after Darla leaves."

Simon looked at Ryder at the mention of her name, and seethed. "I know what you're thinking and I'm not doing it," Ryder said firmly.

THE WHEELS OF CHANGE

"So much for promises," Simon said, gritting his teeth.

"It'll do you good to have at least one woman in your life that you can't sleep with."

Simon looked at his useless legs. "I've got plenty now. You think I'm ever going to be able to have sex again?" His voice rose.

"Now don't start with that self-pity bullshit. That's not the Simon I know," Ryder argued, crossing his arms over his chest. "How do you think you got where you are today, Simon? You think you just landed there?"

Shaking his head, Simon ignored the comment. "You gonna start with your Karate Kid pep talk?"

Ryder tried unsuccessfully to stifle a smile. "Not today, buddy." He looked at his watch. "Listen, Darla's going to be here any minute. You okay to be left alone? I'm going to head back to the office and grab all the stuff for the meeting."

. . .

"How are you today?" Darla asked cheerily as she entered the house, carrying a hockey equipment-sized duffel bag.

"Good," Simon said, avoiding eye contact.

"You sure?" she draped her pink, flower patterned jacket over a kitchen chair and placed the bag on the floor.

"Yep. Sure. Let's get started." Simon clapped, pasting on a smile.

"Alright then," Darla said. "Let's get you out of that chair. We've got a lot to cover today." Her tone was bright, bubbly and Simon couldn't help but smile.

As Simon was wheeled to a large, empty spot on the floor, he felt a strange, but recognizable sensation in his abdomen that was almost painful. "Fuck," he whispered to himself.

"Something wrong?" Darla asked, securing the brake on his chair.

"I need..." He hesitated, feeling bile rise in his throat.

Darla turned so she was facing him. "Is it your nappy?" she said, like she was asking if he needed a drink of water.

He didn't answer, instead, he looked at the floor and fought the lump in his throat. To his amazement, Darla didn't flinch or react to the stench floating in the air around them. She said nothing and carried on like Simon's dignity hadn't just been completely degraded, like the most disgusting human function hadn't just reared its ugly head into Simon's trousers.

Simon watched as Darla wheeled him into the bedroom and swiftly yet gracefully helped Simon lower himself onto the bed. He looked at her, wondering when her nose was going to scrunch up, or when she was going to say, "Let's hope this doesn't go on for long." Like what Nancy would say snidely after performing the same task.

Even when the faulty seam had to be torn open, Darla's expression did not waver. "They trained you well," Simon said as she inched the fresh undergarment onto him.

"Why thank you, Simon," she said happily. "I graduated top of the class."

"You really must love your job," Simon commented under his breath, "to do this." He eyed the diaper apprehensively.

"I've seen and done a lot being a nurse, Simon," she explained. "I could tell you some stories that would make this seem as natural as preparing a salad."

Simon frowned.

Darla changed the subject. "Did you feel your bowels move?"

"Yeah. It hurt a little."

"The nerve endings are getting stronger," she nodded. "This is a good sign." Darla patted him on the shoulder.

He smiled.

THE WHEELS OF CHANGE

. . .

Darla was finished packing away her equipment when Ryder walked in the door.

"Hey, how'd he do?" Ryder asked, as though Simon wasn't there.

"Very well. I'll be sending a report to Dr. Flamborough today," she said, looking at Simon.

"Be sure to get enough rest, Simon," Darla instructed, picking up the bag. "I'll be back in the morning."

When the door closed, Ryder turned to Simon. "So?"

"So what?" Simon tried to ignore the I-told-you-so look on Ryder's face.

"She's good, right?"

"She'll do...for now."

Ryder chuckled and looked out the window. "Sandra was right behind me. Oh! There she is. I'll be back."

Moments later, Ryder and Sandra both came in carrying prepared sandwiches and coffee. Sandra was holding her short purse strap between her teeth, so she could only manage a hello nod to Simon. He stared at the floor, infuriated by his helplessness.

"You guys set up the table for the conference and I'll use this smaller table for the food," she instructed.

Ten minutes later, just as they were finishing setting up the presentation screen on the back wall, the doorbell rang.

"I'll get it," Sandra said. Ryder immediately straightened his shirt and tie. Simon ran his hands through his hair.

The door opened and Mr. Stockton was the first to enter. Ryder shook his hand. "Thanks for coming, Mr. Stockton." Mr. Stockton nodded and adjusted his tie. Sandra was careful not to be next to greet them, so she stood by the table away from view.

113

SANDY APPLEYARD

"Simon," Mr. Stockton grunted. Simon lifted his hand and Mr. Stockton bent down and offered him a slight handshake.

Mr. Wakeman gave a hearty handshake to Ryder and a sympathetic nod to Simon. "How are you feeling?" he asked, approaching Sandra for a handshake.

"Pretty good. No pain. Can't complain." Simon felt his cheeks turn pink.

"Won't be long and Simon here will be back to his old self again," Ryder boasted, slapping him on the shoulder.

"We've got coffee and sandwiches over here," Sandra offered.

"Excellent. We skipped lunch." Mr. Wakeman ogled the food.

"I'll hit the john," Mr. Stockton said.

"Second door on your left," Ryder called.

Mr. Wakeman sat opposite Ryder, Sandra and Simon were beside Mr. Wakeman, saving the head of the table for Mr. Stockton. Mr. Wakeman placed his briefcase on the floor.

"Wow, these sandwiches are delicious, Sandra. Did you make them yourself?" Mr. Wakeman asked.

Sandra giggled. "No. I can give you the name of the catering company."

Simon was nervous. "She was a party planner in a previous life."

Suddenly Ryder spilled his coffee. Sandra grabbed a nearby roll of paper towel, but it was on its last few sheets. "I'll grab more from the closet," Ryder said, taking long strides into the hallway.

To his surprise, he nearly ran straight into Mr. Stockton, leaving Simon's bedroom. Ryder eyed him cautiously. "Did you get lost?"

"No. The toilet paper is out." Mr. Stockton explained. "At home we keep it in the bedroom."

"Ah. No, Simon keeps it in the closet. I'll put some in for you," Ryder

114

chuckled. "Sorry about that. We never thought to check supplies."

"No worries."

Mr. Stockton joined the rest in the living area as Ryder grabbed the paper towel. He looked for the toilet paper to no avail, when he heard Simon's cell phone ringing in the bedroom.

"Dammit," he muttered. When he reached the phone on Simon's dresser, the display read 'Mom'. Ryder sprinted to Simon, handing him the phone, trying desperately to sway the focus off Simon wheeling away from the table for privacy. "So, was anyone else born to be a klutz?" he said louder than expected.

"I was a gangly thing as a teen," Sandra offered, taking a handful of paper towel and wiping up the rest of the mess.

Mr. Stockton sighed quickly. "Let's get this started, hmm? We've got another meeting in an hour."

"Absolutely." Ryder turned on the overhead projector. Moments later, Simon rejoined the table with a blank look on his face.

"All is well?" Mr. Wakeman asked.

"Err...yes, sir."

Mr. Stockton began. "What's your budget for this project?"

Ryder was taken by surprise. They had a whole presentation worked out, the budget was to be discussed last.

"If you'll bear with me," Ryder said as calmly as he could manage, "we'll get to that. There's just a quick presentation we've put together for you."

"I'm not here to see a presentation. I'm here to discuss numbers. We've already seen what we need to see," Mr. Stockton said bluntly, adjusting his tie.

Simon sat up straight in his chair. "Sure. Definitely. We planned on starting with a fifty thousand dollar program consisting of commercials, both local and national, social media advertisements and we've got celebrity endorsement as well."

Mr. Stockton was incredulous. "You plan on doing all that coverage for our entire roster of products with fifty thousand dollars?"

Mr. Wakeman's face dropped. He looked at his colleague and blinked.

"Well...err...we can put more funds on it. That's a preliminary number. A budget," Ryder interjected.

Mr. Stockton shook his head and laughed under his breath. "You play me for a fool."

Simon swallowed. "No, sir." His voice was firm.

Mr. Stockton rose. "Such a pity." He walked to the corner of the room, where Darla had absent-mindedly left her pink jacket draped over one of the spare chairs. He patted the jacket and laughed under his breath again. "Simon, Ryder, Sandra." He addressed them as though he was going to conduct an inaugural speech. "I was willing to see past some of your...shall we say...deficiencies? But clearly you people don't have a grasp on the market we're dealing with." He cleared his throat. "It's terrible that you've been put in this predicament, Simon. I'm a man of my word, but under the circumstances I feel it's in the best interest of Mansfield that we rescind our preliminary contract."

Mr. Wakeman's shoulders squared and his face paled.

"I'm terribly sorry," Mr. Stockton said, giving Simon a non-committal look.

He looked at Mr. Wakeman expectantly. "Shall we?" he said, nodding at the briefcase on the floor.

Mr. Wakeman hesitated. "Y...Yes, of course."

Mr. Stockton exited first. Mr. Wakeman put his hand on the door knob and looked at Simon, quickly apologized, and then closed the door behind him.

Sandra was aghast, her mouth was wide open and Simon had to stifle the urge to order her to shut it or she'd catch flies. Ryder ran to the window and watched them both enter the vehicle. Neither men were speaking from what he could see.

"What the fuck was that?" Ryder said, almost breathlessly.

"What did he do in the bathroom?" Sandra said, as if his trip to the men's room changed everything.

Ryder shook his head. Simon chewed his finger.

"You were out of toilet paper." Ryder tallied the things that went wrong. "I spilled coffee, I don't know." His hands were outstretched.

"From the look on Wakeman's face he was blind-sided," Simon said matter-of-factly.

"He looked like he'd seen a ghost," Sandra agreed.

"I'll call tomorrow and talk to Irene. She'll know what's being said around the water cooler," Sandra offered. "In the meantime, I need to use the washroom. Maybe I'll have a sudden change of heart about important things in there, too." Sandra stomped off.

"What do we do now?" Ryder asked Simon.

"Keep going like we always do."

"We've never lost a deal before, Simon. What's happening?"

"It's called life, Ryder. Shit happens."

Sandra returned a moment later, rubbing her hands together. "Did you say we were out of toilet paper?"

"Yeah. Stockton was looking for some in Simon's bedroom."

"There's half a roll there and more in the cupboard."

Ryder's brows furrowed, and then he shrugged. "Maybe he didn't see it."

CHAPTER 16

Mark and Richard returned to the office just as Lisa was getting ready to pack it in for the day. "Sorry babe, we gotta call the sitter. We'll be pulling overtime tonight," Richard explained.

"It would appear that Max Dunphy has jumped bail," Mark added. "We need the usual. Contact Peggy Beck over at WNYU, get his picture on the news, alert all border crossings, airports, and get his credit cards tapped…and we need his phone records from his home, cell phone and from Mars Construction. He called in sick today from somewhere."

"He's got his cell phone on him, too," Richard added. "You think we can track him?"

"If he was stupid enough to hang onto it."

"Do we need to say he's armed?" Lisa asked.

"We can say he's *possibly* armed, but we have no proof that he's got anything on him. If he is the killer, knives are his weapons of choice," Mark said. "We need to find out if he had any cash on him, and if there are any places he liked to frequent."

"Who posted bail for him anyway?" Richard asked.

"I've no idea," Mark answered.

"On it," Lisa said.

Mark sat at his desk, leaning into the back of the chair, and interlaced his fingers behind his head. "What's the deal with our jumper?"

THE WHEELS OF CHANGE

Lisa typed away as she spoke to Mark through the open door separating his office from hers. "Bob should be done by now."

Mark rose. "Thanks. I'll go have a look-see."

He passed by Richard. "I've gotta go see Bob on the way to Clara Dunphy's. You up for it?"

As much as the thought of visiting the morgue and being in the presence of bodies and their strange-is-a-kind-way-to-describe-him pathologist, Richard was intrigued by the thought of getting to know Clara and Max Dunphy more.

"Sure. Can we grab some grub on the way?"

"Nothing healthy. I'm in the mood for grease and salt," Mark warned.

"Somewhere your cardiologist is screaming," Richard teased. "But he can't hear over your clogging arteries."

"Since when do you wanna go see Bob? Did someone dare you?" Mark retorted.

"Get along, boys," Lisa chided. "And Max Dunphy's picture will make the six o'clock news by the way. Oh, and Clara Dunphy posted bail."

"Excellent." Mark called back. "See you shortly."

...

The pathologist's office was painted a sickly white. Black tiles were placed here and there in an almost illogical pattern on the walls in the examination area. The black rubber trim around the room was so shiny Mark could see the reflection of his shoes in them. There was a large spotlight above the bed where Bob, the pathologist, was examining what appeared to be Michelle Pinchot's body.

Richard fell back, remaining behind the bed, making it look like he had something on his shoe. Mark rolled his eyes. "Hey Bob. Got anything on Michelle here?" he asked without preamble.

"Blunt force trauma to the face and skull upon impact."

"Anything unusual?"

"She's tried it before. Suicide." Bob turned over her wrists. There were scars running both across and lengthwise from previous attempts.

"There are also smaller scars from gashes and cuts scattered all over her body."

Mark scanned Michelle's body as Bob indicated the marks. He shook his head. "She was troubled."

"Very troubled," Bob agreed. "Toxicology came back with a laundry list of anti-depressants in her bloodstream."

Mark looked at Bob. "She was a reporter. How did nobody ever know she had so many issues?"

"People in the public eye can hide lots of truths," Bob explained. "Makeup can cover most scars, even brightly coloured tattoos can be covered nowadays. All the fancy makeup they have for high definition television...you can all but be missing a limb and nobody would know."

"And nobody noticed behavioural changes?"

"They sent her away to Africa. I can run a scan on her hair to see how long she's been on medication, but I don't see the use. She's dead now."

"Well, she liked knives, too, apparently," Richard interjected.

Mark knew where he was going with his comment. "But on herself. I doubt she's a suspect," Mark argued.

"The only way to know for sure is if someone else dies," Bob offered. "You can't kill when you're dead."

...

The outside light was on and they could see the reflection from the television through the living room window. Mark knocked on Clara Dunphy's door and they both waited. A few minutes passed and Richard knocked. "Maybe she's got company again," he muttered.

An inside light was turned on and the glass encasing the front door was illuminated. Clara opened the door in her bathrobe. Her hair was tied back in a messy ponytail and some of the hair poking out the bottom and sides was wet. "Sorry, I was in the tub," she explained.

She let them in and closed the door behind them. "Have you heard from Max?" Richard asked.

"No. Not yet. But he'll call," she said casually.

"What do you mean? Does he take off often?" Mark asked.

"Sometimes." She tightened the cording around her robe. "He's due back to work though, so I don't imagine he'll be gone much longer."

"According to his boss, he called in sick today. Do you know anything about that?"

"Nope. I told you I haven't seen him since last night."

"Do you know if he had any cash on him?" Richard asked.

Clara snorted. "We're not the Cleavers. He has his money, I have mine. We don't ask each other questions."

"Does he have anywhere in particular he likes to go to blow off steam?" Mark tried.

Clara smiled but it didn't reach her eyes. "Like I said. We're not the Cleavers."

"So you have no idea where he goes when he hangs out with his buddies? Does he have any friends you can connect us with?" There was tension in Mark's voice and she picked up on it.

"Look," she said flatly. "None of the places he goes to are where I would want to be. He's a filthy construction worker. I'm a business woman."

"Why are you two married?" Richard asked in disbelief.

"Not that it's any of your business," she spat back. "But I like being married to Max." She smiled too sweetly. "He's a big, burly guy who nobody likes to mess with. He protects me. And there's something about wearing a wedding band that appeals to me," she said, seductively eyeing Mark's left hand.

"Thanks, Ma'am," Richard said. "We'll be in touch."

"Holy friggin marriage of convenience," Richard commented as they headed back to the station. "She's got herself a body guard and he's got…well…who the hell knows what he's got. I think I'll go kiss the ground under Lisa's feet," he said matter-of-factly.

Mark agreed. "Yep. There's some crazy women out there. We've got one who's so loony she throws herself off a building, and another who makes Elvira look like Carol Brady."

"To everything there is a purpose," Richard declared. "I'm sure thankful for my wife right now. Forget about all the sarcasm and name calling when she was in labour with junior."

Richard faced Mark. "And look at you. Shelley came close to having an affair before, but never did. We've got a lot to be proud of."

Mark looked like he was a million miles away suddenly. "Hey, you think the murderer would go after females? Like…ones who cheat?"

"Oh. You're worried about Shelley?"

"Kinda. Yeah."

"Nah. I don't think this is a protest against adulterers in general. These murders are personal. Think about it. Both close range, both victims were caught off guard. This guy knows his victims. We gotta find the connection. Don't stress yourself about Shelley."

Mark wasn't convinced. "All the same. If Max is our guy, he's got a lot to be pissed with women over. I think I'll see if Noonan wouldn't mind keeping watch."

Richard shrugged. "Suit yourself."

…

Nancy ordered the cab to stop at the hotel Barbara said she was staying

THE WHEELS OF CHANGE

at. She paid the driver and exited, waiting for him to unload her luggage. A bellhop immediately appeared at the revolving door and assisted. Nancy looked up at the skyscraper and smiled. Barbara always had good taste.

When Nancy entered the building, the bellhop gestured her to check in at the counter. As she waited for the girl to call up her reservation on the computer, she heard the ping of the elevator behind her and turned around. She did a double-take. The tall man exiting the elevator recognized her instantly and returned her smile.

"I'll be damned," he said as he approached. He took her hand in his soft palms and kissed the backs of them like she was some sacred goddess.

"Ted," she said hesitantly. "I never expected to see you again."

"I'm in town on a conference."

She furrowed her brows. "Conference? I didn't know pastors attended those."

He chuckled. "That's because I'm not with the congregation any more."

Nancy's face scrunched. "Really? I thought you'd never leave the church."

"Ah. Things change. Why don't I tell you all about it over dinner tonight? I'm here for a couple more days. Have you time to spare?"

"Um, sure," Nancy stammered. "I'm here visiting my sister Barbara, but she's visiting someone here as well. I don't see it as a problem."

"Very well, then. How does seven o'clock sound? Would you like to dine here in the hotel, or are you familiar with this area?"

"Here's fine. It looks very classy." Nancy dipped her head around, taking in the surroundings. "I saw the brochure."

Ted grinned. "I'm looking forward to it. We've got a lot of catching up to do."

Nancy blushed. "Well, I should get up and see my sister. She doesn't even know I'm here yet."

Ted nodded and walked to the elevator. Nancy watched him as he pushed the call button and he winked at her upon entering the elevator. She had a sudden chill up her spine, remembering the last time she saw Ted ten years ago.

...

TED

"Simon!" Ted yelled. "Janice is on the phone for you!"

Nancy was in the kitchen cleaning up from dinner when the phone rang. Simon was home from college for Christmas.

"He's not going out with her again, is he?" Ted muttered under his breath.

"Oh, leave him alone, Ted. Janice is a nice girl."

"Nicer than that last one. Did you see how she dressed?"

Nancy rolled her eyes and shook her head. "Really, honey, you're exaggerating."

"Am I?"

Simon came barrelling down the hallway, breathless. "You guys still going to the Mason's for cards?"

"Yes, why?" Nancy asked.

"Janice is stopping by for a bit, and then we're going to catch a movie."

Nancy caught Ted's glance. "That's great, honey." She looked at her watch, averting his glare. "We should get going."

Ted helped Nancy with her jacket and then they walked out the door. When they reached the car, Ted started. "Really, Nancy. I don't like Simon being alone with that girl."

Nancy scoffed, closing the passenger side door. "Simon is an adult, Ted. He's in college for Christ sake." She caught herself saying the lord's name in vain. "Sorry."

THE WHEELS OF CHANGE

Ted let it go for a moment as he started the engine. It was a mere five minute drive to their destination. Before they reached the Mason's street, Ted started again. "You know how I feel about premarital sex, Nancy. I won't have it. It's against everything I believe in."

"What do you think we're having?" Nancy said pointedly.

"Nancy, until Simon is living on his own, he's not an adult. We are. And among consenting adults, it's acceptable to have premarital sex."

They turned into the Mason's driveway and Nancy picked her purse up off the floor with noted vigour. "If you want my opinion, I think it's hypocritical. And we don't even know if Simon's having sex with Janice, anyway, so I think you're worrying for nothing." She looked up at him as he pondered her comment. "Besides Ted, he's in college and away from the house nine months of the year. I can't keep tabs on him."

Ted let his temper flare. "I won't have it in my house! He can do what he wants when he's away, but as God is my witness I won't have him desecrating the holy bible under my roof!"

Nancy laughed and shook her head. "Well, then we have nothing to worry about. It's not your roof he lives under, it's mine."

The vein in Ted's neck was popping out. He stared at Nancy with his eyes bulging. Then he looked down at his hands as though in thought. A moment later he took a deep breath, peered out the window and then focused on Nancy again. "Maybe we should talk about this later. The Mason's are waiting for us."

"I think that's a good idea."

. . .

Simon was watching television when the doorbell rang. He opened the door and Janice stood outside in her long, woollen grey jacket and matching hat. Her blue eyes danced at the sight of Simon, "You look well. Seems you got some sleep since the last time I saw you."

"Thanks. Come on in. It's freezing out there." Simon rubbed his arms as he closed the door. "Did you walk here?"

"No. My dad dropped me off. You think you can give me a ride home?"

"Sure. Mom and Ted should be back by the time the movie's over. You don't mind walking there, do you?" The movie theatre was in the plaza across the street.

"Not at all."

"Good. The movie starts in about an hour. You hungry?"

Simon led Janice into the kitchen. "So, are you still working at Perry's Diner?" he said, opening up the fridge.

"Yep." She pointed to the pitcher of cold water. "Water's fine."

He poured two glasses of ice water and grabbed a bag of pretzels from the cupboard, and led her into the living room, where he switched on the television and they sat beside each other.

"So did you join any fraternities?"

"No. Not really my scene."

"Really?" Janice chuckled, helping herself to a handful of pretzels. "I always pictured you as the frat boy type. You know, partying it up, playing strip poker, stuff like that."

Simon's cheeks turned pink. "I don't drink and I'm too busy hoofing my way to the honour role to be at any parties. College isn't the good-time scene it's cracked up to be. At least not for me."

Janice snorted. "I suppose you're right. When I finished my whole *year* of college, I had more sleep than I did when I was in high school. Classes were boring and the people were snooty."

"Ever think about going back? Finishing your degree?"

"Yeah, if I ever figure out what the hell I want to do with my life."

"Well, that was your first mistake," Simon commented, swallowing a mouth full of pretzels.

"What do you mean?"

"Never go to college unless you've got focus," Simon advised. "I guess your old man was pretty pissed when you dropped out, huh."

"He got over it."

They watched five minutes of a comedy, made fun of how lame the show was, and then Janice looked at Simon contemplatively. "So tell me Simon, what do you do for fun in college?"

His eyebrow rose. "Not much. Study and work part time at the ad agency."

She laughed. "And that's fun?"

"No. Not really, I suppose," he admitted.

Simon looked at Janice and she returned his glance. The air around them had a strange charge, like a magnetic field between them had suddenly been altered. Janice's eyes wandered down to Simon's lips for a second, and then quickly returned to his eyes. He caught the glance.

"Ever meet anyone at school?" she asked. Her voice was soft, like they weren't alone and she didn't want his parents to overhear.

"Not really," he answered, letting his eyes travel down to her lips. "You?"

She shook her head no.

Slowly, Simon inched his way closer to Janice, until he could feel the warmth of her face against his skin. Both of their eyes closed. "What's happening to us, Simon?" she said, as if she had no idea what attraction felt like.

"I don't know." He breathed, placing his hand on her face. His thumb outlined her chin and she inhaled deeply. She angled her head and opened her mouth. Simon could feel her lips on his and he reciprocated. The first contact was just lips. Simon backed away, opening his eyes, searching hers. Janice's eyes were still closed. He opened his mouth again, taking her lips and searching for her tongue in an unpractised motion.

The awkwardness melted away once her tongue met his. They sat on the couch, passionately kissing for a few minutes, when Janice drew back and began removing her top.

"M…maybe we should go to my room," Simon suggested.

Janice did not have to be asked twice. Her eagerness charged Simon, and his initial apprehension went away. He followed her to his room, surprised she remembered where it was. It had been years since Janice had been there. When they were kids, they always played in the basement play room, and as they grew up they usually hung out in the kitchen or watched television as they had been.

He watched as she made her way through the hall, grabbing his hand, like they were in the fun house and didn't want to get separated. She didn't look for the light when they reached his bedroom. The door was closed and Simon could feel Janice pressing her body up against his as he leaned on the door. She laughed in a hushed manner as though they were winning at a game of hide and seek. He smiled and put his hands on her waist.

Janice's hands found Simon's hair and she grabbed a handful, voraciously kissing him. He slid his hand down to her backside and kneaded her buttocks. She could feel his hardness against her body and smiled in the dark. As she stepped back, Simon's eyes had adjusted to the darkness, and he could see her removing her clothes. He quickly removed his shirt and threw it on the floor.

His silhouette was stunning to her, shaved chest, toned pectoral muscles and a flat stomach. She lunged at him in her thong underwear, pinning him against the door, kissing him hungrily. When he moaned, she removed her lips from his and flattened her hands against his chest, feeling her way down his flank until she reached the zipper on his pants. When she unzipped, Simon swallowed nervously.

"Something wrong?" she asked seductively.

"N…no, well, I was just thinking…um…I don't have any…err…condoms or anything."

Janice chuckled. "Left your supply at the dorm, did you?"

"Yeah…um…something like that."

Simon was thankful the lights were off. His face was lit with embarrassment.

"Oh, Simon, baby." Janice breathed, running her index finger down his lips. "Go get my purse," she said before kissing him deeply once more. When she finished, she removed her body from his. "Go," she instructed. Simon opened the door, squinting as his eyes adjusted to the light. As though crossing a street, he looked both ways and spied her purse by the couch. He quickly grabbed it and padded his way back, taking a quick glance in the hallway mirror. His lips were swollen and red, his face was flushed.

When Janice saw him re-enter the bedroom, she closed the door and giggled, grabbing her purse. Simon crept up behind her and began kneading her rear end, kissing her back and neck. She found the foil packet and placed it on the bed.

"Now, let's get these off you," she said, and removed his pants and underwear.

Simon stood in front of her, and for the first time ever, he watched a woman gaze at him as though he was a sexual object. His erection was going limp with the coldness in the air and his apprehension. Janice caught his expression. "Ah, we can fix that in a flash," she said, bending to her knees.

As Janice placed his fullness in her mouth, he felt his heart pound. His breathing was cut off, like he'd just plunged into water. The feeling was unlike anything he could describe. His eyes rolled into the back of his head and his moans and laboured breathing were uncontrollable. She kept sucking and kneading him until he was so afraid he couldn't stop. "J...Janice. I...I can't..."

She knew exactly what she was trying to articulate, and he didn't have the strength to push her back so he wouldn't do the unthinkable in her mouth. Janice sucked harder and faster and Simon lost himself, unbeknownst to him that something like that was also pleasurable to a girl. His fingernails pressed into his hands so hard he swore he drew blood. Simon's cry was so loud when he climaxed, he was hoarse when it was over.

He tried to swallow, but his throat felt like it was covered in sand. "That was incredible," were the words he uttered, but he had no idea how. His breathing was still labored, his chest heaved up and down, and Janice pulled herself onto the bed, taking Simon with her.

Her body was soft and warm, her skin smooth and smelled faintly of honey. She moaned as his weight was completely on her. The sound of her voice against his ear caused him to stir again, and he was astounded by the physical reaction he was having to her. When she began kissing his neck and wrapping her legs around his waist, he was fully aroused again.

He had the sudden urge to touch her, like he was curious if her body would react as his had. Her breasts were pressed up in his chest and he hugged them with his hands, kissing and sucking them and the feeling was marvellous. All his senses were stimulated as he watched and listened to her response to his touch. He watched her nipples harden and elongate from his work and felt himself hardening further.

"I want you to suck me, Simon, and lick," she begged, grabbing his ears and guiding him down between her legs. The thought was a little intimidating at first, but after all the stuff he'd seen on the internet, he had to admit he was curious. He kissed her down her flank and she giggled a little as he reached the inside of her hips. He nuzzled that bony spot with his nose and she arched her back. He tried licking there, too, and she cried out. Simon could get used to this, he thought.

His lips and tongue reached further down. When he reached her thighs, Janice spread her legs further apart, exposing herself fully to him. Since it was dark, the only way he had to explore was with touch. First, he used his fingers. He placed his thumb on her sensitive nub and his middle finger inside her and she cried out immediately. She was so warm inside, the thought of placing his most sensitive part in there made him moan.

"Use your tongue, Simon," she breathed.

He'd recently seen a video on the internet where lovers were doing exactly what he and Janice were doing, and he remembered something about it that he thought to be particularly a propos. He left his middle finger working inside her, but swirled his tongue around her apex. Within one minute, Janice was crying out his name and threatening him physically if he stopped. He was afraid for a moment; worrying that she might crush his head or smother him, or worse, kick him in the throes of passion. But she did none of that. He felt her body stiffen and arch upward and she performed a combination cry/pant until the muscle contractions inside her stopped.

Simon realized that he was fully hard and completely aroused by her climax. Feeling brave, he reached for the foil packet on the edge of the bed and opened it, placing it on. She watched with a finger inserted seductively in her mouth. "You read my mind, Simon," she said, turning over onto her stomach.

"I like it hard, and don't be afraid to slap my ass, either," she instructed. Simon laughed, half hoping it was a joke.

"I guess we can forget about the movie," Janice commented as he slid into her.

"Fuck the movie," he said, surprising himself. His words and thoughts seemed not his own. He felt like he was having an out-of-body experience.

His eyes crawled backward again, and although the sensation was very different from being in her mouth, it was so pleasurable he had to exhale and inhale quickly.

"Oh, Simon," Janice cried. "Oh my god...Simon!" she cried louder. "Oh, FUCK ME!" she yelled, leaning her body repeatedly against his, trying to assist him.

Simon pumped hard and fast into her body, feeling so in control for the first time since they started. He slowed when he felt close to the edge, rubbing her breasts from behind. She moaned and reached for his hands, instructing him to squeeze her nipples. Her mouth opened and he watched her facial expression change into something that looked like pain, but he knew it wasn't.

"Harder! Harder!" she yelled and Simon complied. "I want you to come with me!" she ordered. At first he thought "Come? Where?" and then he remembered, and thought "But how is *that* possible?" Then she clenched her insides, hugging him from within and Simon lost control, climaxing with her.

They both fell apart together, and then she turned over and let Simon flop down beside her, spent. All that could be heard for a minute was their breathing. Simon swallowed and was about to say something, when he heard the door slam and Ted and Nancy began yelling.

...

"Dammit Nancy! What do you know about raising a boy, anyway? I've helped raise an entire congregation of boys!"

"Ted, he's MY boy, he's not some random child you see once a week!"

Simon darted up in bed. "Shit!" His heart began to pound. "They're home early!" he whispered.

"And for the record, he's not a boy…he's twenty two years old, Ted!" Nancy yelled.

Simon quickly switched on his desk lamp and they scrambled around the bedroom finding their clothes.

"Until he leaves the house he's still a boy. You still cook, do his laundry and buy clothes and groceries for him for God's sake!"

"I'm his mother! I try to help him! What am I supposed to do? That's how I show him I care!"

"Sure! I bet you buy condoms for him, too, don't you?"

Nancy's face was red with rage. "That is none of your business!"

Simon and Janice were straightening their clothes and hair when he realized they needed a reason why they were in the bedroom together, alone. He quickly switched on his television and gaming console and threw a controller at Janice, who was smoothing the bed sheets. She looked at him and smiled, realizing his hair told the tale and assumed hers did, too.

"You do, don't you?" Ted sneered. "I bet you he's got a box right in his room that you bought for him," he said, pointing towards Simon's closed bedroom door.

Nancy looked at the ground and shook her head, "You know what, Ted? You're a real piece of work. You have zero respect for my son, and very little for me." She walked towards Simon's bedroom door. "My son is out watching a movie with a friend, minding his own business, and all you can do is pick on him. What's he ever done to you?" Nancy put her hand on the knob as Simon and Janice straightened their hair and tried to look innocent.

"How many twenty-two year olds do you know who are on the honour role? Who come home every holiday? He stays out of trouble, doesn't drink, doesn't have sex and keeps his room clean. What more can I ask for?"

Ted was standing right beside her when she opened the door. Nancy's face registered surprise when she saw Simon and Janice sitting on the bed, presumably playing a game on the console. "Oh...s...sorry honey. I thought you were going to a movie," she stammered, her face was lit up with embarrassment and shock.

The smug look on Ted's face was enough to cause Simon to make a fist. Janice saw it and put her hand over his. Ted walked into the bedroom, clearly not leaving until he saw what he wanted. There was no evidence of any frolicking...except for the condom wrapper left on the floor just tucked under the bed. Ted knelt down and picked it up, hoisting it like a cigarette between his index and middle finger. "Well, that answers my question." He turned it over so Nancy could clearly see what it was.

Simon rose abruptly and pummelled toward Ted. Nancy sprinted forward and stopped him, standing between them with her arms outstretched. She looked at Ted and spoke pointedly. "I think you should leave, Ted."

He chuckled, almost maniacally. "Yeah. I think it's time I did."

That was the last time Nancy and Simon saw or heard from him.

...

As much as Ted was a real pain in the ass when it came to Simon, she missed his gallant attitude toward women, the flowers he brought her weekly, and the way he praised her for staying sober all the years they were together. Nancy couldn't help but also give credit to his faith in helping keep her clean.

After Ted left, Nancy gradually fell back into her old ways. It was less than six months after when she started using drugs again. It was almost like deja-vous. Barbara had called her out to one of Ralph Lavernier's exhibits and into the world of drugs and sex, forcing Nancy back off the wagon.

Nancy knew what she was doing was wrong. She knew deceiving Simon, especially now, was shameful. But she didn't know how else to deal with it. Escaping by getting high was something that she'd always done, and she was never able to get past it, no matter what treatment she received.

She knew Simon would probably get on the first plane and drag her back home if he got wind of what she was up to. The disgrace she felt for herself was enough to knock her dwindling self-esteem down further. Nancy was about to give up and head back to the airport, when she heard a familiar voice call her name from behind.

"Nancy! Oh my God, Nancy! You're here!" Barbara screeched. Nancy turned around and saw Barbara running towards her, with outstretched arms. She hadn't changed a bit. Barbara still looked ten years younger than her true age. Not a stitch of grey hair or wrinkles could be found on her, and her body still remained well sculpted and lean.

Nancy noted the leather pants she was wearing and blurted, "Jesus girl, you still have those things?"

Barbara kissed her on both cheeks, the way celebrities do without actually touching, and laughed. "They're my favourite! How the hell are you?"

"I'm doing well." Nancy gestured to Barbara with her eyebrow raised. "Clearly you're doing well, too."

"Nothing a French-Canadian lover can't do," Barbara winked.

"Let's get you up to your room so we can catch up!"

CHAPTER 17

"Anything on Max yet?" Mark called to Lisa. It had been more than twelve hours since word went out that he jumped bail.

"Idiot left his cell phone in his truck," Lisa reported. "Do you believe that?"

"Great," Mark said sarcastically.

"Noonan and Hobbs went to search when they traced it late last night."

"Yeah?" Mark said. "Was the wife around? Did they ask why his truck was so clean? You could eat off the floors."

"Apparently she was sick in it a few days ago. He had to clean the smell of puke out of it. I guess everyone has their vices."

"Any guns registered in his name?"

"Nope. I'd say our best bet is to monitor his bank transactions and put a tap on the Dunphy's home phone."

"Put a tap on Mars Construction, too. The guy called in sick the other day, he's bound to call again if he doesn't show up there."

Mark's cell phone rang. His brows furrowed. It was Shelley. "Hey babe, what's up?" Mark greeted

Shelley's voice was quivering. "I have to head over to the hospital," she sniffled.

His heart pounded. "What's wrong? Are you sick?"

"No, no, I'm fine. It's Jessica."

"What is it? Where is she?" he said through pursed lips.

"She's bleeding. She may be having a miscarriage," Shelley sighed. "She's not through her first trimester yet, so it's possible."

"I'm on my way." Mark motioned to Richard. Lisa was sitting at her desk, one eye on her computer, the other on Mark.

"She's just at County Hospital. Michael's with her," Shelley added.

"I'll meet you there."

Richard and Lisa looked expectantly at Mark. "Jessica's pregnant...er...she may be having a miscarriage."

Lisa looked sullen. "It's pretty common. I had one, too. She'll be fine."

"I'll be on my cell." Mark saluted them both as he left the station.

...

Mark pulled into the hospital and saw Shelley waiting for him outside the front doors to the Emergency department. When Mark's car door slammed, Shelley began walking toward him.

"How's she doing?" Mark asked, pressing his key fob.

"They're going to run some tests. She's in a lot of pain." Shelley took his hand in hers. Her face was pale and her eyes were red rimmed like she hadn't slept. They walked together to the entrance.

"Is she still bleeding?"

"Yes. She's so scared."

Up until Michael and Jessica married, Jessica wasn't sure whether or not she wanted to have children. Michael came from a family notorious for marrying and having children young. Jessica was never a fan of that. She wasn't the career-driven type, but she also didn't see herself tied down with

THE WHEELS OF CHANGE

half a dozen children before her thirtieth birthday.

"How's Michael doing?"

"He's heart-broken." Shelley looked at Mark earnestly. "You know how badly he wants kids. I think they've been trying a while from the sounds of it."

The thought of Jessica 'trying', no matter how sugar-coated the words were, still brought a twinge of nausea to Mark. "I'll bet." He stared at the ground.

As Shelley lead them through the main doors, past registration and the dilapidated coffee shop, Mark was reminded of his last visit to the hospital when he had a heart attack. The thought sent a chill up his spine. The emergency ward was packed with people, and Mark was thankful he left his hat in the car. His jacket and uniform was enough of a giveaway and he sensed many eyes on him, wondering why on earth a cop was there.

There was the odd baby crying, but generally everyone was quiet despite the waiting crowd. Nobody was moaning except a guy in a corner of the room, holding a blood-soaked rag around his index finger.

Shelley announced their arrival and they were led through a set of double doors and down a corridor. The nurse gave Shelley and Mark instructions on how to find their way to the room where Jessica was. When they reached her room, Michael was sitting in a plastic chair beside an unmade, empty bed.

"Where's Jessica?" Shelley said, unsuccessfully hiding her panic.

"Hey, Mark." Michael paused, rising to shake his father-in-law's hand. "They took her for an ultra sound. I wasn't allowed to go," Michael answered Shelley.

"Jesus. I leave for one minute." Shelley stormed out the door.

Michael stopped her. "Nobody is allowed. I asked."

"The hell I'm not," Shelley said firmly. "I'm her mother."

Michael shrugged. "They went that way." He pointed her in the right direction and re-joined Mark.

137

The tension in the room was palpable. Mark observed the sign on the wall prohibiting the use of cell phones and muttered under his breath. "Dammit. Did you see a payphone around here?"

Michael raised his arm and pointed in the opposite direction he told Shelley to turn. "I think there's one down there."

"Thanks." Mark headed out the door. He reached into his pocket and took his cell phone out. Just as he was about to turn it off, it rang.

A nurse walking towards him gave a stern look and before he answered it. She pointed further down the hall to an area with couches and a television. "Cell phones are allowed over there, sir."

Mark picked up the pace, almost sprinting to the safe area as he answered the call.

Lisa's voice was urgent. "They picked up Max Dunphy."

"Shit!" Mark stomped, running his fingers through his hair. He knew he couldn't leave the hospital. Resenting moments like this, he pursed his lips. "Who's with him?"

"Richard at the moment. Andy's on his way."

"Where'd they find him?"

"Our guys were over at his house installing phone taps. He just showed up."

"Where was he?"

"Not sure. Richard's got him in interrogation." She hesitated. "You want me to patch you through?"

Mark felt a tap on his right shoulder. He turned around. Shelley was standing there with reddened eyes. Her arms were across her chest.

"Not now," he said to Lisa, looking at his wife's serious expression. "I'll call you back."

...

THE WHEELS OF CHANGE

"So..." Barbara said as soon as the bellhop finished delivering all Nancy's things to her room. "What's new?" Her hands slid together as though she was waiting to hear some juicy news.

"Nothing really." Nancy stared at her hands. "Except for Simon."

Barbara frowned. "Now, don't you worry about Simon." she advised, somewhat insensitively. "He's a big boy and he can take care of himself."

"That's true," Nancy smiled. "Ryder's with him and he's got an occupational therapist at his beck-and-call."

"There you go." Barbara patted her on the shoulder. "Now let's have some fun!"

Nancy watched her sister as she walked excitedly over to the small refrigerator in the corner of the suite. "What's your poison?" She opened the door. "Bailey's, red or white whine, scotch or vodka?"

Nancy pursed her lips in thought. Barbara picked up on her indecisiveness. "Still not much of a drinker, are you?"

"Not really." Nancy laughed, feeling anxious.

Suddenly there was an elephant in the room. They were silent. Barbara was well aware that Nancy had been through more rehab than Barbara had been through men. Although they hadn't spoken of Nancy's drug problems recently, Barbara knew merely by Nancy's presence in her life, that she was off the wagon. Their relationship was like an on-off switch. When Nancy was in rehab or off the drugs, she cut off contact with Barbara. Conversely when she was using, Barbara was practically her best friend. The pattern had been going on for most of their adult lives.

Barbara tested the waters. "Simon got you in rehab lately?"

Nancy swallowed dismissively. "No."

"Does he know you're using?"

Nancy shook her head.

Barbara closed the refrigerator door and walked to the large metal door

139

separating the two rooms. She opened it and took Nancy's hand. "Come on."

...

Dr. Bennett opened his chart. "Good morning, Simon."

Simon nodded. He lay on the bed inside Dr. Bennett's office. Ryder sat next to him in the guest chair.

"It looks like things are coming along rather well." Dr. Bennett was pleased. "Darla sent me a report a few minutes ago."

"Yeah. She's stopping by again this morning, right after I'm done with you here."

"Excellent." Dr. Bennett rose and made himself busy with the equipment above Simon's head. "How's business going? You been able to adapt yourself a little?"

Ryder chimed in. "I'm clumsier than he is lately." His thumb pointed at Simon.

Simon snorted.

"It's not funny, man." Ryder was incredulous. "If it hadn't been for me running out of goddamn ass-wipe and knocking over the friggin coffee…"

Dr. Bennett turned around, looking expectantly at Ryder. "What's this?"

"We had a botched business meeting," Simon explained. "Ryder thinks it's his fault."

"It *is* my fault," Ryder insisted. "We should just have it at the office the next time. It's handicap equipped."

Simon was about to scold Ryder for the use of the term 'handicap', when Dr. Bennett interrupted. "Now, I don't know if that's such a good idea just yet."

"Why not?" Simon asked.

Dr. Bennett removed the reading glasses he had perched on his nose.

"Tell you what. We'll see how your treatment goes tomorrow and take it from there." He then hesitated. "That's also dependent on your therapy. If you do what Darla asks, we may be able to allow it."

Simon waited. Dr. Bennett checked Simon's reflexes and mobility in his legs.

Dr. Bennett cleared his throat. "In the meantime, Simon..." He closed the file. "You need to get lots of rest and take your medication. If everything goes as planned, you may be able to get back to work...at least part-time for now, anyway."

"That's great, doc," Simon smiled sincerely. "I'd do just about anything to get back to normal."

The delight in his face was contagious. Ryder patted Simon on the arm.

Dr. Bennett folded the stems of his glasses together and lay his glasses on his chest; he came right next to Simon. The look on his face was practiced, like he had rehearsed giving bad news a thousand times before. "Now, Simon," he warned, his voice was matter-of-fact. "It's important that you understand what normal is as opposed to what it was."

The smile was wiped off Simon's face instantly. He looked at Dr. Bennett and mirrored the serious expression.

Dr. Bennett continued. "What I meant by normal is that your tissues will be healed and no further damage is inherent." Dr. Bennett blinked and glanced quickly at Ryder, then back to Simon. "This may be your *new* normal."

Simon pursed his lips but nodded reluctantly.

"There's still a chance that you may get some functionality back," Dr. Bennett surmised. "But remember there's only a forty to fifty percent probability that that will happen."

Simon looked out the window, like he was a million miles away. "Yeah, I understand."

...

"Hey, Simon," Darla said after Ryder let her in the door. Simon just washed down the last of his coffee and donut.

Darla noticed the empty package of donuts on the counter. "We've gotta get you on a proper diet, I see," she commented. "You keep eating those and sitting in that and soon we'll need a big-wheel sized chair for you."

"Too bad none of our clients make wheelchairs, huh Simon," Ryder joked.

Simon looked at Ryder as though he just called his mother a whore. "I'd like to get the fuck out of this chair if it's alright with you."

Ryder realized he took it too far. "Hey, sorry buddy. My timing always sucks." He grabbed his cell phone off the kitchen table. "I'm gonna get out of your hair for a while. Talk to you later."

Simon nodded, but his expression remained abhorrent. "Later."

Ryder looked at Darla, who winked as if to say 'I can handle it from here'.

When the door closed, Darla broke the silence. "Those donuts are what's getting you so cranky, Simon." She reached into her hockey-sized bag and presented a book to him. "This helped me a lot when I went through a…" Darla sighed, searching for the right words. "Shall we say, chunky phase." She air quoted 'chunky'.

Simon examined the book. The pages were curled and there were pencil markings in the margins. It looked like it had been through the wash a couple of times too, and felt like it weighed more than a sack of potatoes. It was a recipe book.

"What am I going to use this for?" he asked, as if it was the most ridiculous thing he'd heard.

Darla laughed. "After your treatment is over, you're going to need to learn to cook," she explained. "You'll burn very few calories sitting in a chair all day, even less if you have someone wheeling you around." Her eyebrows rose. "You think you're going to have someone deliver your meals all the time?"

Simon hesitated. "My mom doesn't work."

THE WHEELS OF CHANGE

Darla smiled. "And where is she now?"

He exhaled slowly. Had those words been delivered by anyone else, Simon may have rebuked. However, there was something about Darla's attitude that seemed soft and caring, yet realistic. She was not patronizing him or shaming him. Simon did not feel defensive or belittled.

"You'll find most of your family and friends will be there for you. But everyone has a life of their own, Simon. And judging from what I've known of you so far, up until now you've been pretty independent," Darla said, shining her white teeth at him in an earnest smile. He didn't know whether or not to take her statement as a compliment or simply an observation. She was not trying to pat his ego, that he could tell.

Darla rose, wheeling Simon over to the floor. "Now, I bet you're wondering why the book looks so beat up, huh?"

"Kinda."

"Well," she lifted his feet out of the metal supports. "We're going to use this for strengthening," she explained. "First, we'll start with your arms and then, God willing, we'll move to your legs."

Simon frowned and cocked his head to the side, like what she said sounded reasonable. He looked at Darla, who was removing his socks and asked, "Hey Darla, how many of your clients have you seen walk again?"

Darla smiled and took Simon's chin in her hand, as though he was a child asking for a cookie right before dinner time. "That's like asking a soldier how many he's killed, Simon." She let go of his chin. "I never answer that question. It's bad luck."

Darla was flexing Simon's foot, knee and then his entire leg, a sensation that felt very foreign to him. Her movements were soft and fluid, giving the illusion that his leg was made of sponge.

Simon thought for a moment, and then re-phrased the question. "What do you think my chances are?"

Darla moved to his other leg and repeated the procedure. "Honestly, it's really too early to tell," she said, her tone comforting. "Let's wait until after your treatment tomorrow. I'm sure we'll know more by then."

143

He was silent. Watching her work soothed him, the way she handled his limbs so expertly made him wonder how a woman of her scant size could be so nimble with a man nearly twice her weight.

"We're going to try some floor work now. Do you need a rest?" she asked.

Simon laughed. "You're asking if *I* need a rest?" he pointed at himself. "I figured *you* might need one."

Darla smiled. "All in a days' work," she said while she manoeuvred Simon onto the floor.

"How do you do that?" Simon asked as he observed her technique.

"Years of training, Simon."

She laid him flat on his back on the floor and began flexing his legs from the knee to the thigh, asking him if he felt certain movements and where. He felt a pull in his groin and flinched. "I felt that."

"Where?"

"Um…there."

"Painful or a pull?"

"A pull."

"Okay, that's good." Darla lowered his leg back down.

Simon licked his lips and chuckled. "How about this question," he said cheekily. "How many clients have you seen that are able to perform again?"

Darla began lifting his other leg and glanced at him quickly. "Perform?" she asked. "You mean sexually?"

"Yes."

Darla laughed out loud for a moment, like she was slightly embarrassed. "I don't believe I've ever asked any of my clients that before!"

"Ha, that's true," Simon laughed. "I never thought of that."

"However," Darla said, flexing Simon's arm. "There are many ways to make love. It doesn't have to be just through intercourse."

Simon scoffed. "I guess as a lesbian, you would know that, right."

He waited for her to be offended.

"Not necessarily, Simon." Darla switched arms. "You don't have to be a lesbian to learn how to make love to someone without the use of penetration."

Simon was intrigued. Normally by now, he would be licking his wounds from the backlash.

"Making love is a sensual thing," Darla continued. "It occurs not only through your sex organs, but through your mind and heart." Darla shifted to his feet again.

"A person turned on sexually will experience pleasure, of course, and can probably achieve orgasm without a doubt, maybe even several." Darla observed the movement of Simon's toes. "But someone who makes an intellectual or spiritual connection with another person can experience pleasure on so many other levels, even by the simple touch from their lover."

"I don't understand," Simon admitted. "You can have sexual feelings for someone, even without having sex?"

"It's not about the act of sex, Simon." She checked the movement of his toes on the other foot. "It's about connection. Have you ever been in love?"

Simon laughed. "No."

"That's such a shame, really," Darla observed. "People who are in love can go weeks, months or even years without actually having sex or making love and still feel a connection and be properly satisfied, simply by holding hands, cuddling or just spending quality time together."

Simon was quiet, digesting the information.

"It's quite a phenomenon," Darla insisted. "And if two people love one another, they will find a way to make love to each other."

"So what about these newlywed couples who can't keep their hands off one another?" he challenged.

"Well, that's lust, Simon. And it does fizzle out after a while."

"How do you know all this? I thought you said you weren't married?"

"I'm not," Darla stated. "But my parents have been happily married for over thirty years."

"Wow." Simon was impressed. "My parents divorced when I was like ten."

"Such a shame." Darla released Simon's foot. "What happened?"

"Long story…long, *boring* story."

"We've got time." Darla's voice was soft. She retrieved a long, rubbery ribbon-like piece of material out of her bag and brought it over to Simon. "I'm going to help you, but I want you to take this Theraband and place it across the sole of your foot. I'll lift your leg." Darla did this as she explained and Simon carefully placed the band around his foot. "We're going to hold it for ten seconds, lower and repeat five times. Okay?"

Simon nodded.

"So tell me about your father. I've not met him." Darla lifted Simon's leg. Simon struggled for a moment, pulling the band across his foot. "That's it," Darla soothed.

"My father and mother, as I said, divorced when I was about ten." Simon held the band in between his hands on either side of his foot. "Dad's remarried to a woman mom calls 'Betty Boop'."

Darla chuckled. "Clever."

"Anyway, dad started coming home real late from work, you know, spending less and less time at home."

"Ah."

THE WHEELS OF CHANGE

"Grandma started watching me a lot and after a while it was almost like dad phased himself out of the family."

"Did mom and dad fight a lot?"

"Yeah. If dad was home, they fought. I figured that was the reason dad stayed away, but mom told me later that he'd had an affair."

"How old were you when she told you?"

"I don't know. I think I was twelve or thirteen. Dad was long gone."

Darla switched to the opposite leg. "How did your mom take it when your dad left?"

Simon cleared his throat. "Not well. It took her nearly ten years to start dating again."

"Geez. That's a long time, Simon," Darla tutted. "What did she do? Has she ever worked?"

"Yeah. She used to do work-from-home stuff like Avon and Mary Kay. Things like that."

"When did she stop?"

"When we moved to California," Simon explained. "I started making enough money to support her, so she stopped working."

"Really? Didn't she enjoy it?"

"I think she did," Simon said. "She just figured there was no need anymore."

Darla scratched the bridge of her nose and pursed her lips, "I suppose after suffering through a painful divorce, I wouldn't be much interested in work, either. Especially doing something like that." Then she cocked her head to the side. "Although, if you were making enough money to support her, I suppose she could have gone to school or something."

Simon rolled his eyes. "That'll be the day."

147

Darla smiled. "Why is that so strange?"

"My mother isn't the motivated type. Right now she's out hobnobbing with my aunt Barbara and a French-Canadian artist."

"Really?" Darla chuckled, good-naturedly. "I pictured her to be the real maternal kind. I thought she was suffocating you or something. I figured you'd sent her away."

Simon hesitated. He wasn't sure if sharing his mother's drug problem was the smartest thing to do...yet. "No, she hasn't seen her sister in a year or two, something like that. So she went for an open-ended visit."

Darla sensed his discomfort and decided to change the subject. "So what do you do for a living?"

Simon looked at her in shock. He was so used to being well recognized, but he couldn't help but find it refreshing, since he'd made such a playboy reputation for himself, one that he could no longer live up to. "Are you serious?"

"What do you mean?"

"I'm Simon Cross," he said, as if she should know. "Simon Cross Advertising?" He started singing a tune from one of his most popular jingles.

Darla recognized the song. "Oh really?" she laughed. "You did that?"

"Yeah," Simon said. "There are billboards and ads and all kinds of crap with my face plastered to it."

"Really." She lowered his leg a final time. "So you're quite a celebrity around here, then."

Simon hesitated, and then scoffed. "Yeah."

"What's wrong?" Darla reached in her bag.

"I guess I've made a bit of an ass of myself over the years." He stared at the ceiling.

"How's that?"

THE WHEELS OF CHANGE

Simon sighed. "I've not exactly been an angel since becoming successful."

Darla found a bottle of water in her bag and pulled it out. "Nobody's perfect, Simon."

"Yeah, but I'm pretty sure the Pearly Gates won't be open for me."

Darla took another sip. "It's never too late to make a change."

Simon felt frustrated in a way, since Darla had no idea what kind of reputation he'd made for himself. "You believe that, don't you." He said it like it was a statement. Like nobody would believe that that same sentiment applied to everybody.

"Of course I do," she encouraged. "Anyone can change for the better if they put their mind to it."

"It's not that simple," Simon stated.

Darla put the bottle away and helped Simon back up into his wheelchair. "I believe it is, actually." Darla adjusted Simon's feet so they rested comfortably on the steel plate. "Once you begin to visualize a change, any change, and focus on it, there isn't anything you can't do."

"If it's a career goal, yeah, but if it's part of your personality or who you are, you can't," Simon argued.

"That's not true, Simon."

"Yeah, it is," Simon stated firmly.

Darla sat in the chair beside Simon and looked at him. "Simon, I grew up with a severe learning disability. Doctors told my parents I would never amount to anything. Look at me now." She lifted her arms up.

"Well, yeah, a learning disability. You can overcome those. People do it all the time," Simon said, checking himself.

Darla laughed without a trace of humor. "Simon. It took me ten years to overcome it. Thousands of dollars and years of therapy and tutoring, but none of it could have happened if I didn't want it to or if I didn't believe in

149

myself."

Darla pointed at her head. "It's all about drive and motivation." Then she pointed at him, "And you have it. How else could you have risen so far in your career?"

Simon was unconvinced. "But you had support. People liked you. Except for Ryder and Sandra, everyone else sees me as either a paycheck or a goddamn lay." A vein was popping up in Simon's neck.

Darla was silent.

Simon continued, his voice had risen an octave, "You know how I ended up in this mess?" He smacked his legs with both hands. "Someone tried to kill me."

Darla blinked.

"I slept with a married woman and her husband found out." Simon swallowed and took a breath, realizing he'd said enough. They were both silent for a few moments.

Darla spoke quietly. "Simon, do you think you deserved this? Do you blame yourself?"

"I don't feel good about it," he said so low Darla had to strain to hear.

Darla took his hand in hers. "I think once you come to terms with this, Simon, you'll realize you made a mistake, one that you have to forgive yourself for. Once you get there, and see what you can do to change, it will become clear what needs to be done."

"I think the punishment is permanent, don't you Darla?" Simon was persistent. "The old man upstairs made sure I'd never be able to sleep around again."

Darla squeezed Simon's hands. "This isn't punishment, Simon. Everything happens for a reason. It's a lesson or a challenge."

Simon stared at Darla's hands, realizing it was the first time ever that a woman had touched him and not wanted something from him. He looked up at her. "Sure, Darla. God has not only taken my manhood away, but he's also sent someone to me who not only *wouldn't* be interested in me, but who *couldn't* be interested in me, just to see how *shitty* it feels. I call that payback."

...

Janice snorted another hit of coke and watched her sister frolic in the corner of the room with her lover. They were performing some strange pre-coitus dance that looked like a combination of Woodstock and Dirty Dancing. Barbara was wearing a designer dress that looked like it was made of ribbon coiled around her body, just covering all the essentials. Raphael was wearing a three-piece suit that probably cost more than Simon's car.

"Janice, my dear, do you want to hit the lounge?" Raphael asked, removing himself from Barbara's hold. He reached to shut off his iPod on top of the fireplace.

She looked down at her dress, bought with Simon's money on their earlier jaunt downtown. It was an eggplant coloured frock made of lined silk. "Don't you guys want to be alone?" she sniffed the last bit of powder inside her nose.

"Plenty of time for that later." Raphael winked at Barbara who was standing in the mirror, touching up her eyeliner. She looked back at his reflection and mimed kissing him.

"What time is it?" Janice asked, suddenly remembering her date with Ted, her ex-lover she unexpectedly ran into earlier in the hotel lobby.

"It's almost six o'clock," Barbara answered. "I thought we would hit the lounge for cocktails, and then go downtown for dinner and drinks."

"You two go ahead," Nancy offered. "I'll just have dinner and hit the sack. The travelling kind of tired me out."

"Nancy, you're becoming a drag," Barbara whined, painting on red lips, too red for the colour of her dress. "I think tomorrow we'll have some girl time and get to the bottom of that."

Raphael grabbed Barbara and seductively kissed her neck. "Oh, leave your sister alone. Perhaps she just needs some time alone, my love."

"Alright." Barbara placed the lipstick in her clutch purse. "But tomorrow I'm getting you out of here. We're going out on the town."

"Haven't we already seen it?" Nancy asked.

"Oh honey, if you're bored we can go somewhere else," Barbara suggested, hooking her arm on Raphael's. Barbara waved at her sister like she was a queen and winked. "Ta-ta."

...

Nancy waited until she no longer heard Barbara's high-heeled shoes clicking along the marble floor in the hallway and walked back into her side of the suite. She grabbed her purse and pulled out her makeup bag. As she touched up her makeup, she looked in the mirror and gazed at herself. The years had not exactly been kind to her. Her mother's wrinkled eyes and mouth stared back at her, while her sister unfairly inherited her father's timeless features.

She peered down at her body, noting how well she'd kept that up. Years of exercise and dieting, while sometimes were a fad, overall had a nice effect. Nancy credited herself on her attractive teeth, proud that she never lit another cigarette after her bout of pneumonia during a visit to rehab. Nancy had done well, so she thought, and felt she should walk tall when she encountered Ted again shortly.

Nancy placed a few drops of Visine in each eye, concealing any evidence of the small hit she took with Barbara earlier. One last smoothing of her dress and Nancy locked her hotel room, heading to the elevator to meet Ted.

Ted was seated by the bar on a high-backed stool when she approached. "Ah, right on time." Ted gallantly kissed the back of her hand. "Punctual as always."

He opened her arms and looked at her body. "You look wonderful, Nancy." His eyes danced. "Haven't changed a bit."

She couldn't help but blush. Ted was always great with compliments. "You're looking well, too, Ted. Thanks."

Ted was wearing a three-piece suit, but more like a Ralph Lauren than Raphael's taste in men's clothing. His shoes were polished to a gleaming shine and his hair had greyed slightly, but was still as thick as it was ten years ago.

THE WHEELS OF CHANGE

"Please, have a seat. Our table should be ready any minute," Ted said to Nancy.

"Thank you." She sat next to him. "So how are you?"

"That was my opening," Ted joked. "It's been a long time, Nancy." He waved the bartender over. "What would you like?"

"White wine," she answered. Ted smiled. His teeth were still pearly white and his eyes still had that same look of stubborn intelligence.

"May I be so bold to ask…are you seeing anyone?" Ted asked.

"No," Nancy answered, wishing like hell the coke hadn't practically worn off. She could use some courage. She felt like she left her spine in the hotel room.

The bartender served her wine and Ted told him to place it on his tab.

"Are *you* seeing anyone?" Nancy asked, sipping her wine.

"No," he said with the slightest hint of reluctance. "I was, though. Up until six months ago."

"What happened?"

"She met someone else," he explained. "I was working out of town a lot. It was bound to happen."

"You don't seem terribly upset."

"It wasn't serious. It was on and off."

Nancy's brows furrowed as she put down her wine glass. "So, why are you here?"

"Business," he said simply. "I have out of town contacts. I work at a consulting firm."

"What do you consult?" Nancy asked, still confused.

"I'm an organizational consultant. When a business is in trouble, they

153

hire me to come in, analyze, make suggestions, and in some cases I help implement my suggestions."

"How did you go from pastor at a local church to that?" Nancy snorted, and then checked herself.

"You'd be surprised how much experience running a church gives you, Nancy," he said matter-of-factly. "I took some courses and started small. That was eight years ago."

"What made you leave the church?"

"I didn't feel I was helping anyone anymore," Ted said solemnly. "I had a church member who I just couldn't reach. Then another. And then another." His eyes registered sadness even though his mouth was curled up in a smile. "Then I realized I may be better off helping the corporate world."

"Sorry to hear it didn't work out."

"Everything happens for a reason. It wasn't my calling anymore."

"That was quite a leap for you," Nancy nodded. "I thought you would never leave the church."

Ted touched her hand. "I was very headstrong, wasn't I?"

"You were." Nancy shook her head at the memory of their last argument.

Ted changed the subject. "I can't believe we've been sitting here for five minutes and you haven't mentioned Simon once."

"He's doing well. He has his own advertising company in California." She tried to gloss over the predicament he was in.

"Really?" Ted's face lit up. "Why, I never would have guessed. Is he married?"

Nancy answered too quickly. "No, no. He's very much into his business."

"Well, *good* for him." Ted accentuated the word 'good' a little too much.

154

THE WHEELS OF CHANGE

Ted ordered another round even though neither of them had finished their drinks. Nancy felt the tension. But before she could change the subject, Ted asked, "So, you said you were here with your sister? Is that...Barbara?"

Nancy nodded, taking a sip of wine.

"How's she doing?"

The hostess arrived, their table was ready. Ted gestured Nancy to go ahead while they were led to their table. Ted pulled out Nancy's chair and she took a seat. "Thank you," she said, adjusting her dress so it didn't wrinkle too much as she was seated.

The hostess placed their menus on the table and left, noting they still had drinks from the bar.

"Barbara is great," she said, answering his previous question. "She's visiting a friend and invited me to join them."

Ted nodded. "So what do you do? Still working from home?"

"No. I pretty much gave that up when Simon opened his business."

"Ah, you help Simon out around the office, do you?"

"Sometimes." Nancy tried to conceal her discomfort by fiddling with her napkin.

"He's quite successful, is he? Such a shame about the accident."

Nancy's eyes narrowed. "How did you know about that?"

"I was in town, working with a telecommunications company based in LA last month. I left the next day," Ted said all in one breath. "Tell me, did they ever pick up the Mars Construction guy? I saw his picture on the news."

Nancy's nostrils flared. "So you knew about Simon and yet you asked how he was doing? Why did you patronize me? Is this some kind of joke?" She banged on the table with her fist.

155

"Come, come dear. Calm down, there's no need to get upset," Ted said, although his eyes were dancing.

"Don't tell me to calm down!" Nancy shouted. "You've always hated my son and I bet you're loving it that he's down on his luck."

Ted laughed and folded his arms over his chest. "If he's in such a state, tell me, why are you here visiting your sister? Did things get too serious for you, Nancy?"

She quickly rose, placing her napkin on the table. "I'm finished here. I won't listen to another word of this."

As she stormed away, Ted called her back. "Err...Nancy?" She abruptly turned to him. "You've got some powder on your lip, dear."

CHAPTER 18

"What's happened?" Mark asked Shelley as he placed his phone back in his pocket. "Is Jessica going to be okay?"

Shelley fought the tear edging its way out of the corner of her eye. "She lost the baby."

Mark's lips pursed as he put his arms around his wife. "She'll have another one. Lisa even said it's pretty common on the first try. We were lucky with our girls, I guess." He rubbed her back and kissed the top of her head in an effort to soothe her.

"I know that. That part wouldn't be so awful if it weren't for her having to have surgery."

"What?" Mark released Shelley. "What do you mean…surgery?"

"She had an ectopic pregnancy. They have to repair the fallopian tubes." Shelley put her hand in front of her mouth, tears still falling.

"But she's going to be okay? She can still have kids?"

Shelley cocked her head to the side. "I think so. I hope so…" she said, composing herself. "Michael will be devastated."

Shelley leaned on Mark's belly and put her arms around his waist, taking a deep breath. "Let's just think positive. It could be worse."

"That's what I love about you, Shell," Mark whispered, squeezing her.

. . .

"What are you doing here?" Richard said to Mark, while taking a bite out of a donut. "Jessie okay?"

"She'll be fine. She lost the baby but the doctor figures he can repair the fallopian tubes. Shelley sent me here while she's in surgery."

"Driving her crazy, huh," Richard said with a mouth full of donut.

"She said the hospital staff was going to kick me out if she didn't do something about the track marks I was leaving in the hallway," he explained. "I pace when I'm anxious."

"Never knew that," Richard replied sarcastically.

"So what's the scoop on Dunphy?" Mark asked, changing the subject. "I figured you'd be in interrogation with him still."

"He's not talkin' till his *lawyer* gets here." Richard rolled his eyes, mimicking baby-talk.

"Really? I figured he'd have talked your ear off."

"Nah. He feels his rights have been violated since we invaded his home without his consent. The guy's as dumb as a brick. I doubt he's our man."

"I hope you're wrong," Mark warned. "We haven't got any other suspects, leads or any new evidence."

"Maybe he's a *really* good *actor*." Richard thumbed through the newspaper on Lisa's desk. "At least we don't have to tap anything anymore. That'll shut Lipkus up for a bit."

Mark glanced at his watch. "When's his lawyer supposed to be showing up?"

"Who knows," Richard scoffed. "He called his wife. From the sounds of it she was three sheets to the wind, couldn't have cared less."

"Did you offer to appoint him one?"

"Yeah. He says he can take care of it."

THE WHEELS OF CHANGE

"Well, we can hold him for now. I'm going to head back to the hospital and see how Jessie's doing," Mark said. "No point in me sticking around here."

Richard put his thumb up. "I'll be in touch."

. . .

Darla entered the office from the rear entrance, both mentally and physically exhausted from her day, half with Simon, the other half with a client suffering from a brain injury. She placed her hockey bag on the floor next to her locker and entered the combination into the lock. After resting her bag on the rusty floor of her locker, she closed it and headed for the kitchen.

There were some colleagues buzzing around, but since it was late afternoon, the traffic in the clinic was dying out. Darla had been lucky enough to have seniority and hadn't been asked in more than a year to work the night shift for their twenty-four hour operation. However, she saw a friend whom she knew was on the afternoon shift and patted her on the back.

"Grace, darling, how are you doing?"

"Oh fine, I just got here," Grace said, her blonde hair seemed permanently affixed in a bun at the base of her neck. Darla had never seen her with her hair styled any other way. Grace turned around, holding a steaming cup of coffee in her hand.

"How are you doing?" Grace asked.

"Pretty good. Tired." Darla stifled a yawn. "I had an early appointment with Doug Gresham at six, and then I spent the rest of the day with Simon Cross."

"Doug? How's he doing? I treated him when he was here in the hospital."

"He's coming along."

Grace sipped her coffee. "And Simon? What's he like? I've heard all the stories."

Darla poured herself a coffee and sat at the table in front of them, gesturing for Grace to have a seat.

Darla giggled. "He's not so bad."

Grace smiled sheepishly. "Nicole was his nurse on a few shifts when he first had his accident. She said he was such a pig. She asked Dr. Bennett to take her off that floor until he was released."

"A pig was he? Yeah, Dr. Bennett warned me about him," Darla admitted.

Grace lowered her volume an octave. "Can you keep a secret?"

Darla hunkered in closer. "Sure. What is it?"

"I rear-ended him once," Grace blushed.

"You didn't!" Darla was aghast.

Grace waved. "There wasn't much damage, just his license plate." She looked around as if there may be onlookers. "I gave him my phone number in case he changed his mind about repairs. Oh, it was just my work number." Grace waved again. "Heck, Martin would have a fit if he knew I gave my number to Simon Cross."

Darla nodded.

"My cousin met him once. He works for that clothing company, Mansfield? Have you heard of it?"

"Yeah, I think so."

"Rumor has it that Simon Cross slept his way to the top." Grace nodded as if to say 'bet-you-didn't-know-that. "Apparently the head honcho over there didn't know about him and his ways until he came onto one of his assistants during a meeting." Grace looked over to the side, waiting until a co-worker walked past the kitchen before continuing. "Anyway, he got wind of this and dropped Cross Advertising like a ton of bricks."

"So how did your brother find out about this?"

"I told you. He works for Mansfield. He's friends with one of the girls in their marketing department."

"What's he do?"

"Oh. He's in finance."

Darla nodded and changed the subject. "Did Simon ever call you after the fender-bender?"

Grace gasped. "Heavens no!" She swallowed and continued. "Anyway, he never came on to me, but he sure lives up to his reputation." Grace got serious. "Imagine a man in his shape coming on to a woman...a married woman no less! He has no shame!"

Darla shook her head, smiling.

"So has he put the moves on you yet?" Grace asked, serious still. "Be sure to let Dr. Bennett know if he does. Heavens, we'll have to send him a man! That'll make him put his pecker away for a while!"

"No. I doubt he'll be doing that anytime soon. His equipment isn't working."

"Yet," Grace added, warning. "And be sure to watch when you get that hardware out of your mouth. That'll up the ante."

"I don't think we'll need to worry about that anytime soon." Darla lifted her brow.

Grace leaned in closer. "How can you be so sure?"

Darla pursed her lips. "I told him I'm gay."

...

Richard rubbed his eyes. "Jesus, it's been more than six hours. Where the hell is this goddamn lawyer Dunphy's waiting on?"

"I don't know, but Mark should be back any minute now." Lisa looked at her watch. It was nearly ten o'clock at night. "I have to get home. At this rate we'll put the sitter through college."

A few minutes later, Mark's car pulled up. He walked in carrying two large brown paper bags.

"How's Jess?" Richard asked.

Mark set the bags on the reception desk and removed his jacket. "She's fine. Surgery went well. She'll be home in a few days."

"Good."

"I take it Max's lawyer was a no-show?"

Richard nodded, yawning.

"You been in to try questioning him again?"

"Nope. Andy tried earlier though and nothing." Richard nodded towards the bags. "What's this?"

"I've got an idea." Mark picked up a bag. "Grab one and come with me."

Richard followed Mark into the interrogation room. Max was sitting on the chair with his head resting on his crossed arms across the table, the way school children lay their heads down on their desks.

"Hey Max," Mark said like they were old pals. Max lifted his head and wiped a trail of spittle off the corner of his mouth. He didn't say anything.

They both placed the bags on the table and Mark opened the first one. Richard followed, and within five seconds the whole room smelled delicious; McDonald's.

"Hungry?" Mark asked Richard, grabbing a large cardboard container and handing him one.

"Starved," Richard answered, opening the container and wasting no time taking a large bite.

Max eyed them speculatively but he couldn't help watching the food entering Richard's mouth.

"It sucks when your friends stiff you," Mark nodded. "Is that what happened to you today, Max?"

THE WHEELS OF CHANGE

Mark removed another cardboard container out of the first bag and opened it on the table. He placed it halfway between Max and himself. Max didn't know whether Mark was offering him the food or not.

When Max simply eyed the burger but said nothing, Mark started. "Do you need us to appoint you a lawyer, Max?"

Max eyed the burger, then Mark. "Looks like that," he said. Neither man touched the burger. Max swallowed air slowly down his dry throat, still looking at the container.

Richard took a third bite of his burger and asked, with his mouth full. "Where were you the last few days, anyway?"

Mark took the burger and helped himself to a bite, chewing with exaggerated motions. Max swallowed again and his stomach rumbled so loud he had to cough to drown out the noise.

"Hungry?" Mark asked, lifting his burger. Max nodded, looking away.

"Tell us about Simon Cross," Mark said, changing tack. The mere mention of Simon's name brought colour to Max's cheeks.

"That guy's a whore," Max said, like Mark was arguing the point.

"Yeah? He fooled around with your wife, did he?" Mark nodded like he was on his side.

"Fucker." Max chewed his thumb anxiously. "But I wasn't trying to kill him or anything. All I wanted was for him to hit a tree or something. Trash his car. I wasn't looking to harm him, really. If I wanted to I had the chance, I was right in his office. I coulda killed him then if I wanted to."

"Good point," Mark agreed. "You got a good lawyer?"

Mark reached into the second bag and handed Max the third burger. His eyes lit up. "Nah, I don't have no lawyer. Clara says she's gettin' me one, but she's probably busy fuckin' him from what it seems." Max swallowed half the burger in one bite. Bits of bun hung from his mouth and he used his hand to force it back in.

"So where were you the last few days?" Richard said casually, like they were buddies at a poker game. "You had us all worried you'd flown the coop."

Max waved and swallowed. "I wasn't far, just at my mom's. I'm surprised Clara never thought to tell you that. Of course, she'd never call me over there. She hates mom."

"What were you doing over there?" Mark asked, munching on his fries.

"I go over there a lot," he explained. "She cooks."

"Your mom never told you we were looking for you? It was all over the news," Richard asked, sipping his drink from the straw.

"My mom don't own no TV. Hates 'em." Max waved like it was the dumbest thing he'd heard.

Mark and Richard exchanged glances. Mark rose, picking the first bag up. "Alright Max, we'll let you relax for now. We'll get you a lawyer first thing in the morning."

Max saluted them while his mouth was full.

Mark and Richard left the room. When the door closed, Richard asked, "Are you buying his story?"

"Not sure. We'll check out his mom and see what she has to say. In the meantime, we better get him a lawyer and place him in a cell before we have ourselves a human rights issue."

"I have mixed feelings about this," Richard admitted.

"Why's that?"

"Because if it's true, he was with his mom the whole time, then we're going to look like fools. On the other hand if he's lying, we gotta go back to the drawing board."

"I'll give Clara a call and find out where her mother-in-law lives," Mark said.

...

THE WHEELS OF CHANGE

Mark dialed Clara's number and waited. The phone rang six times before she picked up. Her voice was sleepy and slurred. "Hello, Mrs. Dunphy, this is Police Chief Mark Tame. Sorry for the late hour."

Clara took a moment to compose herself. Mark could hear her breathing in deeply and stretching, then she sniffled. "Is Max still with you?"

"Err…yes," Mark said as his brows furrowed. "Did you call his lawyer like he asked?"

"He said he was going to call," she yawned.

"Um…no, he asked you to call when he phoned you from prison?"

"Oh," she said, like she added two and two wrong and Mark was correcting her. "Well then I guess I better call him. What's the number?"

Mark was growing impatient. "Never mind, Mrs. Dunphy. Can you just give me the number or address for Max's mother, your mother-in-law, please?"

"My mother-in-law?"

"Yes," Mark sighed, trying to control his temper.

"Well, what do you want that for?" she hiccupped.

"Because I need to speak with her, please," he said firmly.

Then she said, as if Mark should know, "Well she's been dead for five years."

. . .

"I cannot deal with that woman anymore," Mark whined, throwing Max's file on the desk. "Either she's out of her mind or Max is full of shit. Either way, we need to corroborate Max's story, and clearly neither of them are going to help."

Richard sheepishly handed Mark a slip of paper with a phone number on it. "He knocked on the window two minutes ago," Richard explained. "Said her number's unlisted. In case we wanted to make sure he wasn't

SANDY APPLEYARD

lying."

"Shit." Mark gritted his teeth. "Ever feel like you're a day late for your own birthday party?"

"Yeah," Richard smirked. "That's what happens when you've got too much on the go."

"Tell me about it." Mark looked at his watch. "Well, if we want any cooperation from an old lady, we'd best call her first thing in the morning, not after ten at night."

Richard nodded. "I'll get him into a cell and call it a night."

"Good idea."

Just as Richard got up, they heard a message coming through the squawk box. *"This is officer Noonan. I need backup on Mercer Street."*

Richard and Mark stood to listen. *"There's been a murder, some actor was killed in his trailer."*

Mercer Street was at least ten minutes away; it was closed off at the moment for a movie set. "Hobbs is on that beat," Richard said. Mark nodded and spoke into his walkie-talkie affixed to his shoulder. "Stand fast, Noonan, we'll contact Hobbs and get there ASAP."

"Ten-four."

"Think it's our guy?" Richard said to Mark.

"Must be," he answered. "I guess Max was telling the truth after all. But let's wait and see before we let him go," Mark said under his breath. "Let's not make any mistakes."

Richard nodded.

...

It was a romance movie, starring one of the most eligible bachelors in the movie industry. Drake Scott had been coveted by women of all ages since his debut 'Release Me' hit theatres five years ago. Since then, Drake's films had been box office hits, making him one of the highest paid actors of

THE WHEELS OF CHANGE

his time.

His current flick, 'Just a Touch of Honey', was set for release next year. All the entertainment tabloids had reported that he and his co-star, Jenna Wilder hit the sheets not only on the set, but in reality. Jenna Wilder was married to her high school sweetheart, a man not well known to the camera, Abe Malcolm, for over fifteen years.

There were five trailers along the closed alleyway leading to the movie set. The alley led up to Mercer Street, which was lined with various shops and boutiques. Even though it was early spring, all the store windows were decorated for Christmas. Movie cameras, lights and various pieces of recording equipment was displayed centrally, at a café.

The whole set had been under lockdown since the discovery of Drake's body. Nobody was allowed to leave or enter until the investigation was complete. Mark and Richard were shown to Drake's trailer by his agent, Pamela McCarthy.

"So what's the story, ma'am?" Mark asked Pamela as they entered the set. She was a tall woman in her forties, wearing a pants suit. She resembled a young Jackie Kennedy. Pamela was clearly shaken. Her eyes were reddened and although she was trying to conceal it by hiding them in her pockets, her hands wouldn't stop shaking.

Pamela explained. "We sent him into his trailer for a break in between scenes, we'd just finished a scene where he was walking down the street, looking in the shops. The next scene was going to be in the café, where he would propose to Jenna. About thirty minutes later we sent Amanda in, she does Drake's makeup, and she came out screaming."

"Did he go into his trailer alone?" Richard asked, wondering which trailer was Drake's. Then he saw Noonan and saluted him.

"Yes. Drake likes to go over his lines in between scenes," Pamela explained. "He doesn't like having a page or someone to help him with his lines. He does a lot of improvisation, that's part of his trademark."

"We need to canvass everyone and find out if anyone saw someone going in or coming out of Drake's trailer," Mark said. "We need to get a list of people coming or going before and during recording."

"I'll get Noonan started," Richard offered. "How tight is security,

Pamela?"

She pursed her lips. "Very tight," she said matter-of-factly. "*You* almost didn't get the clear."

"It must have been someone either on the set or well-blended in," Mark surmised. "Is this Drake's trailer?" Mark asked, nodding.

Pamela didn't answer but kept walking up the steps to his extended trailer. It was thirty feet long and had collapsible stairs in the front, side and back. The thing was a monster. It looked like a house fit for a king, on wheels.

"Holy shit, this guy?" Richard said, entering the trailer. Then he checked himself, realizing that Pamela was still nearby. Drake's body was lying across the floor, his legs pinned under him and his arms askew. It looked like he was dropped like a sack of potatoes. "Oh man, Lisa's going to be pissed. She loves this guy's movies."

Mark looked at Richard, irritated. "We'll take it from here." He dismissed Pamela.

"I'll be outside if you have any questions," she said as she walked out.

Richard approached the body, being careful not to step in the pool of blood. The victim had been slashed across the throat. His eyes remained open. He had recently cut, short, sandy blonde hair. The makeup on his face made him look like a waxed figurine, his lip colour was smeared.

Mark went into his pocket and pulled out two pairs of rubber gloves, tossing one pair to Richard. "Check the other exits in this thing. See if there's a sign of struggle."

Richard examined the floor as he inserted his hands into the gloves and grimaced, "Damn, no footprints. I bet he planned this. Perfect day, no rain or precipitation to leave tracks."

"His clothes aren't even wrinkled. Nothing's been touched other than his neck. Even his hair isn't out of place. This guy was slick."

"Well, he shouldn't be too hard to find," Mark said. "He'll be the only guy in the place wearing bloodied rubber gloves."

THE WHEELS OF CHANGE

...

Officer Noonan was met with his partner, Officer Hobbs and two others. They split up and began canvassing all the extras, actors, and any others present on the movie set. In total, there were about forty people that needed to be questioned. Noonan started with a couple of extras. The first few were clean, they were simply waiting for their cue to peruse the store, but one guy caught Noonan's attention pretty fast after asking him a few questions.

"Name, sir," Noonan asked, after clearing the others in his group of five extras.

"Darryl Mattlin."

"What is your function here today?"

"I'm an extra in the café scene."

"Did anything unusual occur today?"

Darryl hesitated, almost jokingly. "Kind of," he said, as though he was about to rat someone out for a joke that wasn't funny anymore.

"What do you mean?" Noonan placed his hands on his sides and looking directly at Darryl.

Darryl chuckled. "I don't know. Some guy paid me fifty bucks for my jacket and gloves," he explained, putting his hands out like it was no big deal. "He said he was with the wardrobe people and they messed up Drake's jacket. He said they were supposed to fit him for something else. He said my jacket was perfect."

"What kind of jacket did you have?"

"It was a nice one. A Mansfield. One of those reversible types, you know?"

"What did he look like?"

"Just a regular guy. Dressed nice like all of us." Darryl gestured to the crowd. "He was wearing a Mansfield ID tag, so I figured he must be telling the truth."

169

"Isn't a nice jacket worth more than fifty bucks?" Noonan asked, suspicious.

"Hey, we're all clothed for free here." Darryl bent toward Noonan and covered his mouth with the side of his hand, like he was about to tell a secret. "We're not allowed to keep the clothes. So I figured hey, why not make an extra fifty bucks today? The pay here isn't great, you know."

Noonan pursed his lips. "Would you be able to describe this guy to a sketch artist?"

"Sure," Darryl said. "Do I get to keep the fifty bucks?"

CHAPTER 19

"Hey, Ryder," Simon said. His voice was gravelly from sleep. "Hand me that jug, man. I'm dying of thirst."

"Sure, buddy." Ryder reached over the bed. "Are you awake?"

"Yeah." Simon smiled slightly. "Did they get everything done?"

Ryder shrugged, pouring water into a Styrofoam cup. "The nurses just brought you back here. They didn't tell me anything."

"Hey, have you heard from your mom lately?" Ryder asked as Simon took a sip.

"Nah. She sent me a text saying she landed safe," Simon explained. "That'll be the last of her for a week or so. Barbara's the social type." He took another sip. "It's kind of a relief. Mom was becoming a little too clingy."

"She seemed that way," Ryder agreed, even though he couldn't help but feel a twinge of worry for whatever she was up to. If Simon sensed the tension, he didn't bring it up.

They both looked over as the door opened and Dr. Bennett entered. He smiled. "Well, there you are, now," Dr. Bennett said cheerily. "How are you feeling?"

Simon handed the cup to Ryder. "Pretty good, actually."

"I figured you'd say that. Dr. Flamborough snuck in just before and just after your treatment to see the difference," he nodded. "It seems your tissues are taking very well to the injections."

"Well that's good," Simon grinned.

"We ran an MRI scan to see if your nerves are firing properly and it looks very promising. Your brain is reacting to stimulus in your legs and feet."

"So what does that mean?" Ryder asked.

Dr. Bennett walked to the window where there was an extra chair in the corner. He picked it up and brought it over to sit next to Ryder and Simon. When he sat, he cleared his throat and began talking animatedly with his hands. "When you react to stimulus," Dr. Bennett looked up at the ceiling in thought. "For example, you see a cookie on the counter and you want to reach for it. Your eyes send a signal to your brain, which is connected to your spine. Your brain sends another signal to your arm, hand and fingers through your spine, telling them to reach for it." He licked his lips. "In your case, when you want to take a step, your brain tells your legs and feet to move. Right after the accident, your spine wasn't sending those signals to your legs, which is why you couldn't move them." Dr. Bennett rose. "The treatment you've received is adding healthy tissues back into your spine, replacing the damaged ones, thus restoring the signals and your ability to move. At least that's what we hope is happening."

"So what does the MRI show?" Ryder asked.

"The MRI shows brain activity when Dr. Flamborough stimulates Simon's legs. Activity that seems stronger after treatment."

"So this is good, right?" Simon asked.

"Of course," Dr. Bennett assured. "We have to wait a couple of days or so while the new tissue replaces the old, of course. But the tests definitely show improvement."

Dr. Bennett looked at Simon. "I've arranged to have Darla come to see you for longer sessions. I feel it's important to get those muscles moving now, while the treatment is still fresh. Is that okay with you?"

Simon nodded agreement.

"I assume things are working out well with Darla?"

"Oh yeah, she's great," Simon said enthusiastically.

"Excellent." Dr. Bennett winked, walking towards the door. "I'll see you back in a week, Simon."

"See ya," Simon said.

When Dr. Bennett closed the door, Ryder turned to him. "So, you like Darla now? Or were you just saying that because you're in such a good mood?" His arms were crossed on his chest.

"Darla's pretty cool. She's well-trained, smart, and she doesn't treat me...you know...like I'm Simon Cross."

Ryder craned his neck and frowned. "How *does* she treat you?"

Simon thought for a moment, sighed and answered. "Like there's hope for me yet."

. . .

Simon woke up and stretched. He felt an odd sensation in his left toe, the one next to the big toe. Reaching down to lift the blanket, he noticed that his toe was cramped. The toe was sitting at a forty five degree angle, pointing away from its natural position. Simon focused on the toe for a moment and surprisingly, was able to move it back to its normal position.

"Hey, Ryder," Simon called from the couch.

"Yeah buddy, what's up?"

Simon looked up at Ryder as he turned the corner, flipping a dish towel over his shoulder. "Check it out."

He moved his toe back and forth, feeling like a show-off. Simon half-laughed, surprised that he could do it.

"Cool," Ryder said. "Now you can play 'This Little Piggy' again. At least part of it."

"Wait 'til I tell Darla," Simon smiled.

Ryder looked at his watch. "Yeah, she'll be here any minute now. I gotta head out, Sandra's got a meeting with Crabtree set up for this afternoon." Ryder stuffed his feet in his shoes. "You still up for conferencing with them at four?"

"Sure."

Ryder grabbed his jacket. "Who knows. Maybe next time we can have the meeting at the office. Doc says if things go well after this treatment he'd okay it."

"That would be nice," Simon scoffed. "I can't stand being in this house much longer."

. . .

Ryder left the door unlocked. Simon sat up on the couch and lifted his legs with his arms, depositing his feet on the floor. He sat and watched his feet, wiggling his toes ever so slightly. To get a better view, he removed his socks, feeling the warmth of his hands and fingers against his skin. The sensation was extraordinary. Simon never thought he'd be so excited for something so simple.

There was a knock at the door and Simon called. "Come in, it's open."

When he looked up, expecting to see Darla, he was stunned when he saw the tall blonde woman standing in the doorway.

"Hi Simon," said Clara.

Simon's eyes bulged and his face lost colour immediately. "What the hell are you doing here?" he demanded.

"I was in the neighbourhood," she explained casually. "Thought I'd stop by and see how you were doing."

"Don't you think it's rather stupid for you to show up here? Considering your husband tried to kill me?"

Clara waved off the comment and removed her jacket, like her being there was really no big deal. "Max? Max is too stupid to kill." She placed her jacket on the hook next to the door.

THE WHEELS OF CHANGE

"So how are you doing?" Clara sat next to Simon.

"I'm a fucking paraplegic...thanks to your husband," he answered pointedly. "Did you come to finish off the job in his place?"

Clara laughed out loud. "Max didn't want to kill you. Besides, if he wanted to finish the job he'd do it himself. He'd never send a woman to do a man's job."

Simon looked at Clara and pursed his lips. "Why are you here, Clara?" He was losing his patience. His tone was clipped.

"I told you." Clara feigned that her feelings were hurt. "I wanted to see how you were doing. When I heard you'd been seriously hurt and it was Max's fault, I've been worried sick."

Simon guffawed. "Really? I find that hard to believe."

"I've been genuinely distraught, Simon," Clara argued.

"Yeah? Fall of the wagon because of me, did you?" Simon seethed.

Clara ignored the comment. "Ah, Simon...so, do things...um...work?"

Simon's face reddened, and he was about to explode at Clara, when the door knocked.

He nodded in disbelief. "It's open," he yelled, trying and failing to conceal his anger.

"Good morning Sim—oh, sorry, I didn't know you had company," Darla commented, closing the door. "That must be your Mercedes parked on the street, then."

Darla extended her hand to Clara. "I'm Darla. Simon's occupational therapist."

Clara was about to introduce herself when Simon interrupted. "She was just leaving."

"I'll just get set up over here," Darla said, sensing the tension.

Clara waited until Darla was out of earshot. "Simon, I've really missed you."

Simon looked at her like she had three heads. "We broke up, Clara. You told me where to go and sicked your crazy husband on me. Although now I don't know who's crazier."

Clara tutted. "I did not *sick* him on you, Simon. It was an honest mistake...him finding out."

Darla was in the background assembling some kind of contraption, trying not to listen to the conversation ensuing mere feet away from her.

"I told you, it was an accident. Simon, if I'd known he would react that way, I would have hidden things better."

Simon laughed without humor. "And yet you're still here, Clara. Don't you think if he finds out where you are, he's going to go ballistic?"

Clara waved. "Relax. He's still in jail. They haven't released him yet."

Darla overheard the word 'jail' and approached Simon reluctantly. "Simon, is everything okay?"

Simon looked over at Darla. "Yeah, everything's fine. Like I said, she was just leaving." He looked at Clara with daggers in his eyes.

"Simon," Clara begged. "Please call me when you're up to it."

Simon shook his head. "I told you I don't want anything to do with you. Please leave." His voice was cold and direct.

"Simo—" Clara said, and then Darla interrupted. "I think it's time for you to leave, ma'am. We need to get his treatment started."

"Treatment? What kind of treatment?" Clara looked at Simon like he was a disease.

"I told you," Darla walked towards the door. "I'm an occupational therapist." Darla opened the door, looking at Clara with upturned brows. "Please leave."

Clara rose and walked toward her coat, hanging on the rack beside the door. Her hips swayed slightly as she looked at Simon. "Maybe he *should* have finished you off," she scoffed, like Simon was a piece of gum she found on her shoe. "You're useless now."

Simon didn't respond. He didn't even look at her. Darla's eyes followed Clara's as she walked slowly out the door. If looks could kill, it would have been a showdown. "Be sure to work him below the belt," Clara seethed. "It looks like he could use some work there. I used to be irresistible to Simon."

"I'll bet," Darla said through gritted teeth.

...

"Interesting friend." Darla attached a smaller pole to a larger one. "I hope there's not too many of her type in your life."

"What do you mean, slutty? Bitchy types?"

Darla laughed. "I just mean that she's not very inspiring."

"Inspiring?" Simon chuckled. "Yeah, Ryder has some burly biker friends down at his shop that are more inspiring than she is."

"So how did you two meet?"

Simon propped himself up on the couch, twiddling his toes happily. "At a conference a couple of years ago. She was nice until she got into the sauce a little while ago."

"Ah. The dreaded fire water. That'll ruin any relationship, surely." Darla stood back, admiring the apparatus. "So, was she your girlfriend?"

"Nah, we just had an affair. I'm not exactly *'boyfriend'* material."

Darla looked at him and frowned. "Why would you say that?" She made an adjustment using a small, metal handle. "You're motivated, you have a good job, you're not bad looking. What's the problem?"

Simon shrugged. "I don't know. I think women look at me differently than they do 'the boy next door' types."

"What do you think causes that?"

"The way I dress…I guess. The fact that I'm successful. Most women I meet through conferences or my business," he explained, lifting his legs back up on the couch. "There was only one girl I met through high school who I ever really had a relationship with."

"What happened to her?"

"I don't know. We drifted apart when I moved here I guess."

"So when did you start feeling like women were looking at you differently?"

"I guess when I opened up my business back in Kansas."

Darla bent down to move the apparatus over slightly, using both her hands on the bars. "Did you ever consider that maybe it wasn't women that were looking at you differently, but that you were looking differently at women?"

Simon frowned and cocked his head to the side. "It's possible. But either way, women started flocking to me when they knew I had money."

"Really? How?" Darla was looking back and forth between Simon and her project as he spoke.

"I can't really remember specifics. But I do remember having many women turning business meetings into sex."

"It takes two to tango, Simon."

"Well, I wasn't getting love any other way. What's a guy to do?" Simon said matter-of-factly.

"You weren't getting love, Simon. Maybe that's the problem."

"Yeah, well, now my problems have changed, I guess." Simon looked at his fingers. "I'm going to be looked at like someone with special needs now. I guess pity is going to take the place of lust or greed."

Darla stood upright and began attaching leather straps to the metal bars. It was becoming clear to Simon that they were going to try strength training today.

THE WHEELS OF CHANGE

"People are going to look at you and see what they see, Simon. It's up to you to show them who you are from the inside. If you shine, they'll see the Simon you truly are. If not, they'll continue to add to the stigma that you will create for yourself. It's all up to you."

Simon looked at her and nodded agreement. "I suppose you went through some similar shit when you came out, huh?"

Darla chuckled. "Not exactly. But we all have trouble with people seeing us as who they want to see. It's up to us to show the world our good attitude so we can dispel any negative ideas they may have already made for us."

"Don't judge a book by its cover," Simon agreed.

Darla winked at him. "You ready to hop on and give this a try?"

"I haven't heard an invitation like that in a while," Simon joked.

Darla smiled. "You might consider getting a restraining order for that woman, too, if you want my opinion."

"Ah, we'll see what happens. If she harasses me again I'll think about it," Simon said. "Thanks for the concern, anyway."

Darla walked over to Simon, bringing his wheelchair.

"You have trouble saying no, Simon. Maybe you should try it some time. You might find your life changes for the better."

Darla held the chair steady for Simon and put her arm across his back as he eased his way in.

"I'll take it under advisement." Simon looked at Darla. She returned the glance and smiled. "There. We're going to burn some energy now, you up for it?"

As Simon sat upright in the chair, he paused, looking down at his groin. "I...I think I have to use the washroom." The look on his face was a cross between confusion and excitement.

"Really? You can feel it?"

179

Simon nodded.

"And you're moving your toes now, I noticed." Darla winked. "Looks like you may be given a second chance after all."

. . .

Simon and Ryder completed the conference call with Crabtree, having updates from them on the direction they were going with their next campaign. When the meeting was over, Ryder disconnected the Crabtree members, but left Simon on the line.

"Hey, Simon," Ryder said. "How'd it go with Darla?"

"Really well." Ryder picked up on the excitement in Simon's voice. "Yeah? What did she have you do today?"

"She put together this support device," Simon explained. "It looks like a treadmill without the movable floor, it's just the two support bars."

"Kinky."

Simon ignored the comment. "I was actually supporting myself while she manipulated my legs and feet. I could feel my feet moving."

"Excellent. Hey, Sandra got the scoop on Mansfield, eh."

"Oh yeah? What happened?"

"Apparently they're in financial trouble or something. Stockton hired some consultant. The guy cut some corners and basically vetoed any new marketing projects until they straightened out their books."

"That's weird. They must have kept that under wraps for a while."

"Yeah. I've heard the clothing market is getting crushed by online sales and discount stores, things like that."

"Maybe we should review their campaign, have them change their product line and target market slightly. Let's play around when I can get back in the office, see what we can offer them."

"Sounds like a plan. You think Doc will let you come in next week?"

THE WHEELS OF CHANGE

"Darla's going to send him another report today. He'll probably call tomorrow morning. I'll keep you posted," Simon said. "You coming by later?"

"Yeah. I gotta go home first and service the wife. It's been a while if you catch my drift," Ryder chuckled.

"You're all charm," Simon commented warmly.

. . .

Nancy walked through the hallway of the hotel, heading for the ice machine. She was terribly thirsty and couldn't be bothered ordering room service again. On her way to the small room where the ice and vending machines were located, a door opened. She moved over to allow space between herself and the exiting patron, when she ran straight into Ted.

He gave her a solemn look. "Listen, I'm sorry Nancy, for the way things went earlier. I don't know what came over me."

Nancy kept walking, showing no interest in him. "That's fine, Ted. I liked you better when you were a member of the cloth. At least then you treated me with some respect."

Ted waited for Nancy, placing his room key in his pants pocket, putting off his walk. He heard the ice clanging down into her glass. When she turned the corner, he gave her a slight smile and peered down at his shoes, like a shy school boy. "Can we talk?"

Nancy sighed with frustration, "Fine," she said through pursed lips. "I've got a little while until my sister gets back."

She led him to her room and he held the door open for her, gesturing her in gallantly.

"What do you want to talk about? I thought we'd covered everything up until you insulted me and my son."

Ted shook his head and bowed. "Once again, I'm sorry Nancy. I know it's not an excuse, but I haven't slept in two days, I've got a meeting tomorrow at six that I'm not prepared for, and I haven't got a clue what I'm going to say to my boss when he calls in an hour."

181

Nancy bit the corner of her nail in thought.

Ted continued. "I'm under a lot of pressure and seeing you, I don't know, I guess it made me realize how much I've missed you and how bad I feel for how things were left between us years ago." Ted's voice was pleading. "It also upset me because I actually did see that you had some powder on your nose. Are you using drugs again?"

She spat a piece of nail across the room and glared at him. "That's none of your business."

"I know. I know," he said sincerely. "I always prayed that you'd stay clean, even after I left the church. It just proves how in vain all my efforts have been."

Nancy was flabbergasted. "What do you want from me, Ted?"

"I just wanted to set things straight is all." Ted walked closer to her. "All these years I always felt bad for leaving. When I saw you in the lobby earlier, I knew it was a sign."

"If you felt bad for leaving, why didn't you ever call me and straighten things out?" Nancy tapped her foot on the floor.

"Because I met Lilly and then you guys moved out to LA. There never seemed to be a good time."

"If it was really bothering you, you'd have done something about it, Ted. I know you, you're a passionate person and very strong in your ways."

Ted chuckled. "Well, you're right about that." He changed the subject. "How *is* Simon doing?" he asked in a concerned voice. "Is he coming around after the accident?"

Nancy sat on the bed, feeling suddenly defeated. "He's having treatments to inject healthy tissue back into his spine. It'll take a while, but I think he'll walk again."

"Really? Well that's wonderful," Ted smiled. "And how's his business going?"

"It's going really well."

"And is he able to look after things…despite his…condition?" Ted said carefully.

"Well, yes," Nancy hesitated. "He has a partner in the business who's helping. Simon should be able to work in the office again soon."

"Good for him." Ted clapped his hands together. "You know, Nancy, I really did think Simon was a wonderful boy. We had our ups and downs, but truly I did love him like a son."

Nancy reluctantly smiled. "I'll tell him you said hi."

Ted inhaled deeply. "Thank you." He sat on the bed next to her, took her hand in his and kissed the back of it. "Do you ever miss me?"

She shook her head no. "I haven't really thought about you in a long time. Things were over between us. We both moved on."

"Ever since Lilly left…I don't know…I wished I was still in touch with you."

Nancy sighed, not wanting to feel anything for Ted. "It's late, Ted. You have work to do and my sister should be back soon."

Ted rubbed her hand. "You're right. I should go."

Nancy walked him to the door. He paused before opening it. "If you change your mind, I'm staying in room 411. I'll be there for a few more days."

She nodded and closed the door as he left. When she closed the door, she rubbed the back of her hand where Ted touched her.

…

"Is the sketch artist done with Darryl yet?" Mark asked Richard.

"Not yet. Another five minutes."

"Okay, we've got to get over to Mansfield right after and find out who this guy is. Did we get any prints on Darryl's fifty dollar bill?"

183

"Nah. Forensics said it's covered in partials. They're too close together, too."

"I figured. But it was worth a try."

"Did you get in touch with Cameron over at the F.B.I.?" Richard called to Lisa.

"Yeah. He's on his way," she called back. "Hey, Mark?"

"Yep."

"Is Jessie home yet?"

"Tomorrow. Doc wants another day with her to make sure."

Lisa put her thumb in the air and answered her phone. A few seconds later, she called to Mark. "It's Judge Caplan. Line two."

Mark picked up the phone. "Good morning, Judge Caplan. How are you?"

The judge cleared his throat. "Morning, Mark. I'm fine, thank you."

"I presume you're calling about Max Dunphy?"

"That's right," the Judge sighed. "You know the rules, Mark. We can't release him now that he's fled. No matter how good his alibi is."

Mark chuckled. "He *was* actually with his mother. We checked it out."

"I don't care if he was visiting the Pope. If he was AWOL, it doesn't matter what he was doing," Judge Caplan said firmly. "He could have been reading to the blind and I'd still hold him."

"I understand," Mark conceded. "How long until the trial?"

"Send him over to Bay Street Penitentiary. If my docket doesn't fill up, we can put him on the stand in a couple of weeks tops."

"Will do, sir," Mark said.

"Take care."

THE WHEELS OF CHANGE

...

Richard knocked on Mark's door and opened it. "Hey buddy. Cameron's here."

"Set him up on Andy's desk. I'll be there in a minute," Mark said.

Richard saluted and left. Seconds later, Lisa brought Mark the composite sketch from the artist. He examined it, realizing this guy was too common-looking. Walking over to Andy's desk, he greeted Cameron and Richard, handing them the sketch. Richard took a close look, there were no distinguishing features. No cleft chin or thick eyebrows, no scars or pock marks. He was a clean-shaven, middle aged, dark haired man who could be anyone's brother.

"Looks like the average Joe," Cameron said.

"Let's hope they don't all look like that over at Mansfield," Mark commented.

"You got a name on the guy who saw him?" Cameron asked, opening his laptop.

"Darryl Mattlin. He hasn't got any priors. They would've screened him before letting him on the movie set anyhow, so we already knew that."

"What about your guy in the holding cell?"

"Max Dunphy? Yeah, he's got some priors. But he's not being released anyway, plus he doesn't fit the profile of our murderer."

"So we should get into Mansfield's database and pull up their employee profiles?"

"You got it."

Without answering, Cameron keyed away on his computer. Within seconds he obtained a list of current Mansfield employees. "Print that off and we'll cross reference those names with the list of extras on the movie set, see if we get a match," Mark instructed.

A few minutes later, no matches were found. "Okay, let's pull up the list of staff over at the bank and at the television network," Mark advised. "This guy's been busy."

When they exhausted all lists and found no matches, Mark ran his hand through his hair. "How did I know this wasn't gonna be so easy."

"We need to head over to Mansfield and see if anyone can identify this guy."

"That would be wise," Cameron agreed. "I'll stay here. You call me when you get anything."

"Excellent."

CHAPTER 20

Nancy sat in the hotel room, surprised that Barbara and Raphael hadn't yet returned. There had been no phone call, no contact whatsoever. Her last hit of cocaine was consumed more than an hour ago in hopes that it would bring her sleep. She turned off the television, picked up the phone on the side table and dialed 0 to get an outside line. Figuring Simon was still up, she keyed in his cell number.

"Simon," Nancy said. "I hope I didn't wake you."

Simon's voice was sleepy but coherent. "It's the middle of the night, mom. Is everything okay?"

"I just wanted to call and see how you were doing."

"I'm doing fine." Simon rubbed his eyes. "Treatment is going well. I can feel my toes again, and the doctor says I can go back to the office tomorrow."

Nancy ignored the good news. "I hope you're not being too hasty."

"No, I think it'll do me good to get out of this house," Simon sniffed. "I've got terrible cabin fever. Besides, I need to get back to work. Ryder can't hold the fort down on his own forever."

"How is business going?"

"We lost the Mansfield account."

"Really? What happened?"

"Long story, mom, but I think we'll get it back. Once I get back to the office, Ryder and I have a plan." Simon hesitated, but couldn't help himself. "Are you staying out of trouble?"

Nancy laughed, as if she knew he was going to ask that. "I'm sitting in my hotel room alone. How much trouble can I be in?"

"Where's Barbara?"

"She and Raphael went out on the town. I expected them back hours ago."

"How come you didn't go?"

Nancy paused. Unsure of Simon's reaction to the truth, she tested the water. "Simon, do you remember Ted?"

"How could I forget?" Simon scoffed. "The guy hated me and the feeling was mutual."

She tutted. "He didn't hate you, Simon. As much as you wanted to believe it at the time, Ted was looking out for you."

"He was a controlling, disrespectful asshole as I remember it," Simon corrected.

Nancy shook her head and changed the subject, frustrated. "So how's the occupational therapist doing?"

"Darla? She's great," Simon yawned.

"Good. Listen, I don't want to keep you up, I just wanted to see how you were. I'll talk to you soon, okay?"

"Take it easy, mom," Simon said, hanging up.

When he put his phone down on the night stand, slightly more alert than when he initially answered it, he wondered why his mother brought up Ted.

...

She looked at her watch, disgusted that her sister Barbara could leave her alone in a hotel room, after asking her to travel out to see her, and seemingly rescue her from the arms of a man who once hurt her beyond what her selfish heart could handle. Nancy began to think about the men she'd had in her life and how they hurt her. She searched desperately for anything to help ease her pain, sniffing the last bit of residue left of her cocaine wasn't enough.

After opening the bar fridge and downing the last mouthful of scotch out of the brown bottle Raphael left, she decided to search Barbara's room. Hey, if they were out having such a good time without her, she was going to use the last of what they had, she figured.

Looking through Raphael's bag, the smell of his cologne reminded her of her ex-husband. James was a loving man, but she never felt like what she did was good enough to please him. Before their second anniversary she was already back into the coke. She managed to stay away from it while she was pregnant with Simon, but it wasn't long after that when James caught her sniffing the white stuff after putting the baby down for his nap.

James worked away a lot. She credited him for his loyalty to her, even though she suspected many times that he didn't remain true. How many times she would go through his things after a trip and find business cards belonging to women, she'd lost count in their ten years of marriage. It didn't surprise her when James announced his intention to marry Betty when Simon was thirteen. Nancy often wondered if they'd met during some of his supposed business trips.

Then came Ted. After James had remarried, it took her five years to get over the heartache of her failed marriage. Ted was a pastor at one of her support groups and there was an uncertain chemistry between them when they had their first one-on-one meeting. One thing led to another and before she knew it, she was seeing Ted regularly and off the cocaine. Simon supported the relationship in the beginning, having found out that Ted was one of the reasons Nancy stayed clean. But it wasn't long until Simon and Ted butted heads.

Nancy came across a snap shot of Barbara and Raphael taken recently, tucked inside the zippered portion of Raphael's bag, and examined it. Why did Barbara always find these casual, young-at-heart types of guys? All Nancy ever found were family-oriented or religious, by-the-book men who only let her play by the rules. Underneath Raphael's passport portfolio was an interesting-looking navy blue drawstring bag. Nancy opened it and her face lit up.

...

Ted sat on the edge of his bed. His left index finger tapped on his left knee and his right hand supported his chin. The table in the corner of the room was covered in papers, empty coffee cups and garbage. He was tempted to clean it up, when he heard a raucous in the hallway.

Rising from the bed, he looked through the peephole and saw nothing, but he could hear a woman arguing with a couple a few doors down. He opened the door and saw Nancy, wasted, trying to reason with what appeared to be a newlywed couple two doors down from him.

"Nancy?" Ted called, with his brows furrowed.

Nancy waved like she knew where he was all along. "Oh, there you are!" she slurred. She walked, or tried to walk, towards him.

"Do we need to call someone?" the newlywed guy asked with outstretched arms.

"I'll take it from here," Ted assured. He walked over to Nancy and helped her into his room.

"Barbara didn't come back." She laughed like it was a big joke.

"She's a big girl." Ted was annoyed. He did a double take at the mess on the table, particularly his laptop wide open on top of all the stuff, and he quickly rose, stuffing all the papers hastily into his empty briefcase lying on the floor.

"I know she is," Nancy argued. "But what the fuck!"

Ted stopped what he was doing and glared at her, "Now it's bad enough that you show up in my room in the condition you're in, Nancy. But I won't have that kind of language in here, too."

Nancy's eyes rolled. "What are you, my father?" she scoffed, like he was being utterly ridiculous. Nancy got up, tripping on her own feet, as she made her way to the bathroom.

Ted's nostrils flared at the mention of the word 'father', reminding him of his failure as a pastor. The state Nancy was in was a further reminder. She was worse right now than she'd ever been to Ted's recollection.

When Nancy returned from the washroom, Ted noticed her glazed-over, bloodshot and lazily moving eyes and heavy eyelids. She sat on the bed and looked at Ted. "Well, I'm here." She gestured to him like he was expecting her.

He was about to speak when the hotel phone rang and Ted lost his train of thought. Nancy watched him as he answered it. After saying hello, he put his finger in the air, indicating he would be a minute, and excused himself to go into the washroom for privacy.

Frustrated at the lack of attention she was receiving overall, she went over to the table where Ted had been busying himself tidying. Sloppily, she walked past his bulky briefcase and accidentally nudged it with her ankle, knocking it over. A flood of paper fell out and she tried to kneel down to pick it all up. Clumsily, she fell over and landed on her rear. Nancy laughed at herself and decided she would work more efficiently from the floor and began the job she intended to do.

At first glance, the papers appeared to be research on Ted's clients. Nancy could hear Ted finishing up his conversation in the bathroom. She came across a bunch of papers that would fit better if they were lined up properly, so she pulled them out and attempted to right them, when a newspaper clipping fell out.

The headline read 'Pastor Missing from Ministry: Fled After Death of Beloved Wife'.

Nancy began reading, slightly sobered by this discovery, when Ted opened the bathroom door and appeared. He looked at her and inhaled, like a boy caught stealing cigarettes from his mother's purse. "Oh, I really wish you didn't find that," he said, suddenly laughing even though it wasn't funny. His laugh sent a chill up Nancy's spine.

Any desire she had to question him was soon quelled.

...

"Well, look who's back!" Sandra called from her desk. She practically jumped out of her chair and ran to Simon. Ryder was pushing his wheelchair from behind.

"Hey, Sandra," Ryder greeted.

She reached Simon and bent down to kiss his cheek, "I'm so happy to see you!" she grinned. "I hear you're starting to get some function back."

"Yep. Darla, my OT, has me training for the Olympics next year," Simon joked. "And not the special Olympics, either," he winked.

"Excellent!" Sandra exclaimed. "I'll be on your cheering team."

Simon took hold of the steel circle around the wheelchair tires and began wheeling himself over to the waiting area. "Place looks great," he nodded, pleased. "Did you talk to Mansfield? Any new information?"

Sandra shook her head. "No. They're realigning some heads there from what I heard last. Looks like some jobs will be lost. I'd move on if I were you," she advised.

Simon waved. "No problem. Just thought I'd ask. You got Crabtree swinging by today?"

Ryder intervened. "Should be here in an hour. You want to review the files?"

"Sure."

Ryder and Sandra exchanged glances. "Err…Simon," Sandra ventured. "UCLA has called a few times in the last couple of weeks."

"Oh yeah? My old stomping grounds? What for?"

"They're looking to place some students for an internship. We could use some help around here until you're completely back on your feet…pardon the pun," Sandra giggled.

"Sure. That sounds like a great idea," Simon said.

Ryder waited for Simon to state his penchant for a hot female intern, but he didn't add anything. "Do you have a preference?" he asked cautiously.

Simon tilted his head and frowned. "Not really. As long as they work hard and sign an NDA I'm fine."

THE WHEELS OF CHANGE

Ryder's brows rose and he smiled, padding Simon on the shoulder. "Look at you, all grown up."

Sandra smiled. "I'll call the college right away and set up an interview. They said they had someone who could start immediately."

"Is the Crabtree file still in here?" Ryder asked Sandra.

She nodded. "On the desk."

Ryder entered the office and wheeled Simon's desk chair away so Simon could fit behind the desk. Simon's wheelchair fit snugly in the appropriate spot. "Like a glove."

"Comfy?"

"Oh yeah. Right at home. It's almost like I never left."

Simon turned on his computer and keyed in his password. "So what's Crabtree thinking? They got a new campaign in mind?"

Ryder opened the file sitting on the desk. "Yeah. They've got a new product line with gemstones." He turned the file so Simon could see the glossy photos. "I told them today would be an initial brainstorming session for ideas, but I'd like to crank it up a notch and give them some story boards today."

"Exceeding expectations. That's our motto," Simon grinned, glancing at the prints.

The jewelry was mostly necklaces and earrings made of white gold with a brilliantly coloured gemstone setting. "Get her jewellery to match her eyes," Simon murmured.

"What's that?" Ryder looked at Crabtree's budget info.

"Get her jewellery to match her eyes," Simon said louder and clearer, yet casual. "First thing that popped into my head."

"That'll work," Ryder commented. "Or to match her outfit." Ryder shook his head. Never mind, that's been done."

They sat silent for a few minutes, quietly thinking, when suddenly Simon

193

looked down at his lap.

"Something wrong?" Ryder asked.

"A muscle in my thigh is spasming. I can feel it."

Simon felt little twinges of movement as he watched the muscle poke in and out of the fleshy part of his inner thigh.

"Pretty awesome," Ryder commented. "I guess it's kind of like each part south of the hips is being slowly reborn one by one, eh?"

Simon shrugged. "Yeah, kinda."

"Betcha can't wait until Simon, Jr. works again, huh." Ryder wiggled his eyebrows.

Simon took a deep breath and pulled himself up higher in the chair. "Least of my worries right now, man."

"Seriously?"

"Seriously," Simon said firmly. "I'm through with women for a while."

Simon hadn't told Ryder about his recent visit from Clara.

"After the shit you've been through I can't say I blame you," Ryder said as the desk phone rang.

Simon scoffed as if to say, 'that's right' and answered it.

. . .

"Simon?" Sandra said, sticking her head in his office. "Carnie's here for the interview. She's the intern from UCLA."

Simon looked at her, surprised. "So fast?"

"They've been waiting to hear back from me."

Simon was suddenly indifferent. "Ryder gone to the bike shop?"

Sandra nodded. "He'll be back in an hour to take you home. Darla

THE WHEELS OF CHANGE

confirmed your treatment for one-thirty."

"Great. Send Carnie in."

A moment later, Sandra returned with the intern. She stood slightly taller than Sandra, wearing a freshly ironed white blouse that was buttoned to the top, and a knee-length navy blue pencil skirt. Her long, straight, sandy blonde hair was tied in a pony tail sitting loosely at the nape of her neck. She was a knockout. Sandra introduced them and Simon gestured for Carnie to sit in the chair in front of his desk.

Simon extended his hand for her to shake, effortlessly keeping his eyes above her nose. "Pleased to meet you."

"Oh, no, sir. It's my pleasure." Carnie smiled sweetly. "I was so happy when my professor told me I'd been selected to be interviewed by Simon Cross Advertising." She paused. "It's a real honor."

Simon folded his hands on his desk and asked. "So what are your grades like?"

"I've been on the Dean's List for two semesters, sir," Carnie said humbly.

Simon winced. "Calling me sir is like putting an elevator in an outhouse," he grinned. "Please call me Simon."

"Sure," she whispered, blushing.

"Do you work part-time?"

"Yes, sir. I work at a local book store on weekends and two nights a week."

"Good." Simon was pleased. "You don't look like the type to work in a fast food restaurant or anything like that."

"No," Carnie swallowed. "My aunt actually runs the bookstore. I was lucky."

"And are your parents helping with your tuition?" He wondered if that was an appropriate question.

"Um, no, actually. My father passed away when I was fifteen and the money he left, my mom put away for my education."

Simon looked at her and was lost for words.

"It's okay, sir." She smiled, but was clearly moved by her proclamation. "He died doing what he loved." Carnie's lips were pursed with pride.

"And what was that?" Simon asked cautiously.

"He was a soldier in Afghanistan." She managed a smile even though her eyes were glassy. "I'm an army brat."

Simon smiled and suddenly felt like he was seeing this young woman through different eyes. He reached his hand out and grasped her hand sitting on the desk, quivering ever so slightly while holding her resume. "He would be proud," he said warmly, in a tone he had never heard before.

Carnie sniffed and bobbed her head respectfully, like she had just been awarded a medal, "Thank you."

He nodded, let her hand go and smacked the top of his desk. "How do you feel about working here, Carnie?"

Her face lit up as her mouth opened. "Oh, I'd love it, sir!...err...Simon!" she gasped.

"You're hired." He placed his hands on the handles of his wheelchair, as if he was going to get up. "I keep forgetting," he chuckled, tapping his chair, looking at Carnie like she just caught him stealing the last cookie.

"The Lord works in strange ways, sir," Carnie said good-naturedly.

"That he does," Simon agreed, wheeling himself out from behind the desk. Carnie opened the door for him, but he gestured for her to go ahead, just as Ryder walked in the front door.

"Hey, Ryder, you're just in time to meet Carnie, our new employee," Simon said.

"Hiya Carnie," Ryder said, shaking her hand.

"I'll see you tomorrow, Carnie," Sandra said.

THE WHEELS OF CHANGE

"Nice meeting you all," she called as she exited the building.

Sandra's phone immediately started ringing, and as she answered it, Ryder walked to the window, watching Carnie enter her car. "Whoa. You'll have a tough time concentrating with that little honey around, huh."

"Nah. She's a sweet girl. Top of the Dean's List," Simon said proudly.

Ryder craned his neck. "Alright, who are you and what did you do with Simon Cross?" he said in jest.

"Shut up and drive me home. Any more lip out of you and I'll hire another intern...to replace *you*."

...

"Darla!" Ryder called from the front door, like they were best friends. "How's it hangin'?"

Simon jabbed him in the ribs for the lesbian joke.

"It's hangin' to the left today," she laughed, playing along good-naturedly.

"You beat us here," Simon noticed. "Sorry we're late. I had an interview."

"Looking for a job, Simon?" Darla chuckled. Ryder unlocked the door and they all entered.

"No, I was interviewing an intern."

"A *hot* intern," Ryder added matter-of-factly.

"A young, hard-working, *orphaned* intern," Simon corrected, with a warning look at Ryder.

Ryder put his hands in the air, surrendering. "My mistake." His eyes were wide, as if to say 'what's his problem?' "I gotta head to the bike shop. Catcha both later."

When Ryder left, Darla turned to Simon. "Have you felt any more sensation?"

197

"Yeah, a little. I had a muscle spasm in my thigh earlier."

"And you felt it entirely?"

"Yep. It was like I was feeling it through a thin blanket."

"Excellent. It looks like the second injection was definitely the turning point. I'll let Dr. Bennett know." Darla was pleased.

As they worked through Simon's treatment quietly, the movements and manipulations came naturally. Simon was deeply focused. He had to fight the urge to simply get up and attempt to walk. His legs were feeling more and more like his, not like they were on loan and controlled by someone else.

"Was it good to get back in the office today?"

"Oh yeah," Simon said, like it was the best day of his life. "I felt like myself again. Or…a different version of myself."

Darla's brows knitted together. "How do you mean? Because of your wheelchair?"

"A little." Simon looked at the ceiling in thought. "I thought a lot about what you said the other day."

Darla chuckled. "I say a lot of things."

Simon pointed at her conversationally. "It was about how I look at people. Instead of how I think people look at me."

Darla swallowed a sip of water. "What about it?"

"You were right. I used to take one look at a person and size them up. Like you, for instance. When I saw you, my first impression was that you had *some* potential." He placed his index finger and thumb close together, as though measuring the thickness of a pencil. "I saw your frame, your face, and before you said anything, I'd formed an opinion of you."

Darla giggled. "Was it a good one?"

Simon blushed. "Not really."

"I admire your honesty."

"Well, you know I think differently of you now," he admitted.

She sipped more water. "Go on."

"Well, Carnie? The intern I hired today?"

Darla nodded.

"I didn't do that with her," Simon said, like he was confused but proud.

"What did you see when she walked into your office?"

"She's tall and looks after herself. Professional. She's beautiful," Simon said honestly. "But I didn't have a physical reaction to her. I wasn't wondering how fast I could get her into bed." Simon paused. "Do you think that's only because I can't physically react to females anymore?"

Darla shook her head. "Not at all. I mean, no, you can't get an erection at the moment, but clearly you wouldn't have anyway. You didn't look at her like a piece of meat."

"No, I didn't." Simon was stunned by this revelation. "And I'm glad I didn't, because I would have made a complete ass out of myself."

"I think having these women out of your life, temporary or not, has caused you to see people, not just women, for who they really are," Darla explained. "There's an old saying: pick three people you want to spend the most time with. Those are the people you will most likely become."

Simon pondered a moment.

"So if you don't have those negative influences in your life anymore, you clearly won't behave negatively."

Darla put her water bottle away. "Not to sound cliché. But I believe everything happens for a reason, Simon. Maybe this accident was a wake up call for you."

"Tell that to Max Dunphy."

"Who?"

"The guy who cut my brake lines. The guy who's married to that woman who showed up the other day."

"Ah," Darla said, feeling more clarity with the situation. "Looks like this lesson couldn't have come at a better time."

Simon nodded apprehensively, looking at the floor, seemingly miles away in thought.

Darla sensed his distance. "What do you say we try out that cook book I introduced you to earlier on?"

Simon's brow rose. "Sure."

CHAPTER 21

Mansfield was an international clothing and apparel company, whose head office was located in Los Angeles. The building was a typical skyscraper, complete with countless mirrored windows and a wrap-around logo on the penthouse floor. Tall and skinny. The logo, which was bright yellow and creamy white, gave the building a birthday-candle-like appearance.

Richard and Mark parked the cruiser at the side of the building, as directed by the valet/security guard keeping watch out front. They were greeted inside by the receptionist behind a glass counter, who gave them both visitors badges despite how obvious their police uniforms were.

"Do you recognize this man?" Mark asked the receptionist casually, not expecting much of a response.

She studied the composite sketch and shook her head. "Sorry."

"Is there someone we can talk to in Human Resources perhaps? Someone familiar with all employees?"

She nodded and raised her index finger, turning toward the phone. A moment later she turned toward Mark. "Evelyn will be down in a minute."

Evelyn, the head of Human Resources, brought Mark and Richard to a meeting room, where she logged on to her employee portal and was given the composite sketch. "This is a large company, over fifteen hundred employees in this building alone. And we have a lot of turnover here. Employees can't keep up with the pace," she explained.

"So you don't recognize him?" Richard asked.

"Not especially." She scrolled through her employee list. "We do have a lot of temps here as well."

"Do they all have to have a badge? The witness said the guy was wearing one, that's how he gained access to the movie set."

She nodded understanding.

Mark eyed the security photo affixed to her lapel. "Do all badges require photos?"

"Only permanent and contracted employees require photos. We can scan the photo database and see if there's a match. If not, I'll ask the receptionist who she's printed blank badges for recently."

Mark and Richard exchanged glances. "And what if all that fails?"

Evelyn shrugged. "Then I'll scan the sketch and send a company-wide email blast to see if anyone recognizes him."

. . .

The database scan turned up nothing as did the second inquiry to the receptionist. "I guess we'll go with plan C then." Mark was disappointed.

"Not to worry," Evelyn said. "I'll flag the email so everyone sees it immediately. I should get quick responses."

"Tell them this guy is wanted for questioning in a criminal case," Richard suggested. "That might light a fire under them."

. . .

Richard dialled Cameron at the office on the drive back. "Cameron, buddy, no dice."

Cameron sighed. "Shit. Back to the drawing board."

"Yeah, not necessarily. Stick around, the woman in HR is going to dig some more and get back to us. Can you hang another couple of hours?"

"Sure. Bring me some grub on your way back. And coffee. Lots of it."

THE WHEELS OF CHANGE

"Will do."

...

"There's an Evelyn Montgomery for you on line two," Lisa called to Mark. "Says she's from Mansfield."

"Got it. Thanks." Mark picked up the phone, impressed. "You weren't kidding. That was pretty fast."

"Yes. Um. I have good news and bad news for you, Chief," Evelyn said casually.

"I'm listening."

"Well, the good news is that twenty people in our Marketing department recognized him as Ken Wakefield."

"And what's the bad news?" Mark asked expectantly.

"Thirty people in our finance department also recognized him as Lawrence Greenfield."

Mark took a deep breath. "What are the chances?" he asked rhetorically.

"Sorry I couldn't be more help, sir."

Mark clucked his tongue. "Well, we'll go with the biggest odds. Give me the story on Mr. Greenfield."

"Absolutely. He's been working with our finance team, doing various consulting jobs. He was working with Harvey Stockton, our head account executive, and our C.F.O. Marvin Gates. I can give you their contact information as well as Mr. Greenfield's."

"That would be very helpful, Evelyn." Mark motioned for Richard to go get Cameron.

Evelyn relayed the information just as Cameron appeared with his laptop, and Richard in tow.

Cameron set his laptop on Mark's desk, opposite Mark, as he took the

203

information from Evelyn.

"Thanks dear, you've been great." He hung up.

Cameron rubbed his hands together eagerly. "So, what have we got?"

"Two names, but we'll go with the most popular first."

Richard's eyebrow rose but he didn't interrupt.

"Lawrence Greenfield," Mark relayed to Cameron. Cameron typed the name in.

"Address?"

Mark relayed the information, and just as Cameron keyed it in, Lawrence's driver's license photo was displayed on the screen. "We need to get our witness back in here to confirm this is the guy. Is Darryl still here?"

"No, but we can email or text him the shot," Richard suggested.

"Good idea. Will you pass that along to Lisa?" Mark asked. Richard nodded.

"In the mean time," Mark said to Cameron, "Let's get the goods on Mr. Greenfield."

Mark and Cameron got some history on him while Richard received confirmation from Darryl. About five minutes later, Richard returned. "Yep, that's affirmative. He's the guy."

"Okay, let's head over to his place and get his story. At the least we need a strong alibi," Mark said.

...

Mr. Greenfield lived in a small town just south of LA. It was a typical suburban neighbourhood, domestic cars were parked in the driveways of single-family homes. The house that Mark and Richard were looking for was on a C-shaped street, or a crescent. They parked the cruiser at the front of the house, which looked barren.

Richard chewed a piece of gum loudly. "No cars, drapes are drawn.

THE WHEELS OF CHANGE

Looks like Larry's on vacation or something."

Mark stepped up on the front veranda and pushed his finger in the mail slot on the door. He bent down and peeked into the tiny horizontal hole leading into the front foyer. "There's tons of mail. Yep, he's been gone a while I'd say."

"We should knock on a couple of doors." Richard suggested.

Mark nodded, gesturing to the small bungalow next door. There was a freshly washed and waxed tomato soup-coloured four-door sedan parked in the drive way. "Easy, killer," Richard said as Mark got his credentials out. "Looks like grandma lives here."

Mark smirked, trying to ignore the comment. Then he knocked on the door. After about ten seconds, an old lady in elastic waist band pants answered the door. Her hair was white as snow and freshly coiffed. "Yes?" she asked, her voice remotely quivering like an old lady's.

"Do you know where we can find your neighbour, ma'am?" Mark gestured to the next house.

"No I'm sorry, I don't." She attempted to close the door absent-mindedly.

"Do you remember when you saw him last?" Mark tried.

"Sir, I have Alzheimer's. Ask me what colour my car is, you'll have better luck." She closed the door gently, like Mark and Richard were door-to-door salesmen.

Richard shook his head. "Better try the other neighbor."

After knocking on the door twice and nobody answered, they left. "Let's head back to the station and give Evelyn a call; find out where he is for work," Mark suggested.

Mark whipped off his jacket as he dialled Evelyn's number on the office phone. She answered quickly and Mark explained the situation. Evelyn responded. "He's supposed to be coming in again next week, but I believe he's out of town working with another company. He's on contract with us and several other companies."

205

"When was the last you heard from him?"

"He was in just last week, working with our Finance department."

"Thanks, Evelyn." Mark hung up his desk phone. "Cameron!" he called.

"Yep." Cameron slipped into Mark's office.

"We need a client list for Mr. Greenfield. Apparently he's on several other contract jobs."

Cameron keyed something into his computer. "Huh," he tutted.

"What's up?"

"You'll be here for a year tracking all these clients down. There's gotta be at least a hundred here."

"Shit," Mark cussed. "Is there a next-of-kin or spouse listed? Someone's gotta know where this guy is. He was under our noses just a couple of days ago for Christ's sake."

"Nope. No spouse or next-of-kin."

"Okay, let's dig deeper. Can you pull anything based on his Social Security or birth certificate?"

Cameron obliged, first trying his social security number with no luck other than data they already knew, and then he punched in Mr. Greenfield's birth certificate information and scrolled through pages and pages of data.

"I hope you've got lots of coffee," Cameron commented.

. . .

Mark was frustrated. "We haven't got time to sort through all this shit, Cameron. What do we do?"

"Let me see if I can track him with his bank records." He keyed more information into the computer and clucked his tongue. "Dammit. His last withdrawal was local. Must have been the day when he was at the movie set. All the other stuff looks to be local as well."

THE WHEELS OF CHANGE

"He must be using a company credit card if he's out of town," Richard added.

"Shit," Mark responded. "Well. Let's take a look and see what we've got here." He pulled up a chair beside Cameron and Richard.

CHAPTER 22

"Look at you!" Darla smiled as she entered the house. Simon was preparing a snack for himself and Darla, courtesy of their kitchen practice the other day. "Wow, you catch on fast."

Simon bowed from his chair. "And check this out," he boasted, lifting his left leg a full inch away from the chair.

Darla sandwiched her hands under her chin, like she was praying, and smiled gleefully. "Oh Simon, I'm so happy for you."

She came over and gave him a hug. When she stood up again, she had an ear to ear smile. Simon looked at her and noticed something different about her. "Hey, you got your braces off," he pointed matter-of-factly.

"Yes. I must tell you, Simon, I feel like a million dollars," she beamed.

"I'll bet." He took a closer look while she held her mouth open for inspection. "Looks great, Darla. Beautiful."

She was pleased with his approval. "Thank you. Shall we do some quick strength training and then stop for a nibble?"

"Sounds great."

Their training was interrupted by the house phone ringing. "I'll get it," Darla said, helping Simon into a sitting position.

She picked up the phone and answered it. "Cross residence, can I help you?"

Simon chuckled. He usually answered it. "Yeah?"

"Oh yes. Certainly." Darla set the phone on the side table and helped Simon on to the couch, and then handed him the phone.

"Simon speaking."

"Mr. Cross. This is officer Quigley calling from the San Bernardino police department."

Simon cleared his throat and knitted his brows. "Yes?"

"Sir. Um. I'm terribly sorry to tell you this, but we found your mother."

Simon's heart started to pound. "My mother? Where? What's going on?"

"Mr. Cross, I think you need to come out here right away."

"Why? What's happened to my mother?"

"I'm terribly sorry son, but your mother is dead."

...

Simon and Ryder arrived at the San Bernardino Hilton and identified themselves at reception. They were sent up to the floor which her mom and Aunt Barbara were staying at. When Simon arrived in the hotel room, he was stunned. Nancy's body lay there in the bathtub, a la Whitney Houston. The Jacuzzi-style tub was three-quarters full of tepid water, and Nancy was floating on top. Her semi-wet hair was splayed across the rim of the tub like a wet blanket. Her eyes were open. She was naked, her clothes were flung on the floor as though thrown in the heat of passion.

"Sorry for your loss, son." Officer Quigley shook Simon's hand. "This is Nancy Cross, right?"

"Yes," Simon said without blinking. Ryder squeezed Simon's shoulder but remained silent.

"I know it's difficult, son, but you were listed as her next-of-kin. We had to call you to identify her."

THE WHEELS OF CHANGE

"Where's my aunt?" Simon asked, pulling himself from his reverie.

"I believe she's down the hall." He gestured to the door. Ryder left Simon and popped his head out. He shook his head, she wasn't there.

The coroner was examining her, paying special attention to her nose. "She had a drug problem," he said, like he was checking it off a list.

"She did," Simon confirmed. He continued to stare at her, like he had been frozen in time.

Ryder kneeled next to him. "You okay, buddy?"

"Yeah," Simon said numbly.

"Did she ever go to rehab?" the coroner asked.

"Several times."

The coroner rose and cleared his throat. "Looks like she died of an overdose. Classic signs."

Officer Quigley nodded agreement.

"No autopsy required."

Simon blinked and stammered. "W…wait. Wait a minute," he said, as though he was trying to put a puzzle together right before it was swept off the table. "Something's wrong."

"What do you mean?"

"She's in the bath," he said, like the officer should understand.

He looked at Simon, puzzled. "Yes?"

Simon blinked and swallowed. "Well, she never took baths."

"Yeah, that's right," Ryder confirmed.

"What do you mean, son?" Officer Quigley asked.

209

Simon spoke quickly, as though every second he spoke was critical. "She was terrified of water, nearly drowned when she was a kid."

Quigley looked at the coroner and frowned. "Well, any chance she might have been so high that she changed her mind or didn't realize what she was doing?"

Simon shook his head, speaking firmly. "Not a chance. She wouldn't even come in the tub with me when I was a boy."

"So you're saying someone put her in there?" Quigley examined the floor. "I don't see water. It doesn't look like there was a struggle."

He looked at the towel bar and saw all the towels were there except for the ones on the toilet beside the tub.

"Check the adjoining room," the coroner suggested.

Quigley went over and came back a moment later. "They're all there."

Suddenly another officer appeared with a writing pad in his hand. "I've canvassed the area, sir." He addressed Quigley, opening his pad to the first sheet and reading from it. "The couple in room 412 say the man in the room beside them had a strange woman in his company. Says she was wasted, on drugs or something, she was looking for the guy and knocked on their door by mistake."

"Can they identify the woman?"

The officer nodded and left the room, returning in a moment with the couple. The woman gasped and nodded, placing her hand in front of her mouth in shock. "Yeah, that's definitely her," the husband confirmed.

"Who was the man staying in the next room?" Officer Quigley asked.

The officer referenced his notes. "Room 411 was registered to a Theodore Greenfield."

Simon's eyes widened at the mention of the name. "Ted? Ted Greenfield?"

"Do you know him?" the officer asked.

THE WHEELS OF CHANGE

"Yeah. He and my mom used to date," he said, shaking his head, confused. "She brought him up recently but didn't elaborate."

Quigley addressed the couple. "Did they have an altercation?"

"No, not to my knowledge," the husband responded. "She was so wasted, she probably passed out in his room."

The coroner and Officer Quigley exchanged glances. "I'll do an autopsy, sir. See if the water in her lungs is pre or post-mortem."

"How do you know she's got water in her lungs?" Ryder asked.

"She was completely immersed when we found her. We had to pull her out to examine her. That's why her hair is all wet," Officer Quigley explained. "If she didn't have any water in her lungs, she would have floated to the surface. It takes days for a body to float if there's water in their lungs when they died."

Ryder nodded, looking at Simon.

"Is Mr. Greenfield still registered in the room?" Quigley asked the officer.

"Nope. Checked out a couple of hours ago."

Quigley looked at his watch. "Odd time to check out," he observed. "Have we got any contact info on him?"

"He used his employer's credit card, but he did leave his address. Santa Barbara."

"Okay, I'll contact Ingram over in Santa Barbara and see if there's anything on him." Quigley said. "Get forensics over here and have them cover this room, the adjoining room and Mr. Greenfield's room."

"Will do, sir."

"We'll release the body after forensics has done a full investigation," Quigley said to the coroner, and dismissed him.

"I'll leave you for a moment, Mr. Cross," he said to Simon. Then he addressed the officer. "Get a statement from this couple, and hunt down the aunt for her statement. See if anyone else saw anything."

"Yes, sir," the officer said.

Ryder looked over at Simon, who was sitting by the bathroom door. "Do you want me to get you closer?" he asked cautiously.

"No, I can do it."

Simon wheeled himself as close as he could to Nancy's body. The small space surrounding the tub didn't warrant a lot of room, Simon could barely reach his mother's hand that was draped alongside the tub. He swore he saw a twitch, but remembered when his grandma died, seeing the same thing, only to be told it was his imagination.

"Do you want me to leave you alone?" Ryder asked.

Simon shook his head. He looked at her in an expression of anger mixed with remorse. "I knew I should never have let her come here."

"Don't blame yourself, man. She would have come no matter what."

"I should have picked up on something when she called. I should have known something was up when she mentioned Ted."

"You're gonna drive yourself crazy trying to figure it out, Simon," Ryder said in a comforting tone. "Wait until they investigate and see what comes of it."

Simon frowned. "You know how these investigations work." He looked directly at Ryder. "She's a druggie. They'll let it slip through the cracks. Especially when they find out Ted's a goddamn pastor."

"You think he did this?" Ryder asked flatly.

"Well, I know my mom would never get into a bath tub, especially a monster-sized one like this. I think she had to be coerced or forced. There's no way she'd get in willingly."

"Maybe she overdosed and then fell in."

Simon gave him a don't-be-so-stupid look. "And why would someone conveniently have a tub full of water waiting for her?"

THE WHEELS OF CHANGE

Ryder was embarrassed. "You're right."

Simon reached out with his hand, barely reaching hers. Ryder quickly applied the brake for Simon and stood back, not wanting to interfere. Gripping the left hand side of his wheelchair handlebar, Simon lifted himself an inch or two off the seat, leaning most of his weight on his feet, which were resting on the steel foot plates. Ryder watched with a combination of worry and admiration as his friend hoisted himself up so he could reach his dead mother's hand.

When he finally made contact, Simon made a throaty sound that Ryder wasn't quite sure was a sob or a grunt from strain. He waited. Simon lifted himself slightly higher, so he could hold her entire palm in his. As he delicately held her hand, he brought it close to his face. Ryder watched as Simon leaned, with both elbows on the apron of the tub and his rear end almost completely off the chair, and brought his mother's tender hand to his lips. He kissed it softly and sniffed. "I'm sorry, mom," he whispered. "I'm so sorry I didn't take better care of you. God will take care of you now."

CHAPTER 23

"Simon! Oh my god, Simon!" Aunt Barbara shouted from the other side of the hallway. Simon and Ryder were leaving as the forensics team had arrived. She ran to him in a cashmere blouse, leather skirt and matching six-inch leather heels. There was a noticeable wine stain on her shirt. When she reached him, she bent down and made cheek-to-cheek contact, mimicking Hollywood-style kisses. Simon could smell the alcohol and cigarettes on her and recoiled slightly. Raphael was behind her with his hands in his pockets, looking like he'd rather be anywhere else.

"I can't believe this! We went out for dinner and she said she didn't want to go with us. She said she was too tired. We left and then came back after dancing. She wasn't in her room, or at least I didn't see her so we left again. When we came back, I looked in the bathroom to find her..." She didn't finish the sentence. Barbara grabbed a tissue that was tucked in her blouse and dabbed her eyes.

"Why did you leave her alone all night?" Simon asked suspiciously. "Why couldn't you just order in and spend some time with your sister? You hadn't seen her in over a year."

"She insisted," Barbara said.

"Where were you all this time? After you found her?" Simon hissed.

Raphael interjected. "We went for a drink. Barbara was distressed."

"I'll bet," Simon said under his breath, disgusted that Barbara partied all night, neglecting her only sister, and then started up again mid-morning, as though news of her sister was the perfect excuse to drink that early in the day.

Officer Quigley approached Barbara in the hallway. "I'll need to get a statement from you, ma'am."

"Can I at least change my clothes first?" she asked, like her wardrobe needs trumped her sister's death.

"That'll have to wait until later, ma'am. Forensics is conducting their investigation. Perhaps the hotel can offer you another room?"

She huffed. "A lot of good that will do. My clothes are in my room."

"The hotel has a boutique, dear," Raphael suggested. "Come. Let's get you some fresh clothes."

Officer Quigley interrupted. "Not until you give us your statement."

Barbara rolled her eyes. "Fine."

Quigley took Barbara and Raphael to the elevator.

"You want to get a room to rest?" Ryder asked Simon.

"We'll wait a bit. I want to stick around in case they find something."

. . .

"Santa Barbara Police Department, Chief Ingram's office. Mary speaking," a voice welcomed.

"Hi Mary, this is Officer Quigley over in San Bernardino. Listen, we've got a situation over here. Do you have anything on file for a 'Ted' or 'Theodore' Greenfield?"

"Hang on a moment, sir, I'll check the system."

There was silence for a few moments as Mary investigated. "Err…I'm sorry, sir, but there's nothing here except a flag on his file. Let me open it and see what it says."

She came back. "It says to contact the Los Angeles police department. The F.B.I. placed the flag on his file."

Quigley paused. "Hmm...okay, thanks, Mary. I'll get a hold of Chief Tame over there and see what the story is."

"Good day, sir." Mary hung up.

Quigley looked up and dialled Mark's desk line.

Mark answered quickly. "Chief Tame here."

"Tame. Quigley over in San Bernardino."

"Quigley. How are you? What can I do for you?" Mark said warmly.

"We've got a woman over here. Died in a bathtub. Looks like an overdose of drugs, but we're investigating. She was in the company of a Theodore Greenfield in the hotel here. He's from Santa Barbara, but there's a flag on his fi—"

Mark interrupted. "Greenfield? We're looking for a Greenfield right now. Lawrence Greenfield. He's wanted for questioning in a murder case."

"You think they're related?" Quigley asked.

"Let me call you back."

...

"Lawrence Theodore Greenfield...come on down!" Cameron boasted. "Dropped his first name and went by his middle name." He continued to speak in a game show host voice. "And why did he do that, Pat? Well I'll tell you, Vanna...his wife died and he fled his congregation of twenty years. Why would he do that, Pat?—"

"Okay, enough." Mark was irritated. "Get me the address of his church, a list of church attendees, congregation, anything you can get me that will help us find out where the hell he is."

Mark called Quigley back and updated him on their findings.

"Okay Mark, thanks. I'll put out a search for all posts and keep you informed."

THE WHEELS OF CHANGE

"I'll do the same, Quigley. Keep in touch."

Mark hung up the phone and hollered to Richard. "Hey buddy, feel like going to church?"

...

Cameron provided them with a list of key people involved in Ted's old church. The head secretary, Lida Brickman, worked for that congregation for over forty years. They decided to knock on her door first. She lived walking distance from Old Saints Baptist Church. The neighborhood was quaint, similar to Ted's, but the houses were cottage-style and appeared to be habituated by retirees and widows. When Mark and Richard pulled up to her house, they peered over and saw grandma-like faces appearing in almost every window.

"I guess they don't get many visits from cops around here," Richard commented matter-of-factly.

As they strolled up the walkway leading to the front entrance, Lida opened the door with a pained look on her face. "Oh Lord, what's happened to Jed?"

Mark smiled. "It's okay, ma'am. We're not here for Jed," he said comfortingly, with one hand in front of his body.

She sighed and looked upward. "Oh, thank God." Then her eyebrows knitted. "Why are you here, then? Has there been some trouble?"

Lida gestured them in and told them not to worry about removing their shoes. "I have to sweep this whole place later. I had my granddaughter's birthday party here yesterday and my great-grandson," she giggled. "God bless him, he walked around holding his cake in his hand practically all day."

"Spread the love," Richard volunteered.

"That's right," she nodded.

Mark and Richard took a seat in her small kitchenette while she started a pot of water. "Coffee? Tea?" she offered in a practiced voice.

"Sure. I'll have some tea," Mark said.

"Same here," said Richard.

"Jed is a special needs boy that lives on the next street over," Lida explained. "He gets out on his parents sometimes and can get himself into trouble. Last year, he inadvertently stole a little boy's bike. It was just sitting in the middle of the sidewalk and Jed, well, he didn't mean any harm."

She stood between Mark and Richard, with her back to the window overlooking the sink. "Of course, everybody comes to me when there's any trouble around here, seeing as I help run the community church." Grabbing three small mugs from the cupboard above the sink, Lida continued. "We're a close-knit neighborhood here. Been like that for as long as I can remember."

"So, what can I do for you today?" Lida asked warmly, pouring water into the teapot and placing a teabag in."

"Do you recall a Ted Greenfield? He used to be a pastor at your church?"

Lida looked up briefly, being careful not to scald herself as she emptied the kettle into the teapot. "Oh yes, Ted? He was a fine pastor. Of course, when his wife died, he fell apart. Poor dear." She nodded solemnly and raised her eyebrows. "Are you here about him?"

Mark ignored the question. "What can you tell us about him?"

Eyebrows still lifted, she inhaled deeply. "He tried very hard to help people, and he was very good at it. But some people, you know, they just can't be helped."

"What happened to his wife?" Richard asked.

"Lilly? Well, she was a troubled soul, too, when she started coming to the church. Ted saw her through most of it, and then, of course, they married. It seems they were just getting settled when she got cancer. It was such a shame, but I guess the Lord works in strange ways."

"How was she troubled?" Mark asked.

THE WHEELS OF CHANGE

Lida took a sip of her tea. "She had a hard life. Her mother threw her father out when she was just a young thing, maybe ten or eleven years old. After that, Lilly got in with the wrong crowd. I don't know exactly what kind of danger she was in, but it was enough to bring her here."

"Why did her mother throw her father out?" Richard asked.

"Apparently he'd been having an affair," she answered. "I never heard it from Lilly, of course. But Ted had a real sore spot for infidelity, that's how come I knew."

"Why's that? Why was Ted sensitive?" Richard stole a glance at Mark, who was squirming at the mention of the word 'infidelity'.

"Well, his father cheated on his mother and from what I understand, her mother ended up in a mental institution because of it. Since then, the mere mention of cheating, well, Ted had radar for stuff like that."

Mark changed the subject, "When did Ted take off?"

"Right after Lilly died," Lida answered. "It couldn't have been more than a month. He was delivering a sermon as usual one day and the next day he was gone. Packed up and left without a word. Left his house and all his things. It's like he disappeared."

"How long ago was this?"

"About a month ago. Maybe two?"

"So he left his house? Nobody's been looking after it?"

Lilly had a crooked smile. "Ted has money. Lilly had a small insurance plan, but it was more from his business."

"What kind of business did he run? I didn't think people of the cloth had jobs," Richard scoffed. Mark gave him a warning look.

"Oh yes," Lilly corrected. "Pastors lead normal lives just like the rest of us. He put himself through college and started some consulting business. I imagine that's what he's doing now. He probably paid someone to come look after his affairs while he was away, I imagine."

"Did Ted seem distraught at all? I mean, besides what would be expected under the circumstances?" Richard asked.

"Like I said, Ted tried to help a lot of people." Lida shook her head slowly. "But in this day and age, some people are so far gone by the time they get to the church, it's too late. You see, Ted was part of a support group, for substance abusers and the like." She pulled a package of cookies out of the pantry next to her. "If you ask me, he got a little too involved," she said like it was a big secret. Her nose was pinched as if there was a funny smell.

"How do you mean?" Mark accepted the cookie Lida offered. "How can a pastor get too involved?"

"Well, Ted saw the most desperate cases and spent practically every spare moment he had with them." Lida took a bite of her cookie after both men began eating theirs. "There have been so many over the years, mostly women. It's almost like he felt he had to be their knight in shining armour or something, you know?"

"Hero complex?" Richard offered.

"Something like that, yes," Lida said in a thank-you tone.

"Lilly, she was pretty bad at first. Suicidal, low self-esteem, eating disorders, there was almost nothing left of her." Lida swallowed her cookie. "And another really bad case was about fifteen years ago. This young, beautiful woman with a young boy, well, she was heavily into drugs. In and out of rehab for years, but she never joined a support group,"

Mark and Richard exchanged glances. "What can you tell us about her?" Richard asked, taking another cookie from the open package Lida left on the table.

"She was raising the boy on her own. Apparently she'd thrown her husband out because he'd had an affair. And of course, like I said, Ted had a soft spot for that. Well, anyway, this girl, Nancy I think her name was, she finally received good treatment here and was part of the support program that Ted ran, when she got herself off the drugs."

"And then Ted got involved with her?" Mark asked, finishing his tea.

"Well, yes," Lida blushed. "I know it sounds strange, but Ted was such a…a sweet man, he was very gentlemanly, you know?" she said carefully,

THE WHEELS OF CHANGE

evidently trying to save Ted's honour.

Mark nodded. "And what happened with her and Ted?"

Lida fluffed her short, curly white hair and poured more tea into her cup. "Well, like I said, he got too involved." She lowered her voice as if someone might be eavesdropping. "Her son, precious thing he was, well, Ted was just too hard on him," she said in a pathetic voice. "Poor boy was doing so well in school and he was helping around the house. A really good kid, you know?" Lida winked. "Ted started on him when he was dating a girl. Well, anyway, they had a row because Ted caught the boy and his girlfriend in his bedroom," Lida said, allowing Mark and Richard to fill in the blanks.

"So he's *really* sensitive about that kind of stuff," Richard said, emptying his cup.

"Yes, sir," Lida said flatly. "Anyway, after that Ted moved out and that was the end of them. Last I heard they moved out to LA." She paused and furrowed her brows. "Say, what police department are you from, anyway? Are you two *from* LA?"

"Yes, we are actually looking for Ted, which is why we're here," Mark answered.

"Has he been in any trouble?"

"We need to ask him some questions," Richard intervened.

"Questions about what?" Lida asked, puzzled. "Is this anything to do with Nancy or her son?"

Mark didn't have the heart to be secretive to Lida, seeing as she had been fully cooperative. "Actually, yes. Unfortunately Nancy died last night in the same hotel as Ted was apparently staying."

The colour drained from Lida's face. "Oh God. That poor woman. What happened? Was it the drugs? Oh, that poor, poor dear." Her hand was in front of her mouth, she was in disbelief.

"We're not entirely sure. The autopsy will tell us the exact cause of death. But a couple a few doors down saw Ted and Nancy together and now Ted is nowhere to be found."

Mark neglected to tell Lida about him also being wanted for questioning in the murders of Jake Campbell, Chase McCann and Drake Scott.

"Oh my goodness. This is terrible." Lida shook her head. "Do you think he fled?" she asked. "I know he had basically no family, that's why he was so deep into the people of the congregation."

"Do you know where he did have family?" Richard asked.

Lida paused for thought. "I think he had a cousin or uncle but he never mentioned where or if they were still alive. Both his parents died in a car accident when he was in his early twenties. He was an only child. The house he left behind was his childhood home; he kept it with the insurance his parents left him."

"So you have no idea where he'd go?"

"I thought maybe he went to look for Nancy. He did speak of her from time to time. I guess that *is* where he went if that was the last place he was seen," Lida paused. "And now Nancy's gone, too. Poor Ted," she tutted. "Where was he working?"

"That's something we're looking into," Mark said, rising. "Here's my card. Thanks so much for your help, Lida. You've been wonderful. If you think of anything else, call me any time."

Richard handed her his card and said, "Ditto. Thanks for the tea."

"Oh, it's my pleasure," she smiled. "Any time you want to visit, I always have tea in the house."

Mark tipped his hat on the way out.

"I wish all grandmas were that sweet," Richard commented.

"Mine was," Mark said as if it was a competition.

"What, did she want you to be a cop?" Richard said, as if to say 'you're a suck-up'

CHAPTER 24

Lisa walked into Mark's office. Both Mark and Richard were there with the files from all three murders on the desk. "The coroner just released Nancy Cross's body. He confirmed she was drowned."

Richard sighed. "And she couldn't have put up much of a fight because she was so full of dope."

"Exactly."

"We need to contact the employers from the first two victims," Mark said. "That's the only way to get full F.B.I. involvement in this. If we can link Ted to all three victims—"

Richard interrupted. "Four, counting Nancy."

Mark continued. "Err…four, then we can get the whole damn team here, instead of pissing around with the media."

Mark looked at Lisa. "Contact the bank and the television network," he instructed. "See if you can talk to one of the big-wigs. We need confirmation that Ted Greenfield was employed there as a consultant around the time of the first two murders."

He looked at Richard. "Then we can link him to those two, and we've got confirmation from Mansfield that he worked there, too."

Richard intervened. "Wait, but didn't that girl Evelyn get *two* names? Don't we need to narrow it down?"

"Get in touch with Marvin Stockton and Harvey Gates over at

Mansfield. They were working with him. Get it straightened out who this shit-head is."

"On it," Lisa said, walking out of the room, and then she stopped, lifting her index finger. "Oh, and I got word from Max Dunphy over at the Penitentiary, he's still whining because he's not been told when his trial date is set for."

"Tell him to speak with his lawyer, he should have been appointed one by now. Judge Caplan said it would be a couple of weeks' wait for trial."

"So, we've cancelled all phone taps for Max Dunphy, and the restraining order for Simon Cross is cancelled, too," Lisa confirmed.

"Yes. As long as Max is behind bars, Simon is safe. We'll worry about reinstating the order when he gets out…if he gets out," Mark explained.

. . .

Simon sat on his couch alone. He had just received word from the San Bernardino police department that his mother's body was being released, and that they were conducting a full investigation, having discovered that she was in fact drowned. Ryder was expected any moment to take him over to the funeral home, to make arrangements for her funeral and burial.

He decided it was time to make the phone call he'd been avoiding, the one to his father. His cell phone sat on the side table, three feet away. Simon scooched himself down to reach for it and pressed a button. The screen came to life. He had a few missed calls but ignored them. As he scrolled down his number list and found his father's number, he hesitated.

All the years he'd known of his mother's drug abuse, Simon always understood that Nancy's addiction stemmed from something his father had done to her. Nancy had manipulated Simon into thinking that James's affair with Betty was the reason she reverted back to drugs. Living with this stigma about his dad always put a wrench in their relationship. Simon felt that James neglected Nancy, not paying alimony among other things, knowing full well of Nancy's several trips to rehab. James's calls were seldom and shallow when they did occur. James never asked how Nancy was doing, he barely asked how Simon was. His life revolved around Betty. The resentment built up in Simon, driving him to let his phone go back into sleep mode.

THE WHEELS OF CHANGE

He swallowed. Simon allowed his mind to go blank as he sat, staring at his phone. It startled him when he heard his land line ring.

"Hello?" Simon answered, surprising himself with the unusual words.

"Simon. Hello." The voice was flat. "It's Aunt Mary."

Mary was Simon's father's sister. She was the only one who stayed in touch with Nancy after the divorce. Mary had always been the neutral opinion in the family, even after James's affair. She loved both Nancy and James despite their turbulent relationship.

Simon cleared his throat. "Aunt Mary. It's been a while," he said, his voice cracking.

Silence.

"Barbara called me," she said in a knowing tone. "I'm so sorry, Simon."

Simon didn't speak.

"I got in my car as soon as I heard," she said. "I'm staying at the hotel up the street."

"Okay," he said.

"Have you made arrangements yet?" she asked in a comforting tone.

"N...no."

"I'm on my way over," she said and hung up.

. . .

Simon lifted himself into the wheelchair, ignoring the fact that he could feel almost every inch of his legs ever so slightly. And he wheeled himself over to the door, disengaging the lock. He got a strange sensation, like his mother was going to walk through the door at any moment and chastise him for something. Part of him missed her overbearing and needy personality already. The other part was feeling guilty because it was glad she was gone.

Since the moment Simon came into money with his business, Nancy always seemed to need more. How do you say no to your mother? Even if you suspected she was using it for purposes other than what she'd stated. Nancy was the only one who supported Simon as he grew into success, and sharing his wealth was a way he repaid her, at least that's what he convinced himself. How many times did she actually spend the money on useful things? Did she ever get her pool fixed? Simon wondered if he was to blame since he never checked up on her expenditures.

The knock on the door broke him from his reverie. He opened the door and wheeled himself away, looking at Aunt Mary for a split second before hanging his head. A welcome to Aunt Mary used to involve a tight bear hug, lifting her slightly off the floor; she was only five foot five and petite. This welcome would not be the same.

"Hi Simon," she said, seeing his solemn expression. Mary bent down so she was level with his eyes, and spoke to him like he was a child. "How are you doing, sweetie?" she asked, leaning forward to give him a hug. He hesitated at first. This was the first time anyone had embraced him since the accident other than Darla in her efforts to lift him without injury. Mary's arms slid naturally around his shoulders as her body came closer to his.

"I'm here for you, Simon," she said. Simon waited to hear her voice crack, fearing he would lose his bearings, too, but she didn't. "We'll get through this," is all she said. Mary's eyes met Simon's. "I told your dad. I figured it was what you'd need me to do."

Simon nodded, looking down at his hands, shaking ever so slightly. "Ryder will be here any minute."

Mary nodded. "Have you eaten anything?"

He shook his head no. She rose and entered the kitchen, searching the cupboards. Simon wheeled over and pulled a pot from the stove top. Mary took the cue and selected a can of chicken soup. Without a word, they began making lunch.

Ryder walked in as Mary put the soup bowl and sandwich plate on the table. He saw Mary and smiled. "Been a long time." He went over to welcome her with a hug. "Glad to see you," Ryder said, unsuccessfully hiding his relief.

THE WHEELS OF CHANGE

...

"It's Quigley!" Lisa shouted. "Line four."

Officer Quigley promised he'd call Mark with any updates.

"Tame here," Mark answered flatly.

"Mark. My investigative team found a receipt shoved into a jacket pocket that our perpetrator forgot inside the closet of his hotel room."

"Oh yeah? What was the receipt for?"

"I don't know if it helps you, but it was for a knife...our guys called the store where he bought it from and apparently it's a hunting knife. You want me to scan and email you a copy?"

"What's the date on it?"

"Err...a couple of days ago?"

"Great. Do that. Thanks, Quigley."

Mark yelled to Richard as he walked by. "We better track this sucker down."

Richard entered Mark's office and raised his eyebrow.

"He's not done yet," Mark said matter-of-factly.

...

"I want a search warrant for Greenfield's house ASAP," Mark said, knocking on Lisa's desk as she hung up her phone.

"I couldn't get in touch with anyone yet to confirm Ted's employment. Everyone is out at conferences or unreachable."

"Get Judge Caplan. I know he's in his office. We need to get into Ted's house right away, I need to find out who's next on his list."

Lisa nodded, punching in Judge Caplan's number. Mark continued on until he reached Cameron. "Have you been able to trace him? He made a purchase a couple of days ago."

Cameron chuckled. "What'd he buy? A knife?"

Mark gave him a warning look. "Oh, shit," Cameron said, his eyes widening as he keyed into his laptop. "He made a large withdrawal a month or so ago, but I already told you about that, right?"

Mark nodded. "Nothing else?"

"Nope. He must be paying for everything in cash."

"Where the hell is his car?"

Cameron shook his head. "Using a rental. Company credit card, local rental place."

Mark was frustrated; he sighed. "GPS?"

"The one he had wasn't equipped."

"Fuck," Mark swore under his breath. "Alright, we need his picture spread across the news." Mark walked back to Lisa's desk.

She hung up her phone. "Caplan's faxing the warrant right now. And I already spoke to Peggy at the news desk, Ted's picture already aired."

"Shit." Mark ran his fingers through his hair. "Call me as soon as that fax comes in."

"So what's the plan?" Richard reached for his jacket. "Are we heading over to Ted's?"

"We have to. He's bought himself a shiny new knife and he's AWOL."

. . .

Simon, Mary and Ryder picked out a simple casket for Nancy, and made arrangements for the funeral to be the next day. Simon figured she would have wanted it to be quick, no wake. He also selected a closed casket so she could be remembered for what she was, not for the pasted-on face the mortuary would have made her.

THE WHEELS OF CHANGE

On the drive back to Simon's place, Ryder drove. Mary sat with Simon in the back seat.

She reached out and took his hand in hers, looking up at him. "Your dad is coming to the funeral tomorrow."

Simon stared out his window, avoiding eye contact. "Why?"

"Because despite what happened between them, Simon, your dad always loved your mom."

Simon nodded. The tension was palpable.

"Your dad loves you, Simon," Mary said. "He misses you."

Simon's lips pursed.

"I know you blame him," Mary whispered. "But it isn't his fault."

Simon looked over at Mary; his eyes were narrowed. "You don't know," he said through gritted teeth.

Mary looked at him imploringly. "Simon, I know you don't want to hear this. But I have to tell you because I don't want you to do anything you'll regret when he comes tomorrow." She looked at the floor. "Believe me. The day you bury your mother is a day you'll always remember."

Simon pulled his hand from hers. "He has no business being here."

Mary looked up and spied Ryder watching from the rear-view mirror. She removed her seat belt so she could sit right next to Simon.

"Your dad wanted you to believe he was the reason she had the problem," she explained. "He didn't want you thinking badly of her." Her voice cracked. "She threw him out anyway, so he figured it was better that you thought she did the drugs because of his affairs."

Simon was silent.

Mary cried. "He never had any affairs, Simon."

Simon looked at her as the colour drained from his face. "Your mother begged him not to tell you about the drugs. But they started long before

229

they met. She started using in high school." She drew a breath. "She got in with the wrong crowd...it happens."

"So why did they both lie to me all these years?" Simon demanded. "Why did she keep making me believe she was better? Why didn't dad ever tell me the truth?"

"I don't have all the answers, Simon." Mary stared at her hands. Then she looked up at him. "But I do know that up until your accident, you were following what you thought was your father's footsteps. Call it Freudian, I don't know."

Simon shook his head. "Yeah, so you have the same opinion of me as everyone else does. Tell me something I don't know."

Mary swallowed, shaking her head. "Simon, what you do in your life is your business. I've always loved you, otherwise I wouldn't be here now," she sniffed. "But I see that you're getting better, and now that your mother's gone, I want you to know the truth, so you won't make the same mistakes again."

They were silent.

"You deserve better, Simon." She took his hand in hers again and he didn't protest. "Your father's a good man...and I always saw a lot of him in you."

Simon pondered for a few minutes while they sat, almost reaching Simon's house.

He looked over at her and pursed his lips, although this time his eyes weren't cutting. "You know you're biased."

Mary chuckled innocently, reaching over to give his hand a squeeze.

. . .

"Simon?" Aunt Mary whispered. He'd taken a nap after going to the funeral home at Mary's insistence. "Simon, I hope you're okay with this, but Darla called while you were sleeping. She wanted to come by for your treatment. I didn't see the harm."

Darla walked to the side of Simon's bed. "Hi, Simon," she said in a voice so low, Simon could barely hear her. "I know this is a difficult time, but it's critical that we keep up with your treatment."

"That's okay," Simon said, grateful for another familiar face.

Simon rubbed his eyes and lifted himself with his arms. "Life goes on." He ran his hand through his hair.

Darla winked. "Good for you, Simon."

"I'm going to run up to the market and get some food. Be back in an hour," Mary said.

"My wallet's over on the dresser." Simon gestured with his head. "Hand it to me?"

Mary shook her head, putting on her jacket. "No need, Simon."

"Did Ryder already give you some?"

Mary shook her head again. "No. I don't need any money, Simon. You're family."

Simon's brows rose. "You're sure?"

Mary winked and walked out the door.

When the door closed, Darla turned to Simon. "She's quite a wonderful lady, isn't she?"

"She's really nice." Simon thrusted himself into the wheelchair. "I didn't expect to see her."

Darla pushed Simon to an open area in the living room. "Why not?"

"I don't know. I didn't expect to see anyone to be honest. Except Ryder."

"Before I say anything else, Simon, I just wanted to give you my condolences." Darla's hand was over her heart. "I feel terrible for bothering you at such a difficult time, but you must understand that if you don't keep up with your treatment, you may never get your legs fully back."

"Oh no, that's fine." Simon extended his hand out for emphasis. "I appreciate you coming under the circumstances."

Darla gently grasped Simon's hand in hers. "If there's anything I can do for you. Anything at all, Simon, please just let me know."

Her sincerity was almost overwhelming. Simon managed a smile. "Thanks."

Darla looked at Simon, seeing a strange expression on his face. He looked a million miles away. "Are you ready to get started?" she asked hesitantly.

He swallowed and said "Yeah," in a whisper.

Darla bent down and put her arms behind Simon to help lift him out of his chair. Simon's hands didn't push from the sidebars. Instead, he lifted his arms up slowly and placed them on Darla's shoulders. She froze. There was a strange squeaking sound coming from Simon's throat. His breathing became erratic. When she heard him swallow, she realized that he was crying.

Darla rested her head on his shoulder and caressed his back with her hands. Simon eased his hands up into her hair as her body came closer to his. The tears began to flow down his cheeks and into her hair as he sniffled and choked with grief. Darla held him tighter and he did the same, trying to catch his breath. As Simon sobbed, Darla rubbed his back and he grasped her hair and let go in a rhythmic, soothing pattern.

"I'm so sorry, Simon," Darla breathed. "I know how much you loved your mum."

Simon said nothing, he choked in a desperate attempt to stop the tears. She held him tighter and he closed his eyes, revelling in his first moment of vulnerability. The feeling of letting go was cathartic. He never trusted anyone enough to cry in their presence.

The land line rang, breaking the spell. "Do you need to get that?" Darla whispered. "No," he sniffed. "Let the machine get it."

Darla pulled back slightly so her eyes were level with Simon's. "Things will get better, Simon. But you need to deal with the loss first."

THE WHEELS OF CHANGE

Simon licked his lips. "I know." He caught his breath. "I just wanted a moment…where I was allowed to need something…and not be asked for something in return."

Darla looked at Simon's reddened, puffy eyes. His cheeks were stained with tears. She blinked. Her hand came up to his face and she stroked it gently, wiping a tear. "Oh, you poor baby," she whispered, shaking her head. "I think the world has you all wrong."

He looked softly into her eyes. "What do you mean?"

"Like you said, people look at you and see money or sex." Darla's eyes were hooded. "But you're just as vulnerable as a young boy, Simon. You had to grow up so fast, you missed a few steps." Her hand ran through his hair, maternally. "Like love and mutual caring." She tapped the end of his nose gently. "And getting to know someone without ulterior motives."

Simon didn't break his glance. "I've never known anyone like you, Darla."

Darla smiled warmly. "I can't imagine."

He smiled back, glancing quickly at her lips. "You're so honest and nurturing. Are you like that outside of work, too, or is this just part of your job?"

Darla leaned back slightly, so there was more of a gap between them. "Simon, I think we both know that we're more than just client and health care provider. I've shared personal things about myself that I've shared with nobody else."

"Like you being gay," he said, like he was marking it off a list.

She sighed and looked down, removing her hands from him. "About that."

Simon's brows furrowed. "What?"

"Speaking of being honest. I wasn't entirely honest with you about my sexual preference, Simon."

He waited.

"Talk around the water cooler at work led me to tell you that," she admitted. "I saw your prognosis and I really wanted things to work out for you, so I told you that to ensure things worked out between us."

Simon thought for a moment, but surprisingly, he wasn't upset. "So you lied to me…for my own good."

"Yes," Darla answered solemnly.

Simon leaned forward and kissed her on the cheek. "Nobody's ever done that for me. Thank you."

"You're welcome, Simon."

. . .

Showing up at Ted's house was like deja-vous. Nothing had changed except his car was parked in the driveway.

Mark pressed the button on his walkie-talkie. "We better call for backup."

Richard removed his gun from the holster. "You think we'll get lucky and he'll be home?"

"Have you won the lottery lately?" Mark answered before summoning dispatch to send some men over to Ted's address.

"I don't play."

Mark pounded on the door. "Ted Greenfield? It's the police. Open up!"

When there was no answer, Mark lifted his gun and tried the doorknob. It was locked as they suspected. Mark stepped back as Richard kicked the door in one thrusting motion. "I've still got it," he said cheekily.

Ted's house was completely vacant. As they entered through the front foyer, they observed that it was clean and tidy, nobody left in haste. The kitchen and living room were adjoining, and everything looked to be in place.

"Check the bedrooms," Mark advised, still walking in his defensive stance, holding his gun up with both hands and pressing his back up against

THE WHEELS OF CHANGE

each wall while checking for movement.

"I'll take the master," Richard said. Two seconds later, they both shouted that it was all clear.

"Basement?" Mark said, looking to see if there was a door leading downstairs. The house was a bungalow, so there was only one floor to check.

Richard and Mark inspected inside each closed door: closet, linen closet and bathroom. "No basement," Richard said. They both placed their guns back in the holsters as they began searching closer for clues.

"Lots of bible stuff," Richard commented, noticing the picture of Jesus with a halo overhead, hanging above the bed in the master bedroom. "You can definitely tell the guy was into church."

"I'll say," Mark agreed, looking through a bookcase on the side wall in the guest bedroom. "Every book is about God and his disciples."

Mark observed the bedroom drawers and found nothing unusual, socks, underwear and all clothing was folded and placed neatly in its appropriate place. They walked into the living room and saw some unopened mail. "Bills, bills, sweepstakes, junk, nothing interesting," Richard observed, scooping up the envelopes lying on the table.

"We'll get forensics to go through with a fine-toothed comb, but it's pretty safe to say his place is clean," Mark sighed, putting his hands on his hips.

Disappointed and frustrated, Mark and Richard walked out the door and decided to peek into the backyard. "No shed, nothing. This guy's about as boring as water," said Richard.

"Well, at least we know," Richard said as they began the walk back to the cruiser. When suddenly Mark turned around and had a second look at the house.

"Wait a minute." He pointed to a window near the roof's peak. "There's an attic."

They both headed back and found the hatch in the ceiling between the two bedrooms. The chain was dangling teasingly as they walked toward it.

235

"I'm losing my touch," Mark said. "I should have noticed that chain before."

Richard pulled the chain and a narrow set of wooden stairs came tumbling down. A plume of dust followed. "Jesus." Mark spat and slapped at his chest.

"Ladies first," Richard joked, motioning to Mark.

"You can kiss my ass on your way up."

The stairs creaked with Mark's weight and as he reached the last step, he pulled out his flashlight and shone it into the room. "Hooooly fuuuuuuck," he said in awe. "It's a fuckin' shrine."

Richard followed Mark as he pulled on a cord, weakly lighting the area with a single bulb hanging above. Richard grabbed two pairs of rubber gloves shoved in his back pocket and handed Mark a pair. "Well, if we didn't know what fucked up meant…we sure do now," Richard laughed, observing the environment.

Newspapers from as far back as fifty years sat in piles on the floor. Magazine articles and old, tattered books lay scattered all over the floor. There were old photographs, hair samples, old glasses, shoes, pieces of old clothing and various other items taken from people that had probably been dead for years.

"The guy's a major hoarder." Mark picked up a scrapbook filled with hair. "What the hell would someone want to do with this?"

Richard shook his head, distracted by an old trunk near the window. "What have we here?" He pulled at the latch. "It's locked."

Mark bent down to feel his way under a table supporting old photo albums. He followed all the way down the length of it and shook his head. "Damn. That's where I used to hide my key."

"I had a box," Richard explained, and before Mark could add a snide remark, Richard stopped him. "A man's jewelry box. I had an obsession with watches when I was a teenager."

Mark chuckled and looked around, spying a small trinket box hidden under a pile of old coats. "Let's see."

He opened the box and found a key inside a pocket on the lid. "Try this." He tossed the key to Richard.

As luck would have it, the trunk opened with ease. "Bingo."

Richard peered in as Mark approached from behind and knelt down. Inside the trunk were piles of pictures, recently taken, of all the murder victims, and various other mementos supposedly from the dead. "Jesus Christ," Mark said. "Are they all there?"

Richard glanced at one and tossed it to Mark. "And then some."

Mark looked at the photos as they were passed to him. "Are these victims or ones on his list?"

Richard didn't answer, but came across one picture and hesitated. "Um...I think it could go either way." He handed Mark a picture with a knowing look.

"Is that who I think it is?"

"Yep. Simon Cross."

CHAPTER 25

Aunt Mary helped Simon into his best suit. "You look very dashing. Nancy would be proud," she smiled.

"Thanks."

Ryder and Sandra walked into the house and greeted Simon.

"Who's looking after the office?" he asked.

"Carnie's there," Sandra said in a comforting tone. "You'll love her, she's been really helpful. Picked up everything, she's a natural."

Simon nodded, adjusting his tie.

"It's perfect, Simon," Mary complimented.

They were all silent on the drive to the funeral home. When they arrived, Simon noted the half-full parking lot. "We're early," Ryder observed, exiting the car. Mary followed as they both retrieved Simon's wheelchair from the back of the pick-up truck.

When Simon was in the chair, he was the first to see the two police cruisers parked on the side street. Ryder followed Simon's line of sight. "Is it customary for cops to be at a funeral?"

"When the deceased was murdered, I guess," Simon commented, watching Mark and Richard approach.

Mark shook Simon's hand. "Mr. Cross."

"Officer."

Richard followed Mark's lead and then they both walked into the funeral home ahead of Simon. "We need to get him police protection," Richard whispered.

"That's why we're here," Mark said quietly. "We'll have Nelson keep vigil afterward, but this is the only respectable way to do it for now. Last thing the boy needs to know today is that his life is in danger...again."

Richard nodded as they took a seat in the back of the chapel.

Sandra wheeled Simon into the chapel while Ryder and Aunt Mary conversed with the funeral director. "I think this spot is for you," Sandra whispered as they reached the first row with a chair missing in front.

"I think I should stay mobile for now," Simon suggested, taking over the wheels. "I'll have to greet people as they arrive."

Sandra nodded. "Sure, Simon. I think Ryder was going to do that for you. But that's a good idea."

"Go ahead, Sandra. Take a seat," Simon said. "I'll be back."

Simon saw Ryder and Mary by the entrance, still speaking with the funeral director. "Did you want to say anything at the service?" Ryder asked.

"No, that's fine." Simon pursed his lips. "Keep it short."

The funeral director nodded and walked into the small office to the left of the chapel, with Aunt Mary following.

Ryder watched a car pull into the driveway. "Darla's here."

Simon saw her exit her car, dressed in a navy blue pants suit. Her brown hair was blown straight, reaching her shoulders. As she closed her car door, the wind caught her hair and she pulled it away from her face in a fluid motion. He watched as she opened the door and adjusted her purse strap on her shoulder.

She smiled sweetly when she saw Simon. When she bent down to kiss him on either side of his face, he took in her light scent. Darla spoke softly into his ear. "You clean up well, Simon."

"You too," he said. "Thanks for coming."

Darla gently grasped his hand and closed her eyes, as if to send a telepathic message to him. "I'll just take a seat," she said, nodding to greet Ryder. Mary joined them and waved to Darla.

The funeral was short, and as the director informed the guests that there was to be a small reception in the basement following the service, Simon felt everyone's eyes on him. As everyone filed out of the chapel, Simon was the last to leave. He saw Aunt Barbara walk straight out the front door without looking back. He craned his neck and noticed Raphael opening the car door for her.

Ryder witnessed this as well. "Don't sweat it, buddy." He smacked Simon firmly on the shoulder. "The people who care about you won't leave."

Simon looked over and saw Ryder's wife, Stacy, sitting alone in the third row. He caught Ryder winking at her and she blinked tightly back with a sweet smile on her face. Simon's heart ached.

Mary helped wheel Simon out of the chapel while Ryder and Stacy paired up with Sandra. James, Simon's dad, approached from those already gathering at the reception.

James kissed his sister on the cheek and patted her on the back.

"Nice to see you," Mary said good-naturedly. "You look tired."

James ignored the comment and looked down at Simon, managing a tight smile.

"I'll leave you two alone." Mary joined Ryder and the rest. They all headed for the reception, leaving Simon and James by the front of the chapel. James sat on the waiting room chair adjacent to the director's office and sighed, clasping his hands together in front of him.

"I'm sorry about your mom, Simon," he said without eye contact.

Simon said nothing.

THE WHEELS OF CHANGE

"I haven't spoken to her in a while. I didn't know…what she was up to."

"How's Betty?" Simon asked, as if he didn't hear the comment.

James looked at Simon. "She's fine." He paused. "She thought it was best if I came alone."

Simon nodded, appreciating his father's honesty. He could've said she came down with the flu or some other lame excuse, Simon thought.

Out of left field, James asked. "Why are there cops here?"

Simon chuckled, guessing Mary left vital information out. "She was drowned, dad."

"I'm aware of that."

"Somebody drowned her."

James looked at Simon. His eyes widened. "What do you mean? Who drowned her?"

"I'm guessing Ted, her old fling. They're looking into it," Simon answered conversationally.

James shook his head. "I thought she overdosed and drowned. I had no idea."

"That's right," Simon said pointedly. "You have no idea."

James digested the new information for a minute, and then looked at Simon hesitantly. "And what...happened to you?" His eyes moved to Simon's legs.

"I guess I'm not very popular, either, dad."

James moved closer to Simon. "You mean someone *did* this to you? Who?"

Simon looked straight into his father's eyes. "Why don't you go crawl back under your rock, dad."

James retracted back, not losing contact with Simon's eyes. Simon looked at his dad and for the first time, he noticed that his father looked older. Unnaturally older. Granted, they hadn't seen each other in over a year, but he'd aged by more than ten years by Simon's guess.

"I guess we're both pretty self-absorbed, Simon." James bobbed his head at his son, as if agreeing to an unspoken thought. "We've both been relying too much on second-hand information."

Simon waited.

"I didn't know anything other than that you'd been in an accident." James licked his lips. "But you didn't know that I was sick, either."

Simon shook his head. "Mom didn't say anything to me."

James interrupted. "Nancy didn't know," he said firmly. "You think I'm going to tell her? Do you think I wanted to be responsible for another fall off the wagon? Nancy could never handle stress." A vein was bulging from James's neck.

"I guess we're both to blame," James said argumentatively, throwing his hand in the air in frustration.

"I didn't know you were in a wheelchair, and you didn't know I had cancer."

"You had cancer? How bad?" he said, feigning disinterest.

"Well, they caught it. But it was a hell of a ride," James said. "Prostate. They removed it and…well, it doesn't matter."

"Are you okay now?"

"So far. I'm older now, son. Age catches up to you and, well, you have to take good care of yourself. I didn't. I was too busy with life."

James shook his head. "Never mind about me. How are you? Can you walk at all?"

"It's coming…slowly. I'm getting the best treatment available."

"Well that's good, son. I'm proud of you. I bet you're doing really well for yourself, too, aren't you?" he said more like it was a statement than a question. "You always could take care of yourself. You sure didn't get that from me."

Simon looked over at his mother's casket. "I don't know who I got it from, then."

James ignored the comment. "Are you seeing anybody? I've never heard about anyone since college. I remember you had a real special thing with that girl that used to live up the street....Janet, was it?"

"Janice," Simon corrected. "Nah, she's long gone. Haven't spoken to her in years."

"That's too bad. But I'm guessing you're too busy with your business and all to be worried about women, right?"

Simon avoided eye contact. "Something like that."

They both sat silent for a while, listening to the chattering coming from the basement. "Do you think we should head in there, or should we just stay here?" James asked, scratching his head uncomfortably.

"I don't think it makes a difference," Simon answered casually. "I've seen all the people I wanted to see."

James wasn't sure how to take that comment. "Listen, Simon. No matter what's happened in the past. I'm still your father. You're my only son." He thought for a moment. "I know I made a lot of mistakes before, but life goes on. We can't dwell on things we did yesterday. Life is about today."

Simon looked at James, surprised at how much he could relate to his father.

"Your mother's gone now, and as much as I haven't been part of your life lately, I'm still here. That's what counts." James paused. "Maybe the women in our life aren't that strong, but us Cross men, we're tough as nails, Simon."

Simon scoffed but managed a small grin. He looked up and saw Darla approaching from the basement. "Simon, I hate to interrupt, but I have to go. I've got a client waiting, but I'll see you later this afternoon, okay?"

"Thanks for coming, Darla," Simon said warmly. "I appreciate it."

Darla leaned forward and kissed Simon on the cheek. His skin started to tingle where her lips were. He reached up and put his hand in the spot, as if to preserve her touch.

When Darla left, James looked at Simon. "I guess I was wrong," he grinned.

Simon's brows furrowed, looking at his dad. "What do you mean?"

"Looks to me like you've got a strong woman or two in your life."

. . .

"It's going to take forensics a year to get through all the crap in Greenfield's attic," Mark commented, looking at the search warrant Judge Caplan sent. "The man is gone, without a trace."

"He's gotta be somewhere local. His passport's not been used," Cameron offered. "And that ten grand he withdrew won't last forever."

"America is a big place, Cam. He could be anywhere. And he could get some low-life cash-paid-daily job to get around if he's desperate."

"True. But he'll make a mistake somewhere."

"And it looks like Simon's last on his hit list, anyway. All the other photos we found, they've matched up to other victims," Richard added. "So what do we do now?"

"We keep Simon in protective custody and hope like hell the bastard fucks up or gets himself killed," Mark said.

"I'll put a flag on all his stuff and see if we get a hit in the meantime," Cameron said. "If he uses any of his cards or puts himself on the map in any way I'll be the first to know."

"Is Nelson over at Cross's now?" Mark shouted to Lisa. Lisa put one thumb in the air, indicating a yes.

THE WHEELS OF CHANGE

Mark suddenly looked a million miles away. Richard gestured. "What's up? Something's on your mind."

"It's too cold too fast." He shook his head slowly, staring into space. "How can we lose all our leads suddenly?"

"Everyone's confirmed it's Ted: the television network, the bank, Mansfield. He'll either come out confessing or he'll fuck up somewhere, Mark. This isn't the end."

"I sure as hell hope not. We gotta find this bastard somehow," Mark said through gritted teeth. "I want to sift through all that shit in his attic myself. There's gotta be something there that tells us his next move."

"Maybe he'll sit and wait until Simon's out of sight." Richard had an 'ah-ha' look on his face. "Think we should bait him?"

"What do you mean?"

"Make it look like Cross is unattended or something. Then be ready?"

Mark's face scrunched up. "We'll give it a day or two and see what happens."

CHAPTER 26

"Simon?" James asked. He was sitting next to Simon in the hospital room, waiting for his son to wake after another injection.

Simon's eyes opened. "Hey dad, thanks for staying."

James didn't respond, but looked up, examining all the monitors around his son. "How do you feel?"

"Fine. How did it everything go? Is mom's body buried now?"

He looked at Simon. "Fine. Thanks for letting me do that. I needed to lay her to rest myself. She was my wife once, after all."

"Is it a nice place?"

"Yeah. You wouldn't have been able to see anything, anyway. Nothing's wheelchair accessible in a cemetery." James changed the subject. "So how long until you know the results of this injection?"

"It's been pretty immediate the last couple of times. Probably by tomorrow I'll know how much has come back."

"Impressive." James cleared his throat. "Is Darla coming by the house later?"

"Yeah." Simon gestured to his dad. "Are you sticking around?"

"Absolutely. I've gotta head back in a couple of days, but until then I'm here."

THE WHEELS OF CHANGE

...

Simon lay in his bed after his treatment with Darla. James was out in the living room, tidying up and preparing dinner for him and his son. He saw his phone sitting atop his dresser and he propped himself up, enjoying the newness of being able to sit up unassisted and rest his feet firmly on the floor. His legs felt like rubber; he knew they were there but if he were to rise, he was sure to quickly fall. Darla assured him earlier that the sensation would dissipate as his muscles gained strength.

James stood in the bedroom doorway. "Need something?"

"My phone," Simon nodded. "I haven't looked at it in days. Needs to be charged."

"I'll get it." James picked the phone up. He pressed the power button and nothing happened. "Yep. Dead as a doornail. Where's your charger?"

"Plugged into the wall over there."

"You going to work tomorrow?"

"Yeah. I've got a million things to do."

"You think the goon outside will let you go?"

"He'll probably follow me. The police chief said Ted's on the loose. Lot of good I can do; he'll cream me in no time."

"Don't think like that," James tutted. "If Ted's smart he's flown the coop for good. Any move he makes, they'll catch him."

"What luck I have, eh?" Simon scoffed. "First I get into an accident and lose my legs, and then my mom dies, now I have some serial killer after me."

James crossed his hands on his chest. "Are you gonna get all poor-me-poor-me again, or are you gonna buck up and get past it?" He took a deep breath. "Everything happens for a reason." He paused. "This?" James gestured to Simon's wheelchair next to the bed. "These are the wheels of change, Simon."

Simon looked at his father like he had two heads.

"Think about it." James sat on Simon's bed. "Since your accident, how much have things changed?"

Simon nodded. "A lot."

"Good or bad?"

"Both...kind of."

"Life isn't all sunshine and roses. When there's something new in your life, it always involves good and bad. It's about balance." James frowned and tilted his head. "People look at you differently now, don't they?"

"Someone told me it's the opposite, that I now look at people differently."

James grinned. "Darla, right?" his index finger was on his lips.

Simon nodded.

"And if you didn't have your accident, you wouldn't have this new perspective, would you?"

Simon sighed. "I suppose not."

James patted Simon on the hand and smiled. "Are you hungry?"

"Yeah."

. . .

Mark lay in bed, tossing and turning. He was just waiting for the phone to ring, knowing Ted would have killed another victim. The urge to call Nelson or whoever relieved him for the night was overwhelming, but he knew it wouldn't be right. The memory of what it was like being checked up on for no good reason stopped him from dialling.

Shelley rubbed Mark's back. "Honey, are you okay? I haven't seen you this restless in a long time."

"Yeah. I'm fine. I'll be a lot better when this case is closed."

THE WHEELS OF CHANGE

Shelley kissed him on the shoulder. "I know, sweetie, but you've gotta get some sleep. You'll be no good to anyone tomorrow."

Mark rose and threw the covers off in frustration. "I'm gonna go make some warm milk."

Shelley raised an eyebrow and seductively ran her hand down her chest. "Can I help?"

Mark winced, grabbing his phone off the nightstand. "Not tonight, baby. My mind is reeling too much." He kissed the air and winked at her. "Sorry."

Shelley winked and lay back down, seemingly relieved. She was asleep before Mark reached the bottom of the stairs. He looked at his phone, there were no calls or messages. Part of him was disappointed. As he pulled the milk out of the fridge, his phone suddenly rang. He almost dropped the carton on the floor. He looked at the screen. It was dispatch.

His heart thumped as he answered. "Tame here."

"Chief. We've got a hit and run over in Santa Barbara."

Mark's face scrunched, wondering why they were calling him if it was for something in Santa Barbara. "I don't understand. I'm in LA."

"Yes, I'm aware of that, sir. There is a flag on his profile in our system, alerting us to contact you directly."

Mark waited.

"The victim is Ted Greenfield."

...

"Is he dead?" Richard asked. Mark was feverishly dressing while talking to Richard on the phone.

"Yes. He was identified by Lida Brickman. Apparently he went back home and saw that his house was cordoned off and went straight to her. It wasn't two minutes later that he was hit and killed by some transport truck."

249

"Why would he be stupid enough to go back home?"

"I don't know. We all said he'd fuck up somehow," Mark grunted. "I want to speak to Lida right away and find out what the hell happened."

"I'll meet you out the front of my house."

...

Constable Nelson peered at his watch and sighed. Someone should have relieved him for the night at least an hour ago. His feet were burning and his back was aching. He had bouts of anxiety and relaxation all day depending on what noises he heard from outside and from the highway. Nelson felt he wouldn't be much good at protecting Simon even if the need arose. He pulled his phone out of his pocket and dialled dispatch.

"Los Angeles police department dispatch."

"Hey Mindy, this is Constable Nelson. I'm over keeping watch at Simon Cross's house. Has Chief Tame or Officer Matthews sent anyone to relieve me yet?"

"Nope. Didn't Mark call you? Ted's been hit. He's dead."

"Really?"

"Yeah. They're on their way over to Santa Barbara right now to check it out."

"Is there anyone around who can come by and keep watch until Mark gives the all clear?"

"Hang on one sec...um...Constable Garner was supposed to stand in for you, but he's gone for the night. I guess it's okay to leave. I mean, the guy's dead, what harm can he do now?"

Nelson pondered a moment. "I'm not sure. I can't leave until the Chief okays it."

"I tell you what. I'll keep trying Mark for you, or I can put a call into Sergeant Lipkus?"

THE WHEELS OF CHANGE

"Oooh, I don't know about that. Chief Tame would be pretty upset if he knew I got the Sergeant involved. You keep trying the Chief for me and let me know what's going on."

"Will do."

. . .

Simon and James were in the house eating dinner and watching the news, when coverage of Ted's death came on. Simon's mouth widened. "Holy shit."

"What's the matter?"

"That's Ted. That's the guy who drowned mom."

"Jesus Christ."

They watched for a few moments while the reporter showed the area where Ted was hit and the truck that hit him.

"Well, I guess you can send that poor boy outside home now." James gestured to Nelson's shadow shining in on them. "He's been standing on the front porch all day."

"They sure he's the guy?" James asked.

"He was the last one with mom. He's wanted for questioning on other cases as well. That was an easy out for them, I suppose. Far as I know they haven't even gone through all the evidence."

James shook his head and rose. He opened the front door and nodded at Nelson. "The man's dead, son. I think you can go home now. We're safe."

Nelson thought for a moment and then tipped his hat. "Thank you, sir. I appreciate it. But I can't leave until the Chief says so."

James waved him off. "Ah, we're okay. Unless his ghost is gonna come after us, I think it'll be fine," he chuckled good-naturedly.

Nelson smiled and looked down, not sure what to do. "I insist," James said, seeing Nelsons' pale face. "Go on home, son. I'll vouch for you."

251

"Okay, sir. Thank you. Good night." Nelson walked off the porch.

James closed the door and sat beside Simon. "He's a good boy. Trained well."

Simon nodded and heard a funny beep in his room. "What was that?" James asked.

"My phone's charged."

"I'll go get it for you."

He returned and handed Simon the phone. Simon pressed the power button and started going through all his text messages. When he found nothing pressing, he moved on to his voice messages. There were a few people that left him condolences, but nothing unusual. He was about to listen to the last one, when he heard dead air on the recording. His brows knitted together as he strained to listen.

"Something wrong?" James asked. Simon lifted his index finger, indicating to give him a moment.

He listened and his eyes widened. "I need to get in touch with Chief Tame."

"What is it?"

"It's a message from mom."

...

Mark knocked on Lida's door. He realized it was extremely late and he would wake her, but it was urgent enough to warrant a midnight visit. A few minutes later, Mark knocked again. "Car's in the driveway," Richard commented, peering over.

"I'm coming," she said from inside, switching on the exterior lights. When she opened the door, she didn't look surprised. "I figured I'd get a visit from you," she chuckled. Her hair was slightly dishevelled, like she'd only gone to bed a little while ago, and she had wrapped herself tightly in a white terry-cloth robe.

THE WHEELS OF CHANGE

"Come in," she said, shivering from the midnight chill in the air. "Some tea?" she offered.

"Sure," Mark said, and cut right to the chase. "What can you tell us about your encounter with Ted tonight?"

"It was very brief," Lida answered, filling the kettle. "I asked him to leave and go turn himself in, since he knew he was wanted for questioning." Lida searched for the tea bags in her overhead cupboard. "I told him even though he wasn't part of the congregation anymore, he was still God's child, and he should do the right thing."

"And what did he say?" Richard asked.

"He said he would, but was concerned that the house had been cordoned off," Lida explained, and then she turned toward Mark and furrowed her brows. "It was like he didn't expect that they'd find him. Like he wasn't even missing. It seemed like he had no recollection of what had happened since he left Santa Barbara."

"How did he get here ?" Richard asked.

"I think he took a cab or he walked. His car wasn't here."

"How did he look?" Mark asked.

"He looked...different." Lida shook her head. "He changed his appearance, but I couldn't put my finger on what he did. Maybe it was his hair...hmm...I can't be sure."

"How did he sound? Was he aloof? Nervous? Did he threaten you in any way?" Mark asked.

Lida sighed. "No, he wasn't threatening at all. He sounded normal, just like I said, he seemed to have no recollection. It was like if I were to tell him, he'd be shocked."

"Did you see the body?" Richard asked, accepting the tea.

"Oh yes. I heard the tires squeal from the road. It was like a thousand fingernails scoring a chalkboard. I ran out the door and saw his jacket and knew right away it was him."

SANDY APPLEYARD

"Did you go over and make sure?" Mark asked.

"Yes I did. A few others from the church recognized him, too. Almost the whole congregation lives within a six-block radius."

"Who called the police?"

"Well, I don't know. They showed up not even three minutes later. The station is just across the highway."

Lida offered the boys cookies, the same box from the other day. "You know, for years we were fighting to get a set of lights for that intersection. Even Ted helped us with the petition, he encouraged all the worshippers to sign it. I don't know what ever became of it, but I'm sure this will change things."

Suddenly Mark's phone rang. "Tame here," he answered gruffly.

"Chief Tame? Simon Cross. Listen, I have a message here you might be interested in listening to."

"What is the message?" Mark rose and indicated for Richard to follow him into the living room. Richard lifted his finger up to Lida, and she nodded for them to go ahead into the living room for privacy.

"My mother tried to call me, I'm guessing right before Ted got to her and she must have left her phone on or passed out before she could speak, I'm not sure."

"What does the message say?" Mark held the phone out so Richard could hear as well.

"I'm calling from my land line, so I'll play the message for you." Mark and Richard waited while Simon cued it for them.

There was silence at first, and then a sound akin to the phone being dragged along the floor in her pants pocket. The noise stopped and then there was rustling in the background. It sounded like Ted was taking a bath and all was well. He started talking.

"Oh Nancy, I'm sorry it had to end this way. You and your whore of a son will soon be dead. (sigh) Then my job will be done...for now. I'm only one man, and I can't be expected to take care of all the whores in this world. Just the ones I know of." His

254

THE WHEELS OF CHANGE

voice was getting louder. "*I tried to help you and the others, but you didn't listen! (smacking the side of the tub) Dammit! (shouting) I can't help everybody! I tried! For twenty five years I tried!*

And then the one person I could help, God took her from me. Lilly was nothing like you, she was a fighter. Not like you and your weak son...(laughter)...oh, no. But Simon, well, I wasn't the only one who saw through him. Too bad someone got to him before I did. But now that he's better, I'll get him. Now that his mommy is gone, who will protect him? The best part is...nobody will find me. I've got a nice insurance policy...oh you wait, Nancy. Don't fret. You'll meet your son in hell soon...I'll make sure of it."

Simon came back on the line. "Then there's just some movement before Ted leaves and it goes quiet again."

"Err...thanks Simon. We'll have to check into a few things and get back to you." Mark was completely confused and distracted. "Please keep that message. We'll have to format it for evidence."

"Will do."

Richard was flabbergasted. "What the hell does he mean by an insurance policy?"

"I don't know." Mark put his phone back in his pocket. "We need to go through the stuff from his attic and see if he had anything with him when he died. He took all his belongings with him from the hotel. He had to put his stuff somewhere."

"We need to go see the body."

255

CHAPTER 27

"Simon, how are you?" Darla said, entering the house. "You look very fresh."

He grinned. "I am. I told Ryder we should do a pool for what day I'll take my first step."

Darla was impressed. "Really?"

"Yeah, the last injection really was the comeback I think." Simon looked down at his legs. "Check it out." He lifted himself right up out of the chair, about a foot in the air, and then he sat back down and lifted his feet straight up off the steel foot bar, one by one.

"I think we can order you a walker, you're just about ready." Darla laid her equipment down. "We should even start having you come into the clinic for your treatments."

"Will that mean you won't be my therapist anymore?" Simon tried to hide his concern.

"Of course not," Darla insisted. "I'm your therapist until you fire me or don't need me anymore," she chuckled.

Darla's brown hair had grown in the time she'd been treating Simon. Her braces were off and she had this glow about her that Simon couldn't seem to ignore.

"So how are you doing?" Darla assembled her walking machine. "I mean, besides the obvious."

"I'm doing okay. Dad left this morning. He'll be back to visit with Betty in a couple of weeks. They don't live far away thankfully."

"And how do you feel about that?"

"Pretty good."

"I heard on the news that the man they were looking for is dead. Does that mean the case is closed?"

"I guess so. They took my phone away for evidence and that's the last I heard. Apparently they're still looking through all his stuff."

Darla adjusted the last piece of the contraption. "Why your phone?"

Simon looked at his hands. "They had to analyze the last message my mom left me."

Darla sensed a tone in his voice. "Was that hard? Was your mother's voice in the message?"

"No," Simon whispered.

Darla looked over at him. "And you're disappointed that there isn't a voice recording for you to remember her by," she said quietly.

"Kind of."

Darla walked over to Simon and knelt down. "Simon, although it would be easier if there was a physical remembrance of your mother for you to hold on to, you don't need it." Darla took Simon's hand in hers. "Memories of your mom will forever be in here." She slowly and gently patted his temple with her other hand. "And in here." She lifted the hand she was holding with hers and slowly placed it on his chest. "That's where love grows. And that's where it stays. Always," she promised.

The sincerity in Darla's eyes stirred Simon. He lifted his free hand up and softly stroked her cheek. He looked at her with softness in his eyes and whispered to her. "I don't think you can be my therapist anymore."

She smiled and cocked her head. "You don't like me anymore?"

The corner of Simon's lip twitched. "No," he blushed. "I don't like you anymore." He took the hand that she was holding on his chest and slowly placed it on her chest, gazing at her longingly.

Darla smiled and sighed. "Well then," she said quietly, returning his glance. "I guess the Lord does work in strange ways, doesn't he?"

Simon didn't answer, nor did he break his gaze.

"It's the accent, isn't it?" she joked, breaking the silence.

"No," Simon guffawed. "It's you."

Darla took a deep breath, changing the subject. "I suppose I've got this contraption working." She nodded towards it. "You want to give it a go?"

Simon cocked his head and winked. "I'm ready."

Darla rose and Simon wheeled himself over to the walking machine. He pulled himself up out of the chair with Darla's help, and she attached the straps. Simon wrapped his arms around the bars like a child going across monkey bars. His muscles were well-toned from weeks of work, and his legs had regained much of their muscle tone as well. Simon had never been in greater physical shape despite his affliction.

"That's great, Simon. When you think you're ready, try adding more weight to your legs," Darla encouraged, standing at the end of the bars, just like a mother waiting for her child to make it to the other side of the jungle gym.

She watched him put one foot in front of the other slowly, but with little effort. Then in the last few strides, she observed the colour come back to his fingers slightly, as he eased more weight onto his legs. Darla was about three feet away from him. Simon looked up at her and smiled as he took the last step almost completely on his own. As he reached her at the end of the bars, he had an ear to ear smile.

"You took that last step by yourself, didn't you?" she beamed.

"I did," he admitted. She looked at him and leaned upward, so they were nose to nose. He closed his eyes, drinking in the moment. It was the first time since the accident that he'd been able to stand up in front of a woman, or anybody for that matter, and feel the warmth of skin next to his.

THE WHEELS OF CHANGE

He took her face in his hands, leaning on the bars with his elbows, and slowly kissed her chastely on the lips. "Thank you," he said, letting go of her face.

"My pleasure, Simon," she whispered with hooded eyes.

Darla looked down at his lips and kissed him back with more emphasis. There was a smacking noise when their lips lost contact. Simon looked at her, confused, and leaned in to kiss her once more. He turned his head to the side and she reciprocated. At first, the kiss was quick like the others, but then Simon went back one last time and opened his mouth, meeting her tongue. They kissed passionately as Simon felt things he hadn't felt in months. There was an immediate tingling sensation that started in his chest and belly, and moved down to his groin. A familiar pull occurred and Simon smiled, kissing her deeper.

He remained close to her, but snuck a peek below when the kiss was over. He looked up to the ceiling and opened his eyes wide. "Oh thank you, Lord."

Darla gave him a knowing look and joked. "My sentiments exactly."

...

"So we've combed through all the newspaper clipping and clothes?" Mark addressed Richard as he helped in the forensics department.

"Yep. The clothes aren't helpful, too dusty and contaminated for any DNA."

"Hmm. What about the hair?"

"Ran it through DNA and it belonged to his wife. The lab said it was younger hair, so he must have kept it after giving her a haircut or something."

Mark scrunched up his face. "Weirdo."

"Did we match all the pictures up with the victims?"

"Not all of them yet. Some are older, so we think they're just relatives. He must have mixed some normal ones up with the others to make it look

259

less obvious."

"He must have been stalking the victims. How the hell else did he get such close shots?"

"That's my guess," Richard agreed. "Did they do an autopsy on the body?"

Mark frowned. "No need. He died instantly when the transport hit him. Head injury."

"What did the driver have to say?"

"He said Ted was running, ran right into him. He wasn't looking where he was going."

Richard's brows knitted. "Was he running from something?"

"He probably didn't want to be recognized by anyone in the neighborhood. Having Lida know where he was was probably enough."

. . .

Mark was tossing and turning in bed again. Shelley was less than enthused this time. "What's the problem now? I thought the case was closed."

"Something doesn't sit right." Mark sat up in bed. "I gotta make a call."

"At this time of night?" Shelley squeaked. "Can't it wait until morning?"

Mark didn't answer. He grabbed his cell phone off the nightstand and headed downstairs, closing the bedroom door. "Sorry, baby. I won't be long."

Richard answered the phone on the fifth ring. "I'm glad you can sleep," Mark said sarcastically.

"I wasn't sleeping," Richard answered, catching his breath.

"Well, must be nice."

Richard swallowed. "What's the problem?"

THE WHEELS OF CHANGE

"Meet me over at the station. I want to go through that damn trunk again. We've missed something."

Richard was incredulous. "What the hell are you talking about? The guy's dead."

"It's too easy," Mark insisted. "Too many loose ends."

Richard sighed angrily. "Fine. I'll meet you there."

. . .

"You're relentless, you know," Richard whined, opening the door to the forensics department.

"At least you got laid," Mark scoffed. "I haven't slept a wink or done anything but toss and turn in bed for weeks."

"That's your problem," Richard scolded. "It is what you make of it."

"Fuck you."

Richard craned his neck. "Tou...chy." he remarked. "Where's this trunk that's got you in knots?" He looked at the back of the room.

"Over here." Mark walked towards it.

All the pictures had been removed and bagged and were lined up in rows, labelled alphabetically and by approximate date. The trunk itself sat on the table with the lid closed; it was labelled as well. Mark perused the pictures and Richard chided him for not wearing gloves. "I'm not in the mood," Mark warned.

"Clearly." Richard looked at the pictures from the other side of the table, away from Mark.

"They didn't find anything on him?" Richard asked.

"Wallet. That's it."

"And all his ID was in it? Cards? Nothing unusual?"

261

Mark shook his head. "Nope."

They continued searching through the pictures, recognizing the faces of the dead. They came across a few framed photos that were bagged but not yet labelled. "What's this?"

Richard rolled his eyes and threw Mark a pair of gloves before Mark opened the bag. He grunted disapprovingly and put them on. He pulled out what appeared to be a small family portrait. Observing the faces in the photo, Mark looked closely at what he recognized as Ted's face. Richard came up beside him.

"Is that Ted?"

"Looks like."

"Why is there a hole beside his head?"

"The picture is pretty old. It could be just wear over time."

Richard took the tiny picture out of the frame and observed that it was a puncture mark. The edges on the back of the picture were sticking out, like the hole had been forced.

"Weird," he commented. Mark picked up another framed photograph. In that one, Ted looked slightly older. "There's a hole beside Ted's head again."

"Another puncture mark?" Richard asked. "I know my buddy in elementary school cut his father's face out of all his pictures after his parent's divorce."

"His father's right there. And there's his mother," Mark pointed.

"Did he have any siblings?"

"A sister. But she's right there."

The other two framed pictures were of Ted and a dog, and Ted holding a trophy of some sort. Mark scratched his head. "Is that all the pictures?"

"Looks like."

THE WHEELS OF CHANGE

Mark walked over to the trunk and bent down. "Help me lift this thing up."

Richard obliged and they both turned the trunk over. Mark knocked on the bottom of it and had an 'oh-well' expression on his face. They righted the trunk, so the bottom touched the floor. Mark tapped on the top of it, where the keyhole was and made the same face. Then he opened it right up and looked down to the floor of it.

"My grandmother had a cedar chest similar to this," Mark explained. "The bottom was made of the same material as crates are made from."

He knocked on the bottom and his eyebrows lifted. Although there were no perforations in the bottom, like the old cedar chests had, it appeared painted over. The whole inside of the chest was painted brown, to give it the appearance of a box. Mark punched the bottom of the chest really hard, creating a large hole. "Paper mache."

They carefully ripped the whole bottom of the chest floor out, using their hands. "I hope these assholes aren't being paid overtime," Richard commented.

Mark ignored him as he found a small plastic bag underneath the paper mache lining. He pulled it out and took it to an empty table, dumping the contents.

Both men sifted through the pictures. "Look for another family portrait," Mark instructed. All the pictures were loose. At first, they were just ancient photographs of what Mark guessed were Ted's ancestors. Then they came across a picture of Ted and another identical picture of Ted. "Why would he have two of the exact pictures of himself? Did they take duplicates back then?"

Mark shook his head, his brows furrowed. The words *insurance policy* crept into his head. His heart began to pound as he looked feverishly through the pictures. Then he found it. "Shit!" he hissed and then spoke desperately as he headed towards the door. "Call Nelson. Get him back to Cross's house. And get him back up!"

CHAPTER 28

Simon sat alone at his kitchen table, looking for realtors over the internet on his laptop. He knew he had to sell Nancy's house, and dreaded the thought. Ryder offered to take care of it, but Simon, feeling empowered with his budding mobility, wanted to do it himself. His lips were still tingly from Darla's kiss earlier. The land line rang and Simon wheeled himself over to the side table to answer it.

There was nobody there. When the dial tone returned, Simon looked around the room. He wheeled himself over to the living room window and opened the drape slightly. The driveway was clear. Simon still had no vehicle and had no plans to purchase one in the near future. He shrugged and returned to the kitchen table.

The moment he returned to the realtor page on his laptop, his cell phone rang. He rolled his eyes and reached for it on the other side of the table. It was Ryder.

"Hey buddy, I'll be over shortly, I was just helping Stacy tidy up from dinner."

"That's okay. There isn't much to cover, anyway. McProcter's a new client," Simon said evenly. "Shouldn't take more than an hour. We can even go over it in the morning."

"Nah. I was kinda hoping to come in a little late tomorrow."

"Oh yeah? Pulling a late one tonight?" Simon joked.

"Err...actually..I've been meaning to tell you something, but there hasn't been a right time."

THE WHEELS OF CHANGE

"What's up?"

"Stacy's pregnant."

"Nice," Simon smiled. "Congrats."

"Thanks. Anyway, she's had nasty morning sickness," Ryder explained. "I wanted to stick around tomorrow to make sure she's okay."

"That sounds fine. I'll see if Carnie can come pick me up in the morning."

"Cool. Anyway, I'll be over in about twenty."

"See ya."

Out of habit, Simon went over and made sure the door was unlocked, knowing Ryder would be there. Ryder had a key made a while ago, but Simon had gotten into the habit after so long.

He wheeled himself back over to the table and reached for the water glass he'd poured himself earlier. When he knocked it over, he suddenly had a flashback, the Mansfield meeting that went sour. He remembered Mr. Stockton going into his bedroom for some reason, apparently he was looking for toilet paper, but after Sandra reported that there was ample supply in the bathroom in plain sight, it occurred to Simon that Stockton had no reason to be in his room.

So why did he go in there?

He cleaned up the water from the table and wheeled himself over to the bedroom. Passing the bathroom on the way, he peered in and saw the toilet paper dispenser in the corner. Frowning, he continued to his bedroom and switched on the light. His unmade bed was in the middle of the room for easy access. He wheeled himself over and feeling brave, pulled himself on the bed.

Simon's legs and feet were crossed over Indian-style. *What was Stockton doing in my room?* Then he saw it, the Mansfield basket that Ryder brought him when he was in the hospital right after the accident. It sat in the corner of his room, right by the door in plain view. The clothing items were no longer stacked tightly in their original display, but appeared thrown in a harried manner. Simon scrunched up his face and shook his head.

He heard a click coming from the living room and pulled himself back into the wheelchair. When he reached the living room, expecting to see Ryder, he furrowed his brows at the empty room. Turning back to the living room table, he removed the wet paper towels from where he spilled the water and wheeled himself into the kitchen to discard them. As he bent down to pick up a loose piece, he heard someone behind him.

"Hello, Simon," said a familiar voice. "Do you remember me?"

Simon tried to turn around, but there was a knife at his throat. "I thought you were dead," he said, surprised.

"Hmm. So did everybody, apparently," Ted chuckled. "Sorry about Nancy," he said as though he screwed up a birthday cake order for her.

"I bet," Simon said snidely.

Ted jutted his head down to get an exaggerated view of Simon's legs. "So I guess you're...um...out of commission with the ladies, eh?" he tutted.

"Why? Did you want to have a go?" Simon said, grabbing his crotch.

The mention of sodomy stirred Ted deeply. He tightened his grip on the knife, causing Simon to choke. "Now we won't have any of that kind of talk, understand?" Ted seethed.

"Why are you here, Ted? If you're gonna kill me, kill me," Simon said, making his hands go limp at his sides, like he was helpless.

"Well, I want to savour the moment," Ted explained. "I did save the best for last."

Simon scoffed. "How come I'm the best?"

"Well, you've been a whore the longest," he said simply. "Since you were in college, if I recall correctly."

"Look whose got a potty mouth now?" Simon teased.

"I'm afraid there's no other word for filthy ingrates like you, Simon."

THE WHEELS OF CHANGE

"Why am I a filthy ingrate?"

"Because you've made it your life's work...sleeping with married women. I don't like adultery, Simon. It breaks up families."

Simon laughed in disbelief. "I've never broken up a family, Ted. Anyone I've slept with, they did it for their own reasons," he advised. "And none of them had children, so explain to me where I've destroyed a family?" Simon added. "Besides, not all of them were married...and how do you know all this shit about my life? How is it any of your business?"

"As your pastor, it was my business to look out for you, Simon."

"You were never my pastor, Ted."

"You had a living, breathing member of the clergy right under your nose and you still did all those nasty things!" Ted spat. "How could you!"

Simon smirked. "You're crazy."

Ted pulled hard on the knife and Simon put his hands on the exposed flesh, feeling the wetness of blood slowly flowing from the wound. Simon choked as he felt Ted's hot breath against his ear. He whipped his hand up, grabbing a handful of Ted's hair and tugged as hard as he could. Ted let go of Simon's neck and took a step back. Simon swirled himself around so he was face to face with Ted.

"You're a feisty one," Ted observed, smoothing his hair. "All the others were much easier."

Simon ignored Ted. "So how'd you pull it off? How'd you make everyone think you were dead?"

Ted grinned. "Ah, you see, I've had this planned a while, Simon."

"So you're not only crazy, but you're also clever?" Simon said facetiously. "What are the odds?"

Ted was rattled. He put the knife in the air, letting the light from the fluorescent light catch it. A small bead of Simon's blood was still on it. "I'm here to use this, Simon." Ted warned. "It's up to you how *quickly* I use it."

. . .

"Nelson's on his way, sir," Lisa reported. "And I've sent everyone else on patrol in the area over as well."

"Excellent," Mark said. "We'll intercept."

"One question. How is he not dead? Who is in the morgue?" Lisa asked, pushing her hands through her hair and watching her switchboard light up intermittently.

"Twin brother."

"Fuck," Lisa whispered. Mark heard her profanity and his eyes widened. He couldn't help but chuckle since it was so out-of-character for her to swear.

She sensed the silence as shock. "Sorry."

"That's okay," Mark chuckled. "I needed a laugh."

Lisa blushed. "Don't tell Richard. I'll never hear the end of it."

"Don't worry." Richard appeared and took a seat in the guest chair at Lisa's desk. "I won't tell him his wife has potty mouth under pressure." He winked at Richard.

"Thanks," Lisa said sarcastically. "So he killed his twin brother, too?"

"We don't know that," Mark clarified. "He just walked out in front of the transport truck. Who knows what really happened. Ted had money, he might have paid the driver off, who knows. There were no other witnesses until after he was dead."

"So you think Ted's headed for Simon's house?" Lisa asked. "Isn't that suicide?"

"He had pictures of himself and his twin brother in the same box with all his murder victims," Mark explained. "It's likely it'll be a murder-suicide to end it all. He's stupid if he thinks he's getting out alive."

"Well, he's crazy, so who knows what he's thinking."

THE WHEELS OF CHANGE

"We'll keep you posted," Mark said.

"Be careful."

...

Mark and Richard reached Simon's street and remained three or four doors down with the rest of the cruisers. Two patrol cars stayed on either end of the street, blocking off any incoming traffic. Mark addressed Nelson first. "Did you get a look inside? Is Ted in there?"

Nelson nodded. "Yeah, he's been in there for a few minutes."

"Is he armed?" Richard asked.

"He's just got a knife from what I can tell."

Mark nodded. "Okay, this part should be easy," he assured. "Simon is in a wheelchair, so we don't need to worry that he'll be in the same line of fire as Ted."

"Where's SWAT?" Richard asked.

"Gibson's already assembling his weapon across the street."

Mark peered over and noticed there was a cookie-cutter house closely resembling Simon's directly across the street. Mark spoke into his walkie-talkie. "Gibson?"

"Sir."

"When you get a clean shot, take it," Mark advised.

"Sir," Gibson confirmed.

Mark's walkie-talkie chirped. "Sir, we've got a Gus Ryder here. He says he's a friend of Simon's."

"What does he want?"

"He's supposed to be meeting with Simon."

"Tell him to go home, we're in the middle of a fucking take down here!"

"Sir."

. . .

"What the hell is going on?" Ryder insisted. "I thought the freak was dead!"

"I'm not at liberty to disclose any information about the case, sir."

"Who the hell is in there with Simon?"

"I'm going to have to ask you to leave, sir."

"Arrest me," Ryder said, and walked back to his truck. He pulled into the donut shop one and a half blocks away from Simon's street and parked there. Ryder got out and walked to the street behind Simon's.

He walked down the street, peeking behind each house, until he could see Simon's backyard from the front of the house. There were no cars parked in the driveway thankfully, so Ryder strolled onto the property and pulled the latch to get into the back yard.

He pulled himself up the chain-link fence and saw Simon's back door. Climbing the fence, he cursed himself for having such large feet, and again for wearing giant biker boots. Trying to be as quiet as possible, he finally reached Simon's side of the fence and jumped down. What was working for him was the fact that it was dark. What wasn't working for him was the neighbor's dog, who had just discovered him and began to bark.

Ryder scooched down behind Simon's rosebush that Nancy helped him put in two years ago. He was thankful she knew how to garden, and the thing was as hardy as ever. The back exterior light was switched on from inside the house, and he saw an unfamiliar face observing the yard through the small window.

"Bastard. I'm coming for you," Ryder whispered under his breath.

. . .

"Well, I think it's just about time to say goodbye, Simon," Ted said, like he was leaving after a welcomed visit. "It seems your friends, the police, have discovered me."

Simon tried to buy time. "I thought you were everybody's friend."

Ted laughed maniacally and then stopped, deadpan. "Walk," he demanded, his face red.

Simon scoffed. "What?" He was incredulous.

"I said WALK!" Ted yelled, coming towards Simon with the knife. "WALK...OR DIE!"

"Why do you care if I walk or not?" Simon asked sarcastically. "I mean, aren't I getting what I deserve?"

"I want to see you walk so I can cut your throat like a man!"

"Oooh, instead of the coward that you *actually* are?"

"WALK, GODDAMMIT!" Ted repeated. Veins were popping out of his neck and a line of spittle escaped as he shrieked his command.

Simon shook his head and tutted at Ted, like he'd been a naughty boy. "Taking the Lord's name in vain...isn't that a sin, Ted? But I guess you don't really care much about God anymore...seeing as you're killing his children, right?"

'WALK...YOU WHORE!!!!" Ted screamed and walked toward Simon, just as there was a bang and Simon turned his head to see Ryder breaking through the back door, foot first. Simon backed away as Ryder tackled Ted. They both fell to the floor as Ryder tried to choke Ted, lying on top of him. Ted managed to hang on to his knife through the struggle, so he slashed Ryder's arm, cutting through his clothes and grazing the skin underneath slightly. Ryder reacted by taking the hand holding the knife and forcing it down repeatedly, until Ted let go of it.

Ryder then punched him in the face, still sitting on top of him. From Ryder's sheer girth, Ted was unable to fight back, seeing as Ryder was at least fifty pounds heavier than he was. Simon wheeled over to the knife and kicked it away.

"The cops are outside! Run!" shouted Ryder, forgetting that Simon couldn't actually run.

Simon wheeled over to the door as two cops entered. He recognized Mark and Richard right away. Mark headed straight to Ted and instructed Ryder to step away.

"Ted Greenfield, you're under arrest." Mark slipped handcuffs onto his wrists as he rolled him over onto his back. "Anything you say can and will be used against you in a court of law."

Richard helped Ted up off the floor and led him out the front door. Mark observed the deep gash on Simon's throat. "There's an ambulance just outside. Come with me."

Simon watched Ted walk out the door and Ted turned toward him. "May God be with you," he said, as if he'd done nothing wrong and Simon was to blame.

Simon looked at him like he was the biggest joke. "God has always been with me. Even when I lived with the devil, apparently."

Mark jerked Ted's arms, forcing him to keep walking.

"Come on, buddy, let's get you some stitches." Ryder pushed Simon's chair out the door.

"Thanks, man."

Ryder watched them put Ted in the back seat of a cruiser. "There's a special place in hell for people like that. Maybe he'll die in prison."

Simon stared at the back of Ted's head for a moment. Ryder patted him on the shoulder, "Come on. You'll be safe now."

...

ONE MONTH LATER

Simon sat in the first pew with Darla. Judge Caplan was about to hand down the verdict and sentence for Max Dunphy in the attempt murder case against Simon. Clara was sitting in the second pew on the opposite side, Simon glanced at her. She gave him a dirty look, like he'd just called her mother a whore, and turned her head back towards her husband.

Darla caught the glance and muttered to Simon. "Charming, isn't she?"

He scoffed and shook his head. Darla took his hand as she saw Judge Caplan return to the stand from his chambers. "All rise," the bailiff called.

There was shuffling as everyone stood, including Simon.

"The jury finds Maxwell Clarence Dunphy guilty in the attempted murder of Simon Cornelius Cross."

Darla looked at Simon and mouthed 'Cornelius?'

He elbowed her in the ribs.

Judge Caplan continued. "Mr. Dunphy is sentenced to ten years in a federal penitentiary. Court is adjourned." He smacked the gavel on the desk and rose from the podium, returning to his chambers.

Simon watched Clara walk over to Max and kiss him on the cheek coldly. Then she walked away.

"Well, there you have it," Darla said. "How do you feel?"

"Relieved. Wait'll Ryder hears." Simon kissed her on the cheek. "Shall we?" He gestured for her to go ahead. Darla waited for Simon to grab his four-pronged cane and slowly follow her down the aisle. They linked arms on the trek down the long path to the courtroom door. It took Simon longer than a normal person, but he did it gracefully, feeling thankful that he got his legs at least partially back.

As they exited the courthouse, Simon was met by reporters who immediately shoved a microphone in his face and asked, "So, Mr. Cross, how does it feel to know both the men who tried to kill you are behind bars?"

Simon answered to a young male reporter. "I'm relieved and glad it's over. Thank you."

Clara exited the courthouse and the reporters immediately flocked to her. Simon and Darla took that as their queue to leave. "You hungry?" Simon asked Darla.

"Not really."

Just as they were about to walk away, Clara unexpectedly approached. "Simon," she called.

He turned around, still linked to Darla's arm. Clara reached them and stopped, with a sly look on her face, like she had a big secret. "I sure hope things work out for you," she said snidely. "But if they don't," she stroked Simon's free arm. "I sure hope you'll come to visit."

Darla let go of Simon and walked over, directly in front of Clara, lifted her arm up and ploughed her with a right hook to the face. "Enjoy your conjugal visits, bitch!" she shouted.

With the force of Darla's hit, Clara was knocked right over. She grabbed her face with her mouth wide open in shock. Darla took a step back and spat on her. "You get tired of the old ball and chain, then go fuck a prison guard!"

Simon watched Darla with widened eyes. Darla winked at Simon and linked her arm around his again. "Let's go have some lunch."

"I thought you weren't hungry."

"Somehow I seem to have worked up an appetite."

The End

A NOTE TO READERS:

Thank you for reading my work. I hope you enjoyed it. If you did, it would be most appreciated if you could take a moment and place a quick review on Amazon. These days it is very difficult to get reviews if you're a little indie author like me, and hey, if you only write one sentence, then that's one sentence more than I would have received otherwise. It may even make a difference, but you won't know until you try.

ABOUT THE BOOK

Her husband is dead. Her daughter doesn't speak. The town she's raised her child in is being set aflame and nobody knows who is responsible or why.

Sherry is alone, facing her worst fears while the town pulls together to keep everyone safe. She prays the culprit will be found before it's too late, but her instincts predict otherwise.

When a new face arrives in town, Sherry realizes she isn't the only one who has lost, and more importantly, that there is much more she could lose.

EXCERPT

A breeze drifted into her room from the open window. Sherry pulled the blankets up tighter to her chin as she slept. Her hand swept absently through the empty spot beside her. The crease in the mattress still held Chris's shape but hadn't been warmed by his body in months. Often, her dreams included him, but lately they turned cold and dismal.

Tonight's dream was no exception. The lilies that lined her garden were quickly wilting. Grass that was once green lay yellowing and crispy on her lawn. As she floated into her home the dreamy haze surrounded her, clouding her view of Baker's Farm beyond her house.

As she proceeded through the kitchen, Sherry could feel the hair on her forearms suddenly stand up. The chill felt down her spine was juxtaposed by the inherent heat enveloping her. Looking downward she gasped; smoke was billowing around the room. It followed as she made her way to the upper floor. The smell scorched her lungs as she strived to get to the room at the end of the hallway, where her daughter lay.

To her relief, Denise was sleeping soundly, undisturbed by the flames licking up the sides of her bed. Following her instincts, Sherry reached to scoop her daughter up and run, but something stopped her. Under the cloud of gray smoke at her feet was a man's hand. It pulled at her ankle, preventing her from reaching out.

Suddenly, Denise's eyes fluttered open. As she witnessed the flames and smoke engulfing her room, she cried out. But her cries fell on deaf ears; it was as if all the wind had been taken from her. No sound would come. Sherry tried to break free from the hand, grasping her seemingly from the depths of hell, but her attempts were futile.

Sherry watched as her seven-year-old continued mutely screaming for help, when suddenly the screams were replaced by the shrieking beeps of an alarm. Bolting upright, she pounded her fist on the alarm clock and wiped her face. It was beaded with sweat and her sheets were soaked. "Jesus Christ." She swore, pulling her feet down onto the cold wood-planked floor.

Swallowing, Sherry managed to catch her breath. The house was quiet. All that could be heard was the chirping of morning doves as they prattled

THE WHEELS OF CHANGE

amongst the trees, waiting for sunrise. Staring at her shaking hands, Sherry observed the tan line where her wedding ring once rested. Looking at her jewellery box, she walked over and sat at her dressing table, glancing into the antique mirror.

The face that was once framed with smiles and laughter looked back at her, shadowed with grief and anxiety in the form of wrinkles and shadows. Her body, that had once been touched tenderly, would never again feel love or new life. Feet that would never dance with a partner again, lay flat against the hard floor. She took the wedding band from the box and placed it on her finger; giving herself permission to pretend for another day.

Hearing a voice, Sherry rose and padded over to Denise's room. She heard the voice again and walked faster. Could this be it? Has the day finally come? Sherry asked herself, trying to calm the fluttering in her belly. Her heart sank as she opened the door and saw her daughter, lying fast asleep, with her talking Elmo doll wedged against her body, chattering inadvertently.

Sherry chided herself for believing. Today wouldn't be the day. And probably tomorrow wouldn't be, either. But one day she knew it would happen. One day it wouldn't just be in her dreams.

CHAPTER 1

The leaves on the trees were green and lush with spring. Morning had greeted them kindly with warm sunlight and a fresh breeze. Sherry winded her window down further and rested her hand on the door of her beat up Eldorado, letting her fingers weave through the air as she made her way up the long country road to the school.

Long, brown ringlets bounced up and down, riding the wind as it flowed through her hair. Sherry looked back and saw Denise's hair doing the same and she smiled proudly.

"I put peanut butter sandwiches in your lunch today, darlin', with the crusts cut off, just the way you like 'em."

Denise continued straightening her bear's outfit, without a response to her mother.

Turning into the school, Sherry waved to her friend Martha, who was dropping off her son. "Oh, look, there's Luke." she pointed.

277

Denise spotted Luke; Martha's son, and waved to him politely. Unfastening her seat belt, Denise bent forward, stepping out of her booster seat, onto the floor of the car, where her mother waited to embrace her. "Bye bye sweetie. I'll see ya later."

Denise kissed her mother and walked into the school without looking back, being careful that her bear was safely tucked away by her side.

"How's she doin'?" Martha asked, giving Luke a playful goodbye tap on the bottom as he joined Denise in line with the rest of the class.

"Good. No more fever. Dr. Baker gave her the good stuff." Sherry crossed her arms over her chest.

"She's got a little glint in her eye today, doesn't she?" Martha noticed, walking up to Sherry's side.

"Yeah. She almost smiled at me on the way here."

"It'll come." Martha said as if by rote, pulling her purse over her shoulder. "It's been almost two years now, hasn't it?"

Sherry nodded, not looking up, "Come summer."

"She been up to the Baker's farm lately? Ned's built a conservatory for the butterflies."

"Yeah. That's how I found out about the bear." Sherry explained matter-of-factly.

"The bear?"

Sherry looked up and pointed at Denise's little purse and the bear sticking out of it, like a lone traveler secretly placed in her luggage to avoid entrance fees. "Rainy Day Bear. That's how I found out she wanted the bear for her birthday."

Martha's brows furrowed, "And how did you find out about that?"

"Because she told one of the butterflies."

...

THE WHEELS OF CHANGE

"Great scot!" Ned Baker shouted, darting out of his chair, "Who is this little princess strollin' up the walkway?" He looked over at his wife, Kate, who was sitting on the porch in her wooden rocker, knitting what appeared to be a baby bonnet. "Hand me a lollipop," he instructed, "one o' the ones with the candy in the middle….the good ones." He smiled, gesturing her to hurry.

"Ned, for heaven's sake," Kate scolded, reaching behind her to the large pink plastic candy bowl they kept on their porch for passers-by, "Better ask her momma first."

Denise and Sherry were walking up the gravel pathway to the house, carrying a basket full of torn stale bread. "We came to feed the ducks again." Sherry explained, scooting Denise up towards Ned, who was walking proudly down the hill towards the young girl. His knees bent further with each step, stooping down to Denise's level. When he reached the little girl, his toothy grin and proffered lollipop forced an ear-to-ear smile across Denise's face.

"Absolutely, love, they've been waitin'." Kate rose, setting down the knitting on her rocker, "you can help feed the butterflies, too, if you can spare the time."

"Absolutely, Kate. I'm sure she'd love to."

"How ya doin' today, sweetheart?" Kate's arm was over Sherry's shoulders, "You looked downright pale this mornin'."

"I'm fine. Thanks again for gettin' hold of Doug so fast yesterday. He's a lifesaver."

Doug, Ned and Kate's son, was the town doctor. Sherry called him yesterday after receiving a call from Denise's school, reporting that she was burning up with fever.

Kate gestured Sherry into the house, "No trouble, dear. Can I get you a tea?"

"Sure. Have you got chamomile?"

Kate reached for the box of chamomile tea in the cupboard above the sink. "Sarah was by earlier; the beauty parlour must have been slow today."

"Did she come for your cinnamon rolls? I swear this baby of hers has given her the nose of a hound."

"Yeah, she took my last one. Ate my apple dumplings, too. I'll make a fresh batch later." She waved casually, scrunching her nose.

The kettle began to boil and Kate poured two small mugs full. "Doug says Dr. Graham thinks Denise is goin' to hit a tippin' point soon." Kate said cautiously, handing her the tea.

"He says it won't take much. She's come a long way in the last year." Sherry agreed.

"What do you think it'll take?"

Sherry scoffed, taking a sip of tea, "If I knew that I could pull her out of treatment."

"Sorry, love, I didn't mean to pry." Kate placed her hands on Sherry's and changed the subject, "You hear they're puttin' in a new hospital?"

"No. It's about time. Poor Doug's been tellin' me for years that the hospital's too small."

"That's right. This town's grown twice its size in the last ten years."

"I remember," Sherry said, "When they built the Food Mart over there on Carlaw Street. Ned just about had a coronary."

Kate grinned, "I've never seen that man run so fast." She shook her head, "Nothin' stops him when it comes to this farm. It took him a week to get 'em to buy their goods from us."

"Now that Marty and Liz run it, you guys can't keep up with 'em."

"Yep. We've got more cattle, pigs and chickens now than I've ever had...even since I was a girl."

"So where's the hospital goin'?"

Kate turned away from Sherry quickly, fumbling through the drawer, looking for her oven mitts. "Just up the way here." She mumbled, pointing

THE WHEELS OF CHANGE

absently at the overhead window.

Sherry's brows furrowed, "Up the way where? Closer to me or the other way...towards Sarah's place?"

"Er....on the other side of the farm."

"What do you mean? Over towards the main highway? Where the...where the road's been closed?"

"It hasn't been made official." Kate turned to face her, speaking apologetically. "They may put it over by Sarah's. Ned says they're still negotiatin', but I wanted you to know. So you wouldn't be surprised if it came about."

Sherry sat silently for a moment, "How long?"

"Ned said the town is goin' to hold another meetin' in a month's time. I didn't want to tell you but Ned said it's for the best. He made me promise I'd tell you after Denise's birthday; he didn't want ya upset for that."

"I guess it was goin' to happen some day." Sherry sighed regretfully, "They can't keep that road closed forever just for me."

Kate walked over to Sherry and took her hands, "Maybe it's a sign, sweetie." She rubbed the back of Sherry's hands with her fingers. "God's tellin' ya it's time to let go."

281

ABOUT THE AUTHOR

Thank you for reading my work. If you've made it this far I'd say that's a good sign! My writing career began back in 2006 when I was up to my elbows in dirty diapers, caring for my two children. I always had a desire to write something but up until then I didn't really know what to write.

Inspiration struck and it took me two years but I finally wrote my first book: a fifty page memoir, and I was so excited about it. After my second book, another memoir, was self-published, I realized there was something more to it than a hobby. I've been writing ever since.

Giving up my full-time career in the corporate world was not an easy decision to make. But coupled with personal reasons and the drive to do something really meaningful, was the ache of creativity that has kept me motivated for the last nine years.

I hope this book gave you something to think about, entertained you and made you laugh at least once, because that is what I strive for when I write.

Seeing as you've read most of my bio I'll insert the mundane stuff now. I'm a married Canadian who lives in Niagara Falls with my husband, two daughters and a loving, eleven pound cat. If you would like to see more of my work it can be found at www.sandyappleyard.com.

Also, please leave a brief review if you enjoyed it!
Here is the link:

Happy Reading!

Made in the USA
Charleston, SC
22 January 2015